DESERTED PROPHECY
ORACLE SERIES, BOOK 2

Jaemi Lee

Bamboo
Publishing

Deserted Prophecy
Oracle Series, Book 2

First Hardback Edition: 2022

Copyright © 2022 by Jaemi Lee
All rights reserved.

Hardback ISBN: 978-1-956501-03-2
Paperback ISBN: 978-1-956501-04-9
eBook ISBN: 978-1-956501-05-6

Cover art by Joshua Deni Prakoso (@jdprakoso)

The characters and events in this book are fictional. Any similarity to actual persons, living or dead, is purely coincidental.

To everyone who continued to believe in me.
To my younger self.

And to all my fans and readers.

1
FAMILY

Elliot pressed circles against his wrist. The marking of the oracle had been throbbing ever since they'd departed Ruglow, and it was only growing stronger.

The travel from Ruglow to Valquent was not a short one. Elliot felt the hard ground through the soles of his boots. Even the grass beneath him felt harsh. Whatever cushion he'd had in his boots had vanished, leaving him with an ache that thrummed from his heels to his ankles and knees.

Each step weighed him down, reminding him of how much he was failing as the oracle, reminding him he hadn't kept his duty in mind as he'd pranced around the lower lands. How long had it been since he'd left Mistfall? One month? Two? Three? How long had it been since he had last seen his family? Or even Xeno? Elliot's stomach shot up to his throat every time he thought of his companion. He hadn't seen him since he was captured and separated from Minari and Chloé back in Venin.

Elliot had had to keep himself from screaming when Minari had told him he'd left Xeno in Mistfall. He gripped the blanket so tight that his knuckles turned white. His eyes stung from fresh tears. Guilt overwhelmed him. An elf was an ovis's trusted partner for the rest of their lives if they ever decided to leave the wilderness and live amongst the elves.

And he'd ruined that trust.

Minari had assured Elliot that nothing was wrong in Mistfall. He'd told him that his family just missed him, so he had left Xeno with them in hopes it would quell their loneliness. He had also left Redd behind because Alder had told Minari he no longer needed to observe their progress. The demigod of earth believed in them and trusted them to fulfill the prophecy.

Elliot recalled Vylantra's words. He'd been tasked with putting a stop to the rise of the Necromancers and Mykronos, the Dark God. He needed to find four warriors and the lost hero, who was supposed to be Myru's most trusted keeper.

When Elliot had met Chloé, there was a strong sense of companionship, as if they were two friends who hadn't seen each other in a long time. When Elliot met Mimi, he didn't have the same reaction as Chloé, though Mimi had admitted to feeling the need to protect Elliot. And while his memories of first meeting Luka were fuzzy, the ethereal had confessed he knew who Elliot was; he'd sensed Elliot's magic core when he was in Oasis's dungeon but couldn't act on it due to Namir's control over him.

Three of the four warriors were found, meaning Elliot

needed to find one more warrior and search for the lost hero.

Elliot was positive he would know who the last warrior was when he found them.

When Elliot had asked Minari about their childhood friend, Lily, he could only smile. But the smile did not reach his eyes. It looked forced. And all Minari said was, "She's doing fine," before handing her dagger back to Elliot. He was fortunate Luka had been able to retrieve it before it was lost forever.

Minari's voice broke Elliot out of his thoughts. He looked up from his feet, meeting the faces of his worried friends. He hadn't realized his pace had slowed. They were a good fifteen feet away.

Minari made his way over, Xander's reins in his hands. "You're pale. Why not ride Xander?"

"I'm fine," Elliot said. He turned away, not wanting to face Minari's judging eyes.

"Do you want to rest?"

"No, we should keep moving. We've been traveling for days and still haven't reached Valquent."

Minari didn't respond right away, but Elliot could still feel his gaze. "You shouldn't push yourself, Elliot."

Elliot pressed his lips together. He breathed in through his nose before letting it out from his mouth. "I'm fine. We should keep moving."

"Ell—"

"I *said* I was fine!" Elliot slapped a hand over his mouth. He hadn't meant to yell.

Minari's shoulders slumped. "Okay, we'll keep moving, but you have to ride Xander. Get on."

Elliot stared at Minari. Minari stared back at him. His

9

shoulders were straight, and his stance was firm. He wasn't going to budge from the topic.

Elliot sighed. "All right. I'll ride."

Minari smiled. "We're close to Valquent. Chloé was just saying we're about two days away. Stay strong."

Elliot grunted as he mounted Xander. He tapped the ovis's sides, leading him to the rest of the group.

Elliot didn't speak to anyone for the rest of their travel.

It was nearing sunset when the city walls of Valquent came into view. The cream stone walls appeared golden as they reflected the light of the setting sun. The group was exhausted from their travel, but their eyes lit up as soon as they saw their destination was within reach.

"Finally!" Chloé said. "I can finally take a bath."

Elliot took a glance at the nix. Her curls were matted compared to when they'd first met. Her hair had once been bright pink, but now it was dull, and stray strands poked out haphazardly. Her shoulders were now hunched forward rather than straight, and her clothing had shifted in color since the start of their travel.

"You took the longest bath out of all of us," Minari said.

"Just because I take longer baths doesn't mean I feel any cleaner," Chloé scoffed.

Minari rolled his eyes. "Okay. Whatever you say."

A sudden sense of déjà vu washed over Elliot. He watched as Chloé puffed up her cheeks and smacked Minari's shoulder. She was mounted on top of her mare while Minari was on foot, which allowed her to perform the action with ease. The situation between the two, bantering with Chloé mounted on a horse . . . Elliot had seen it before. He felt the corner of his lips twitch upward. It was when they had first left Blanc Grotto after being held in a dungeon by Chloé. The two didn't get along at all at the time, but Elliot could see how close they had gotten.

The bickering between them wasn't that of two people who hated each other; rather, it was that of two people who trusted and were fond of each other.

"We should take a pause here. Owen and I should cast an illusion spell on Mimi and Sage," Luka said. "It would not be wise to proceed otherwise."

Mimi pressed himself against Sage, their arms touching. "Only until we reach an inn?"

"Correct. Only until then," Luka assured him.

"Do not worry. You will not feel any discomfort, just the slight itch of your skin," Owen said.

"As long as I don't stink like a human, it's fine with me," Sage said. He scrunched his face. "Remind me to erase this from my memory. I never want to remember myself as a chimera who had to *disguise* himself as a human."

"At least it's temporarily," Mimi said.

"Very well. I can promise you two shall now emit the aroma of humans," Luka said.

Luka and Owen stood in front of Mimi and Sage. Luka drew his sword and pointed it toward Sage. The feathered wings atop Owen's head started to glow. A small translucent orb began to radiate at the tip of Luka's sword.

Luka's mouth moved, but no sound came out of him. His eyes briefly flashed gold before the orb pierced through Sage's body.

The soft glow surrounded the ox's body. The strands of his hair shifted to a deep black, and his height shrank. His muscular body was replaced with a slimmer build, though it was still toned. His clothes transformed into a simple white top and black pants, and the open-toed sandals he wore morphed into black boots. The bronze cuff on his ear vanished, leaving his ears bare.

The light dimmed before disappearing.

Sage scratched his arm. "When you said I'd only feel a little itch, I think you meant a lot."

"It is best if you withhold yourself from scratching," Owen said. "Your body will get used to the transformation in due time."

Luka repeated the action with Mimi. The younger chimera grew about two inches in height. His pale sand hair turned light brown, and his skin warmed to a peach tone. His golden eyes shifted to chocolate. Like Sage's, his clothes transformed into a similar white top and black pants with matching boots. The snake cuff on his ear vanished.

Luka sheathed his sword. "And with that, it's safe to proceed."

The surrounding trees became sparse, revealing the open area around Valquent. The scenery surrounding the city contrasted with what Elliot had seen throughout the journey from Ruglow. He took in a deep breath, appreciating the fresh and open air that entered his lungs. It revitalized his energy.

The grass grew rich in color. The dirt road was soon replaced with stone. Red and white flowers spread across the fields. The trees' trunks were wide and full with branches. The biggest difference was the new appearance the leaves had taken. They were indigo, and if Elliot squinted, he could see them sparkling, almost as if they were emitting an aura.

"What are you looking at?" Minari asked. "You've been staring at the trees."

"They're blue."

Minari glanced around. "What's blue?"

"The leaves."

It was Minari's turn to squint. "Um . . ."

"Are you looking with your right eye?" Elliot asked.

Minari gasped, eyes wide as he turned to Elliot. "Did you just try to crack a joke?"

Elliot chortled. "Yes and no."

He knew Minari wasn't too fond of being reminded he couldn't see out of his left eye. It was a reminder of what had happened to his father, but something in him wanted to lift the mood. It had been too long since the two elves had been relaxed around each other without having to worry about responsibilities.

"You know what I would make Redd do to you if he were here."

Elliot immediately covered his hair. "My hair is already a mess!"

"Perfect nesting material." Minari shrugged.

The two elves stared at each other.

The younger elf tried his best to force his lips closed, but he sputtered and cracked. He laughed, tears prickling at the corners of his eyes. The weight that was on his shoulders disappeared as he relished the moment with Minari.

"I've missed this," Minari said. "You've been all doom

and gloom ever since we left Ruglow."

Elliot wiped his tears away. His stomach was tight and sore from laughing. "I have been, haven't I?"

"This is a better look on you. You're already looking better. Whatever was bothering you, don't let it weigh you down. We're in this together, through thick and thin, so confide in us when you need to."

Elliot smiled. Minari was right. He looked over at the others. He didn't know how long they'd been eavesdropping, but they looked at him with smiles on their faces. It seemed like Minari wasn't the only one who'd noticed Elliot's demeanor, and it relieved them to see Elliot in a lighter mood.

Elliot was truly fortunate to have met Chloé, Mimi, Sage, Luka, and Owen. They were his family now, and he would cherish them in his heart forever.

2
TROUBLE

Elliot dismounted from Xander once they reached the edge of the bridge. The guard outside Valquent gave them a puzzled look. It was obvious he was aware of who Chloé, Luka, and Owen were. Chloé was a member of the council, and Luka and Owen were ex-captains of Oasis. The guard didn't bat an eye when he looked at Mimi and Sage. But when it came to Elliot and Minari, the guard stared. He didn't stop them from entering, but Elliot saw the shift in his posture.

The guard tightened his grip around the hilt of his sword, and his back straightened. His chin stayed forward, but his gaze followed the two elves. It wasn't until they'd passed the gates that the guard stopped focusing on them.

"Isn't that . . . ?"

"Why is she with . . . ?"

"Why are they also with her?"

"*Barbarians.*"

Suddenly, everyone around Elliot disappeared, allowing the people of Valquent to close in on him. Their bodies pressed against his back. Their fingers grabbed his arms. Their shouts pierced through him.

The air grew thick and hot, and Elliot found it hard to breathe.

He tried gasping for air, but no matter how hard he tried, there was not enough oxygen flowing into his lungs. His chest ached and tightened. The edges of his vision darkened as the world spun.

Elliot collapsed onto his knees, pressing his palms against his ears. "Stop. Stop. Stop. Please," he whispered.

"Elliot!"

The screams disappeared, leaving a low ringing echoing in Elliot's ears. His heart thudded loudly against his chest. The shadows in his vision cleared.

"Elliot, look at me."

Minari's voice was muffled underneath Elliot's palms, but he could still make out the request. The older elf tightened his hold on Elliot's shoulders.

"Elliot?"

Elliot slowly lowered his hands, placing them over his knees. They throbbed against the hard gravel. He looked up.

"Are you with me?" Minari asked.

Elliot nodded slowly before he looked around. Chloé, Luka, and Owen were spread apart, trying to keep the on-lookers from getting too close. Mimi and Sage were looking at Elliot, concern written across their faces.

Mimi had a small child with him. The chimera held the

boy by the arm, keeping him away from Elliot. The boy looked confused, wanting to reach out to Elliot. He had his arm outstretched, reaching for him. He had a pale complexion and freckles across his cheeks. His ginger hair covered part of his eyes, and the top of his head reached Mimi's waist.

"Mom! Mom, look! He has pointy ears!" the boy said.

"Chris, get back here!" a woman from the crowd called out. She had the same ginger hair as her son. It was curly and reached her shoulders. She glanced at Elliot and Minari before looking back at her son. "Chris, be a good boy and come back. Stay away from them."

"But Mom! He—"

"*Christopher!*"

The boy flinched at the tone of his mother's voice. He looked up at Mimi before looking back at the older woman. Mimi slowly let Christopher's arm go, allowing the small boy to scurry back. He hugged her legs, burrowing his face into her skirt.

"Come, we need to leave," the woman said quickly as she dragged Christopher from the scene.

Elliot turned back to Minari. "What happened?"

"That boy ran from his mother and tried to get to us," Minari started. "I was going to stop him, but you suddenly collapsed. It was a good thing Mimi was there to stop him."

"Miss Gemme, could you please explain why there are two elves with you?" a man asked. He had gray hair and leaned against a cane. "Are they not supposed to have your family's collar to mark they are domesticated?"

"He's right! You basically led stray animals into Valquent! And that boy. If he'd gotten any closer, who knows what would've happened to him," a man standing by Owen said.

Elliot's body tensed. His memory flashed back to when he and Minari were in Blanc Grotto, back to when a smaller nix had rushed up to them in an attempt to protect Chloé from them. The young nix had assumed Elliot and Minari were threats.

But this was different. The small child had been curious. He'd wanted to take a closer look. He hadn't seen them as a threat, but the others did. They were afraid of them.

Christopher's mother had refused to step any closer to them, beckoning her son to return to her. She hadn't had the courage to protect her son from potential harm. She had hoped he would listen and return to her.

The older humans saw the elves as bloodthirsty killers.

A race that danced around the bodies of the dead. A race that would smear the blood of the fallen across their faces. A race that would eat the flesh of their prey. But it wasn't what the elves were. No. That was far from it.

And no one knew of this but them.

"These two are my friends," Chloé said. "And I expect them to be treated as equals."

The older man stared at Chloé as if she had lost her mind. His eyes bulged, and his mouth gaped. "Miss Gemme, did they bewitch you somehow? Surely you do not think this. This is blasphemy."

"We should get away from them, else they'll bewitch us too." The man shoved his shoulder against Owen before turning and walking away.

"If this is what you think, then the council should reconsider its members." The older man bowed his top hat to Chloé before turning away.

There were murmurs amongst the crowd before they dispersed, completely ignoring the group as if they weren't there.

Minari helped Elliot up. His knees still throbbed, but it didn't bother him too much. Xander twitched his ears. The ovis nudged his muzzle against Elliot's cheek.

"Looks like Xander was worried about you too."

Elliot stroked Xander's head before shifting his attention to Chloé. The nix smiled at him.

"You okay?"

"I should be asking you that. Are you going to be okay? What they said earlier . . ."

"Don't worry about that. It wasn't the first time I've heard someone mention the council. There were a lot of people who didn't agree with me being on it in the first place with me being so young." Chloé crossed her arms. "It hasn't gotten much better since I joined, and I've learned to just ignore them. They can say whatever they want. Enough about me. What happened earlier? You just fell and started mumbling to yourself."

"It was worrisome," Luka said. "Your complexion paled, and we were afraid you had become ill."

"I'm fine," Elliot said. "I must have just gotten dizzy."

Minari placed his hand against Elliot's forehead. "You don't feel warm."

"The inn I was planning on taking us to isn't too far from here. I usually stay there when I come for council assemblies," Chloé said.

"The faster we get out of here, the better," Sage said. "I

want to take this skin off."

***

"Miss Gemme."

Chloé had just received the keys to four rooms at the Twin Seasons Inn when a voice called out to her.

A Valquent officer walked over. He wore a navy uniform with gold line embellishments going across the sides. A cape was draped off his left shoulder, and there was a sword at his left hip. He pulled off his cap, revealing his blond hair. He placed a hand over his chest and bowed his head. "Miss Gemme, I heard whispers and rumors that you'd been spotted inside Valquent with a group of unknown elves. Though it pleases me to see you are unharmed, it's concerning to see you are in the company of elves. Some believe they cast a spell on you."

Chloé put on a smile. "I can assure you that I am not bewitched, and these are my friends, so I would appreciate it if you could tell the townspeople and your colleagues the same. I do not wish to experience any trouble during our stay in Valquent."

"And how long do you plan on staying within the city, Miss Gemme?"

"Why? Is there a concern I need to know about?"

The officer glanced behind Chloé, narrowing his eyes upon seeing Elliot and Minari, before looking back to the nix. "Word of your arrival spread, and the council has summoned you to an immediate assembly. They sent me to find you and escort you to Nexus Hall."

Chloé frowned. She did not like the sound of that. The council hardly did impromptu assemblies, and when they did, it was usually for more dire situations. It took a great deal of effort for her and the Azure family to attend any impromptu assemblies because of how far the grottos were from the city. The last impromptu one had been when Trox was raided by bandits, and they'd needed to tend to the townspeople and find whoever was responsible.

"It's urgent, Miss Gemme."

"I just arrived. Could I have some time to rest before leaving?"

The officer looked around as if making sure no one was watching them. "I can give you enough time for you and your group to see your rooms, but I cannot give you much more than that. Please understand."

Chloé sighed. "All right. Then please wait here until I return. I will not be long."

The officer bowed his head once again before placing his cap back on. "Of course, Miss Gemme. I will be waiting."

3
BELIEVE

Chloé, Elliot, and Minari walked into the third booked room. Like the other rooms, it had all the bare necessities. Two beds were pushed up against the walls, with a small round table in the center. Each bed had its own wooden nightstand next to it, and a door that led to the bathroom was on the left side of the room. Though the space was simple, there was a large window. Chloé enjoyed staying in the Twin Seasons Inn. Even though it didn't have electricity running in the rooms like other inns, it was multistory. The rooms on the third floor had large windows in comparison to the ones below. There were times when she simply enjoyed watching through the pane.

Luka and Owen were in one room, and Mimi and Sage were in another. All four rooms were next to one another down the long hallway on the third floor. Windfall and Xander were kept in the stables at the back of the inn.

"Are you in any trouble?" Elliot asked.

Chloé blinked at the question, pausing at the doorway. The thought hadn't come to mind that *she* would be the topic of the council assembly. She had merely assumed it was to get her up to speed with the previous assemblies she had missed. "No, I don't think so."

Elliot bit his lip. He brought his hands together and scratched at his fingertips. His fingers were raw with peeled skin and dried blood. Why hadn't she noticed that before?

"Sometimes this happens. I'm sure it's just to update me on any recent events, especially with Oasis's disbandment. They might be wondering what they should do with the Outlawers."

"Outlawers . . ." Elliot mumbled.

"This is the first I've heard of them," Minari said. "Though I can take a guess based on the name."

"The Outlawers are a group of chimeras who defy the regulations we have on them. They are allowed certain areas to live in around the kingdom. If they leave and enter other lands, then they are deemed part of the Outlawers." Chloé took a pause. Saying it out loud made her realize how awful it must have been for the chimeras. Their land was small—a fraction of what was given to everyone else—and there were many of them. There was no way they could live in comfort with how cramped it must have been for them. No wonder the Outlawers had formed. It was essentially a cry for help. "Oasis was in charge of them. Since they're gone, I'm sure it's a question of who will handle them now," Chloé finished.

"But you plan on freeing the chimeras, right?" Elliot

asked.

"That is something I'm going to have to bring up, and today's assembly seems like a good place to start." Chloé smiled. "Don't worry, I'll be fine. I'll be back before you know it."

Minari placed a hand on Elliot's shoulder. "You heard it from her. I'm sure Chloé is no stranger when it comes to these meetings. Believe in her."

Chloé's cheeks warmed. Having someone believe in her wasn't something she was accustomed to. Because of her young age, no one believed she could do a good job of being a council member. It came with heavy responsibilities and decision-making. With her being significantly younger than the other members, many thought her lack of experience would hinder her. She did her best to show she was confident and sufficient for the role, but having someone tell her they believed in her made her feel . . . happy.

Chloé turned away and cleared her throat. "Well, I'll be off now." She quickly left and closed the door behind her.

She took a deep breath, leaned against the wall beside the door, and blew out her breath through her lips. Placing a hand over her chest, Chloé felt her heart thump. She tried to slow it down, thinking about anything but the comforting words Minari had said, thinking about anything but the softness of his eyes and the smile on his face when he'd looked at her. She shook her head and patted her cheeks. She shouldn't have let something like that rile her up so much.

Chloé took another deep breath before she pushed off the wall and walked over to her room. She slipped the key into the lock and opened the door.

The specific room she'd booked for herself had a single bed, though instead of a twin like the other rooms, it had a queen. She collapsed on the bed, throwing her arm across her eyes. Fatigue spread through her body. She really did not want to attend the council assembly. The sun had already set, and hunger was starting to settle in. But she knew the officer was downstairs waiting for her, and she had already told him she wouldn't take long.

With a huff, she sat up and shook her head, attempting to rid her eyes of tiredness. "Guess I should get this over with."

When Chloé returned to the entrance, the officer was still waiting, as promised.

"Miss Gemme." The officer lifted his hat and bowed his head. "Shall we head to Nexus Hall?"

"Yes, I am ready."

The lamps around the city were switched on, and they now illuminated the streets. The fire heaters were also set aflame, which allowed the trip to remain warm. The streets were unusually empty. During this time, the night market should've been preparing, but there were blankets over the stalls, and not a single person was by them.

"Here we are," the officer said.

Nexus Hall was secluded from the other buildings. The front of the building curved in like a semicircle, while the other three walls were squared. The structure was made out of brick and had a tall white stone staircase that led up to the double wooden doors. The building had always felt cold to Chloé. It was never welcoming, just like the other members, and the lack of life around the city only amplified the feeling.

Chloé took a few steps up the stairs before turning back

to the officer. "I don't think I caught your name."

The officer smiled, the creases reaching his blue eyes. "Gale. Yuan Gale."

"Officer Gale, thank you for escorting me."

Yuan bowed. "Of course, Miss Gemme. Good luck." He lifted his hat and nodded before leaving.

The corners of Chloé's lips perked up. Good luck? It would've been lucky if she weren't part of the council at this very moment. She would've much rather have been eating a delicious meal and resting at the Twin Seasons Inn.

Chloé rested her palm against the door. A circle formed around it and pulsed with a white light three times before it disappeared and the door handle clicked. With a turn, she pushed it open.

A fire pit was in the center of the hallway. It was lit with a blue flame, indicating an assembly was in session. She walked past it, her heels echoing off the polished white floors. She kept her head high and shoulders straight as she reached another pair of wooden double doors. Unlike the silver handles attached to the doors that led inside, the handles in front of her were gold. Chloé assumed it was to make the council feel they were of importance since silver and gold were not available to the lower class. It was still rare even for families who were of higher status.

Chloé knocked on the door before reaching for the cold handles and letting herself in.

4
CORNER

Stares surrounded Chloé as soon as she stepped through the double doors. It was her first time entering the room while the council was in the middle of a meeting, so the lights were already switched off. The gazes sent chills down her spine.

There was a U-shaped table in the center of the room. It had every seat filled except for two; one was meant for her, and one was meant for Ragnar, the ethereal council member. Licht and Emilee Azure must have been in the area when the impromptu council assembly was called.

"Chloé, it pleases us to see you were able to make it," Licht said.

Chloé did not like the way Licht's wine eyes sparkled at her.

"Chloé, please stand in the center," Sasha said.

Sasha Clifford was one of the eldest human members on

the council. Her brown hair was combed neatly into a tight bun at the back of her head. The wrinkles on her forehead were prominent as she furrowed her brow. She flipped through pages of notes before aligning the bottom edges of the sheets against the desk and straightening them into a neat pile. Removing her rectangular navy glasses from her nose, she placed them on top of her head. She glanced at Chloé, her brown eyes cast on her. She frowned and motioned Chloé to move. "Gemme, please stand in the center."

Chloé's stomach fell to the floor. Her feet were glued to the ground. Her mouth dried. Her palms broke out in a sweat.

Chloé swallowed.

She was the subject of the assembly.

"What—"

"It would be in your best interest if you saved your words for later," Sasha interrupted. "We've been waiting for quite some time now, so if you could please hurry on up and do as you're told, it would be greatly appreciated." She snapped her fingers, gesturing toward the center.

Chloé bit the inside of her cheek. She did her best to hide the trembling in her body, but she knew the other members were aware she was nervous and anxious. Those who stood in the center of the council's table were heavily interrogated and usually found guilty.

Chloé gripped her skirt, staring at the unlit candles that formed a circle around her. Standing in the center made her feel like an ant ready to be squashed underneath someone's boot. Chloé had never felt so insignificant.

The guards turned the knobs on the lamps until they barely glowed. With a snap of Licht's fingers, the small candles by each of the council members, and the ones by Chloé's feet, sparked to life. Harsh shadows were cast against the council members' faces.

Sasha placed her glasses back over her nose. "Thank you for the candle flames, Licht. Now that Chloé Gemme has finally joined us, we can proceed with this assembly."

"Do we need to waste any more time?" Baron asked. He ran his fingers through his black-and-gray hair. He was the same age as Sasha and her husband. "It's obvious enough what transpired here, and we have the culprit right in front of us."

Chloé bit her lip. She wanted to speak, but she knew better. She was not allowed to say anything until she was asked a question or given permission. If she let anything slip beforehand, it would be used against her, and they would probably deem her guilty on the spot.

"The people of Valquent already feel uncomfortable with the heavy baggage she brought into the city," Allen said. He leaned his cheek against his fist, his blond hair falling over one eye. "My wife is waiting for me at home with dinner already made. I'd like to finish this as fast as possible."

"Just because your wife made you dinner doesn't mean we should be hasty about this," William said. William and Allen were brothers and part of the Russell family. William was older than Allen by three years.

"But we've pretty much agreed to a decision, right?" Allen said. "What else is there to discuss?"

William tapped his fingers against the table and leaned against the backrest of his wooden chair. "Who is going to replace her?"

"Do we need someone to replace her?" Gwenevere

asked. She held her fingers close to the flame, observing her freshly done manicure. "She is so young that her input doesn't even matter anyway, especially with those things she brought in with her. How can we trust her judgment?"

"I find the company she brought into Valquent strange," William said. "I agree with Miss Percey."

Allen rolled his eyes. "You are just agreeing with her because you're trying to score brownie points."

Sasha cleared her throat. "Allen Russell, keep personal comments to yourself."

Allen shrugged and shook his head.

"Chloé may indeed be young, but if she were to be removed, then only my husband and I would represent the nixen. I find the representation unbalanced," Emilee said. Her turquoise eyes pierced through the darkness. "I do not agree with the decision of removing her."

"I will have to agree with my wife," Licht said. "And there is no one else amongst the nixen who could replace her."

"Surely there has to be at least one other family," William said.

"Other than the Gemme and Azure families, the rest are miners or artisans," Emilee stated.

Baron waved a hand. "If that's the case, just pick one and get them to be part of the council. They will automatically become an aristocrat."

Emilee narrowed her eyes. "That is an insult to us if you think we can just pick any family. Our families have been part of the council for generations. You cannot expect us to just pick another family willy-nilly and expect them to have the same resources and knowledge."

"Maybe we should keep her in the dungeons. She can *technically* still be part of the council, but she won't have free rein over the kingdom," Gwenevere said. She moved her hand away from the candle and leaned back into her seat and crossed her legs. She tucked her curly caramel hair behind her ear. "This way we won't have to worry about the unbalanced representation between humans and nixen."

"Perhaps it's time we ask Chloé Gemme if she has anything to say to defend herself," Sasha said. She pushed her candle forward. "Chloé Gemme, you may speak. You are allowed a single statement of defense."

Chloé opened her mouth before closing it. She had so much to ask. First, she didn't even know why she was being interrogated. Second, she was lost in the conversation between the other members. She was certain she hadn't done anything to jeopardize her position. She had clearly told Licht she was going to be on temporary hiatus to explore Etheria. Entering Valquent with others should not have raised any red flags. Both Mimi and Sage had been disguised as humans using Luka's and Owen's magic, so the only concern would've been Elliot and Minari.

"What, cat got your tongue?" Allen mocked.

Chloé clenched her fists. Allen had always dismissed her comments during council assemblies, so it was no surprise he didn't care if she was trying to collect her thoughts or not.

"Let the young lady speak," Baron said. "She is always respectful to you. You could learn a thing or two from her."

Allen scoffed. "Did you forget she brought *elves* with her? I don't think she deserves respect, especially not from anyone here."

31

The temperature in the room dropped. No one uttered a word. It was as if everyone was holding their breath, waiting for someone to break the ice. No one looked around; they were suddenly mesmerized by the sheets of paper in front of them.

"I want to know what charge I am being issued with," Chloé said. If everyone was going to pretend they weren't in this room, then she would be the one to remind them. No matter what they were saying, she was still a council member, and she deserved to know.

Allen cocked an eyebrow. "That is your statement of defense? Wanting to know what you're being charged with?"

Gwenevere chuckled. "Little nix isn't even aware of her situation."

"Did you not hear what I said earlier?" Allen asked.

Sasha pulled the candle back. "That is her statement of defense." She clasped her hands together, fingers intertwined, and placed them on the desk. "Chloé Gemme, you are being charged with neglect of your council duties, conspiring with Oasis, and threatening the safety of the kingdom of Etheria by allowing two elves into the walls of the capital. It was your duty as an aristocratic nix and council member to control any elves that breached the boundary between their mountains and our lands. Seeing as a small child was able to be within a mere few feet of these barbarians, we cannot allow you or the elves to roam free."

Chloé's eyes widened. *Those* were the reasons she was being treated like a criminal? They weren't even true. She looked toward Licht, expecting the older nix to make a statement, to defend why she hadn't attended the past council assemblies. He knew of the elves and the reason. Surely someone of her own race would defend her. But to her horror, Licht remained silent. He only looked at her. His lips were pressed into a straight line. She glanced over at Emilee, but she only shook her head, pressing her fingers against her forehead.

They weren't going to defend her. Even after trying to persuade the council members that it was unfair to have only the Azure family represent the nixen, they didn't care to shield her from lies.

"Multiple witnesses saw the interaction between the elves and the child and overheard your demand of treating the elves as equals. We cannot have someone with these kinds of views on the council," Sasha said. "Chloé Gemme, you are young and naive. It is unfortunate that as of today, your powers and position as a council member and an aristocratic nix will be revoked." Sasha pushed her candle forward once again. "Those in favor of nullifying Chloé Gemme's powers and position?"

Allen pushed his candle forward first, Gwenevere and William following shortly after. Baron, too, pushed his forward. Chloé looked at Licht and Emilee with pleading eyes. They were her last hope. She *needed* them to object to this verdict. She had so much she still needed to do as a council member. She'd promised to bring equality to both elves and chimeras.

Chloé's world crumbled as she saw Emilee push her candle forward. Licht had his fingertips against the saucer of the candle, but he didn't move. Instead, he smiled at Chloé.

"I have a suggestion," Licht said.

The council members snapped their heads toward Licht as if they hadn't been expecting an objection, not when it was obvious removing Chloé would have been in the council's favor.

"And what is this suggestion?" Baron asked.

"Chloé informed me she had the elves under control a while back. Oh, and that she was going to be on hiatus from council duties for about a month or so because she wanted to explore Etheria."

Sasha narrowed her eyes. "Why did you withhold that information from us?"

"It must have slipped my mind." Licht smiled. "It's not like that child was hurt, right?"

"There were numerous witnesses—"

"But which one of them actually saw what happened, William?" Licht asked, his voice dropping. "The child, as you saw, was unharmed. His mother clearly just didn't like what was going on."

Allen scoffed. "Of course you would defend her."

One corner of Licht's lips curled. "Allen Russell, I am more than twice your age; therefore, I have more than twice the experience you have. I suggest you hold your tongue."

"Was that a threat?"

"Merely a statement."

"So, you want Chloé to remain on the council?" Baron asked.

"Not only that, but why not have her bring the two elves back here? We can determine with our own eyes if they were tamed by her."

"Eyewitnesses stated they didn't see Chloé's magic-binding chokers on them," Gwenevere said. "They pose a substantial risk without their collars, and you want them to be here?"

"That can all be arranged, I am sure." Licht smiled at Chloé. "Return here with the two elves tomorrow at six in the evening. What do you say?" He pushed the candle forward, allowing her to speak.

Chloé took a deep breath. Her knees threatened to give out, but she kept her feet firmly on the ground. She formed her lips into an O shape before exhaling. This was the chance she needed, and she would not waste it. Chloé smirked. "Yes, this can all be arranged."

5
SORROW

Elliot kept his gaze on the door for a while after Chloé left. Minari hadn't lifted his arm. Minari's words echoed in Elliot's mind. It wasn't that Elliot didn't believe in Chloé; he just had this feeling in his gut. It twisted uncomfortably, preventing him from completely staying calm over Chloé's summons.

"Hey," Minari said. He squeezed Elliot's shoulder. "You okay?"

"Yeah . . ."

"Feeling hungry? We could grab everyone and head down to the dining hall."

Elliot shook his head. He felt drained, and he knew he wouldn't be able to stomach anything. "I think I want to sleep."

"All right then." Minari removed his hand from Elliot's shoulder and took hold of his wrist. The older elf lifted it so

Elliot's fingertips were at eye level. "But could you tell me what's going on? I've never seen you pick your fingers before."

Elliot pulled away, hiding his hands against his chest. "I don't know." He didn't know why or when he'd started to pick and peel, only that it kept the fraying nerves at bay.

Minari was silent before letting out a soft sigh. "What happened after we got separated in Venin? Inside Oasis's hideout . . ."

"Nothing happened," Elliot mumbled, his voice barely audible. Flashes of Charlotte appeared in his mind, and he shut his eyes. He desperately pushed the memories away, not wanting to recall what had happened between him and one of the captains of Oasis. He didn't want to recall her sinister smile, the lies she'd forced him to say, or the torture she'd made him endure.

Elliot didn't want to remember.

"I'm sorry. I didn't mean to upset you."

Elliot took in a shaky breath. "I want to rest. You can head down and eat with the others."

"I didn't mean to upset you."

"I'm not upset. I just—" Elliot bit his lip. "I'm just going to rest, and I know you're hungry, so . . ."

"All right. I'll be back after dinner. I'll bring some soup up for you in case you get hungry later."

"Mm."

Minari placed the key to the room on the left nightstand. "I'll leave this here if you decide to join us. Just lock up when you leave."

Elliot nodded, but he didn't move from his spot until he

heard Minari leave, the door clicking shut. His body snapped into motion, leading him toward the left bed. He kicked off his boots and crumpled onto the sheets. He curled up, bringing his knees to his chest. Exhaustion was quickly spreading across his body, and he allowed his eyes to close.

Elliot jolted up. His heart raced, thudding loudly against his chest. He looked around frantically, trying to see anything in the dark room. "No, no, no, no," he muttered under his breath. Why was he here? He crawled, hands gliding across the floor until he reached the wall. He stood, palms still resting against the cold stone.

Elliot continued onward, using his left hand as a guide as he pressed it against the wall. His leg bumped against a large, solid object, causing him to lose his balance. He yelped, tripping forward. He flung his arms forward, attempting to catch himself.

His body collided with something warm. Elliot heard a grunt and immediately froze. He bounced back, touching the unknown object in front of him. His heart raced. He had hoped he'd heard wrong, but it felt like someone's leg.

But it wasn't just anyone's.

It was Minari's.

Minari was here.

But why?

"Min-Minari?"

Another groan.

"What are you doing here?" Elliot wished he could see, but the room was pitch-black. He shifted his hands, moving up Minari's body, pausing when his fingertips met something wet.

A hiss came from Minari.

Elliot pulled away. Minari was bleeding.

"Minari! Minari, are you okay? What happened?"

The door to the chamber opened, and the loud creaking of the hinges sent chills down Elliot's spine. The light creeping in from the doorway allowed Elliot to see the damage done to Minari.

His friend had a gaping wound on his side and a gash on his shoulder. Minari was deathly pale. His lips were cracked, and his matted purple hair clung to his forehead. Sweat beaded down his temple. His scout's uniform was in tatters. His daggers were missing. Minari's eyes were shut, his brow furrowed in pain.

"Ah, so you're finally awake."

That chipper tone. Elliot knew it all too well.

He slowly turned his head, hoping it would be anyone else, but to his dismay, he came face-to-face with Charlotte. Charlotte, who he thought was dead. But maybe everything had been a dream. Maybe escaping Oasis and reuniting with everyone had been a dream—a sick and twisted dream. Perhaps they'd injected him with a substance that allowed his mind to project something so realistic that he'd truly believed it'd happened.

Elliot stood, blocking Minari.

Charlotte tilted her head. She had her quiver in her left hand and a bow in the other. "Were you thinking you could protect him?" She inched closer, her boots clicking loudly against the floor.

"D-don't touch him!" It was difficult for Elliot to speak. It was as if his throat were closing against every word he tried to say.

Charlotte chuckled. "Don't touch him? I already have. While you were taking a nap, I had him answer some of my questions."

Elliot paled. He turned back to Minari. Charlotte had tortured Minari while he was sleeping? But how? When had Minari been captured? How long had Elliot been out for?

Charlotte stopped, now only a few feet away from them. "Mistfall. Oracle. Prophecy. Do those ring a bell?"

"No!" Elliot reached for Minari, shaking his shoulders. "Minari, tell me this isn't true!"

Minari gasped and grunted. He reached up, taking hold of Elliot's wrist. Minari's grip was weak. He opened his eyes slowly, and Elliot's heart sank. Both of Minari's eyes were now gray.

Minari looked forward, eyes unfocused. "Elliot . . . ?" Minari turned his head in Elliot's direction. "Elliot? Are you all right?"

Elliot's breaths came out in spurts. His hands shook. His lungs ached. His body was heavy. The world spun, and his mind went blank. He couldn't think. He couldn't feel. Nothing mattered anymore. Charlotte knew everything. There was nothing left for him to protect.

He had failed as the oracle.

He had failed the prophecy.

He had failed to protect everything he held dear.

6
SUPPORT

Elliot gasped for air, eyes shooting open. His chest was tight and heavy, as if someone had placed a boulder over him and left him to suffocate. His head turned side to side, eyes scanning the surrounding room. The room was dark, but he could make out the mahogany wood walls. He could smell the light, musky scent of the sheets and blankets around him.

He was in the Twin Seasons Inn in Valquent.

Or so he hoped.

Flashes of the dream kept Elliot on edge. He could still vividly see how injured Minari was, how much Charlotte enjoyed seeing the two of them suffer. The fact that she *knew* about Mistfall, the prophecy, and the oracle made Elliot's stomach turn. He had told lies when he was held captive but hoped they had seemed truthful enough for them to believe him. The last thing he wanted them to know was how to get to Mistfall.

Elliot pushed the memories of the dream away, thinking about anything else. He collapsed back onto the bed, turning on his side. His mind wandered to his family, Lily, and Xeno. How were they doing? Were they thinking about him? Did they miss him? Was Xeno eating well?

The sudden sound of the door creaking open and the clicking of heels against the hardwood floor made Elliot's heart jump. He had forgotten that Minari had left the door unlocked when he'd left for dinner.

Elliot was facing the wall, his back to the room. He held his breath, keeping his body still.

The clicking came closer and closer, and the feeling of dread grew in his chest. Elliot shut his eyes, willing whoever was in the room to magically disappear.

"Are you asleep?"

Relief instantly washed over Elliot. He melted into the bed, no longer stiff with anxiety. He leaned up. "No, I'm awake. When did you get back?"

"Not too long ago. I ran into the others downstairs, and they told me you were up here." Chloé had a tray of food in her hands. It held a bowl, a loaf of bread, a cup, and a small candle. "I figured you hadn't eaten yet. Are you up for dinner? I had the kitchen make potato soup."

Elliot placed a hand over his stomach. He wasn't hungry, per se, but the idea of eating didn't repulse him. He nodded.

Chloé placed the tray on the table. She reached for the oil lamp in the center and turned the knob, illuminating the room. She took a seat in one of the two chairs.

Not bothering with his boots, Elliot made his way to the

other chair. His stomach grumbled at the scent of the fresh soup. The color was creamy, and it smelled delicious. He took a scoop, giving it a few puffs before putting it in his mouth.

"Good?" Chloé asked.

"Mm-hmm." Elliot took another spoonful. He reached for the bread and found it pleasantly warm.

"Is it still good? I specifically requested a fresh batch."

"It's still warm. Thank you." Elliot smiled.

"Of course!" Chloé placed her elbows on the tabletop. She laced her fingers together and rested her chin against them.

Elliot continued to eat. The silence between them was comforting.

It wasn't until Elliot finished his meal and sipped his water that Chloé broke the silence.

"I have some bad news."

Elliot pulled the drink away. "What is it?"

Chloé chewed her lip. "The council . . . They want me to bring you and Minari back with me. They want to see if you two are a threat."

"Is it because of what happened today?"

"Partially." Chloé leaned back, slouching against the chair. "It's also because you two are elves and aren't wearing my binding chokers."

Elliot rubbed the back of his neck. "Was it a bad idea to take them off?"

Chloé shook her head. "No. As long as we can prove you don't need it, it will help the fight for equality for all races." She smiled. "I can't fight for equality while having you two under my command. It would be contradictory." Her expression shifted. "I'm afraid . . . I'm afraid of what they might do to you."

Elliot stretched his arm out in front of him. "Give me your hand."

Chloé blinked before sitting up and placing her small hand over Elliot's.

Elliot placed his other hand on top of hers, enclosing it. "I know how stressful this might be for you, but I want you to remember that you aren't alone. Not only am I here, but everyone else is too. Minari, Mimi, Sage, Luka, Owen . . . I want you to rely on us. When the burden becomes too heavy and you can't bear it alone anymore, come to us. I know I may not be able to do much compared to the others, but I'm pretty good at listening."

Chloé's eyes started to well, and a blush crept across her cheeks. She turned away and tried to pull her hand out of Elliot's grasp, but he tightened his hold. He smiled as he saw the slightest tremors from Chloé's shoulders. Silent tears fell down her cheeks.

Chloé must have been immensely worried over the fact that the council had given her the sudden request. Though Elliot did not know what Chloé was going through as a member, he understood the weight of responsibilities that were asked of her by others.

It was difficult, but having the support of friends always helped ease the burden.

7
COMRADE

Luka sipped his tea, tuning out the ambient buzz whirling around the dining hall in the Twin Seasons Inn. It was crowded with traders and travelers. But word had spread quickly; not one party sat at any of the tables near them.

Luka and Owen had recast the illusion spell over Mimi and Sage before venturing downstairs, so it wasn't those two who made them nervous.

Minari sat across from him, tearing the loaf of bread in half before taking a bite. The loud crunching echoed throughout the hall.

The elf did not care about the stares or murmurs that were cast at him. He continued to eat as if he were the only one in the room.

"Humans have interesting ways of eating," Sage said. He picked up his spoon, eyeing it. "Why use this when you can just lift the bowl to your mouth?"

"Table manners," Owen answered.

Sage scoffed. "Why does it matter? The whole point of eating is to feed yourself. How you do it shouldn't matter."

Mimi elbowed Sage. "Just do it. We'd stick out too much if we didn't use them."

Sage scratched the back of his neck. "Having this stupid itch is already bothersome. And now I have to worry about table manners?"

Mimi rolled his eyes. He held his spoon and used it to taste his chicken soup. His face scrunched up. "It's so . . . flavorful."

"It smells just as much," Sage commented.

Minari was about to take another bite of his bread when he paused. He straightened his back but kept his eyes on his food.

A hand slammed down on the table, causing the bowls to jitter.

"Hey, you, *elf*. Who said you can eat our food?" A large gruff man leaned his hip against the edge of the table. He crossed his arms, puffing his chest out. His black-and-gray beard had crumbles of food mixed in its curls.

Minari stayed still, not saying a word and not making eye contact.

"Did you hear me talking, or are you deaf? Or maybe you can't understand what I'm saying." The man looked over at Sage. "Why do you lot subject yourself to this scum?"

Luka pressed his knee against Sage, signaling him to stay quiet. He could tell from Sage's clenched fists and stiff shoulders that he wasn't afraid to sock the older man.

46

Luka cleared his throat. "Is there something about him that bothers you?"

The man cocked his eyebrow. He shifted his lips, moving a toothpick from one side to the other. "What 'bothers' me is there's an elf in this inn. This inn does not allow elves."

"And what gives you the right to determine that?"

"Aye, Scott!" another man shouted. "Maybe they're trying to sell the elf off! We ought to get in on some of that coin."

Scott's eyes lit up. He pulled the toothpick from his mouth. "I know about chimeras being sold, but an elf would probably bring in more money. Is that why he's with you?"

Luka stared at Scott, his eyes narrowing and lips pulling into a frown. "You think we would stoop so low as to sell living beings for money? You humans disgust me."

"What did you say to me?" Scott pointed his chin at Luka. "You think just because you're an ethereal that you're above us or something? Humans run the lands here. We make the rules. You're lucky you can even stay in this kingdom."

Minari suddenly stood. The chair legs scraped loudly against the floor. Scott opened his mouth but shut it as soon as his eyes locked with Minari's.

The elf's glare was cold and sharp. His lips were pressed into a line. If looks could kill, Scott wouldn't have had the time to even take another breath.

Scott's face scrunched before he spit in Minari's face, but the elf stayed unmoving, gaze still locked on the bald man. "Don't think this is over." Scott shoved his hands into his pockets before stomping off to join his party.

Minari rubbed the back of his hand against his cheek, staying silent. He took his water cup, chugging it before slamming it against the table. He turned to leave, but he wasn't going back upstairs.

He left the inn.

"Where is he going?" Sage asked.

"Hmm," Luka mused. "I will go check on our friend. Don't worry about waiting for us to return. Feel free to retire for the night."

Luka weaved through the crowd of people. They had all started to disperse once Minari had left the dining hall. But Luka was quicker, his legs allowing him to take long strides.

The front of the inn was empty, and it didn't take long before a few patrons joined the ethereal outside.

"Where did your friend go?" Scott asked.

Luka sighed. Sometimes humans could be so bothersome. "As you can see, he is not here."

"Obviously. Didn't you leave to find him?"

"No, why would I do that? He is more than capable of taking care of himself. I merely left to get some fresh air."

"Why, you! Are you mocking us?" Scott balled his hands.

Luka sighed. Humans tended to be hostile, especially when it came to riches. Greed easily swayed them.

"What's going on here?" An officer approached the inn. Luka recognized him as the same person who had informed Chloé of the impromptu council assembly.

Scott immediately relaxed his fits. "Nothing."

The officer raised a brow. "Then what's the ruckus about?"

"We don't want any trouble, officer," Scott said, shrugging.

"If you've had too much to drink, then perhaps it's best

to retire or return home. It's late, and I don't want to have to drag you to the cells."

Scott glanced at the others with him before shrugging. "Don't have to tell us twice. We don't want any trouble."

Luka smirked, watching the suddenly tamed humans retreat inside. The way they behaved when in the presence of authority was like night and day. He was thankful the officer had been there. It would've been tiresome if Luka had had to deal with Scott and his friends himself. Using too much of his power left his body weak and his eyelids heavy, and having to still sprinkle his magic on Mimi while he was inside and Luka was outside was already putting a strain on his core.

"I don't smell any alcohol on you," the officer said, approaching Luka. "Were they harassing you?"

"You could say that."

The two stayed silent, neither of them moving. Luka wondered why the officer hadn't left yet. He wanted to find Minari, but not when the officer was around.

"Do you plan on returning to the Snowy Hills?"

"What?" Luka tilted his head.

"Luka Yunmei, you and Owen Ko both left Oasis. All the officers around Etheria know this. It is unusual for any officer of an official guild recognized by the king himself to leave."

"Ah." Luka turned, fully facing the officer. "I plan to return home eventually, so yes."

"Is there a reason you are with Miss Gemme? Actually, I find your group . . . rather strange."

"Though it is not discouraged to be curious, sometimes curiosity is best left being curious."

49

The officer blinked, his mouth opening and closing. He broke into a chortle. "All right, I can tell when I'm not wanted. Well, have a good night." He lifted his hat, giving Luka a small nod before leaving.

Luka unlatched the lock to the stables, allowing himself through. The stables ran deep and long, with fifteen stalls on each side. Luka spotted Chloé's mare near the center stall, but he did not see Minari's ovis near her.

His eyes scanned the stalls, head turning back and forth as he walked deeper into the stables.

He spotted the large animal at the very end. He was secluded, shoved into the corner stall away from the other animals, and could be easily missed by the stable boy if he didn't realize there was another animal besides the ones in the front.

Luka found Minari resting against the ovis. The elf was nestled against the ovis's body. His eyes were closed, fingers intertwined and hands against his stomach.

"How did you find me?" Minari asked, eyes still closed.

"Chance." Luka remained outside the stall, not wishing to disturb the two.

Minari's purple and gray orbs cracked open, peering at Luka through the darkness.

"Xander was in here without food or water. I had to feed and water him myself."

"It's unfortunate your steed was treated in such a way." Luka wasn't surprised. There was no hiding the fact that the innkeeper didn't care to take care of anything of Minari's. The stall Xander was in was empty and didn't seem to be well kept.

Minari sat up, twisting his body to stroke Xander's fur. "I needed to get away before I stabbed someone. He was lucky my daggers were in the room."

Luka smiled. "I do not blame you. They were obnoxious."

"Obnoxious. Ignorant. Annoying."

"Humans are one of a kind. It's a wonder what Azar was thinking of when he created them."

Minari chuckled. "I'm going to have to tell Alder he needs to knock some sense into his brother."

Luka's eyes widened. "You are on close terms with the demigod of earth?"

"In a way." Minari stood, stretching out his arms. "You're talkative. This is probably the most I've heard you speak. It's usually the others who talk until their mouths fall off."

Luka covered his lips with the back of his hand, stifling a chuckle. "There are times I would much rather listen than interject. It's a good way to gather information, though I find a lot of the gossip around the kingdom to be just that: empty gossip."

The sudden tug of Luka's core reminded him he was still using his magic on Mimi. He pressed a hand against his chest, slowing down the flow of stamina leaving his body. He still had time, but just enough to return to the room. He hoped the rest of the group had retired in case any accidents occurred.

Minari eyed Luka curiously. "Something wrong?"

Luka cleared his throat. "I should probably return. I can feel my power draining from casting the illusion spell. It takes a toll on my body if I am too far from the subject."

"You didn't have to look for me."

"No, I did not, but I wanted to."

"Thank you."

Luka's lips curled upward. "Of course."

Luka had observed the way Minari tried to shoulder Elliot's burdens, doing anything he could to bring the younger elf's mood up. Ever since the Oasis incident, the oracle's mood had shifted to one full of darkness and hopelessness. Sometimes Luka would catch Elliot looking over his shoulder as if someone were following him. He would catch Elliot groaning in his sleep from nightmares. The elf barely had an apetite most of the time.

The elves were extremely young compared to the ethereal, and they were traveling into a land unknown to them. Luka wanted to be the one to alleviate any unnecessary stressors.

It was the least he could do to amend for his actions while he and Owen were a part of Oasis.

And the least he could do as a warrior of the oracle.

8
ACHE

Minari leaned against the wall, left leg propped up to support his arm. It was still early morning, and the sun was barely starting to crack into the sky.

Minari twisted the small object around in his left palm a few times before running his thumb across the carvings in the wooden pendant. He had yet to return the birthday gift to Elliot.

He'd wanted to at first, when Elliot had first awoken in Ruglow, but he'd decided against it. It wasn't right to return the gift when he couldn't even admit the truth. Minari wanted to hide the fact that Lily was a Necromancer for as long as possible.

But Elliot deserved to know.

The longer he hid the truth, the worse it was going to be.

"It's going to have to be sooner rather than later, huh?"

Minari whispered to himself.

He tucked the pendant back into his coat.

"And I need to be there by six tonight," Chloé said.

"I don't like the sound of this," Minari said. He crossed his arms. "It sounds like a trap."

"Unfortunately, we don't have a choice." Chloé frowned. "They don't trust you two, but I can use this as a chance to show them that elves deserve the same treatment."

Minari's rest had been interrupted by a sudden knock on the door. He had been awake for a while, simply staring at the ceiling, before his thoughts were broken by the noise.

Elliot stirred awake from the unexpected noise. He looked around the room with groggy eyes before looking at Minari and plopping back down in bed, pulling the covers over his head.

Minari chuckled. Elliot was slowly becoming not a morning person.

The older elf listened closely to the voices on the other side of the door. His ears picked up the quiet murmurs of Mimi's whispers and Chloé's sighs. Though he only heard two distinct voices, he sensed more bodies beyond the door.

The elves were greeted by Chloé, Mimi, Sage, Luka, and Owen when they entered the room. Chloé seated herself at the small table while the others gathered around.

It took a solid twenty minutes for Elliot to make it out of bed and into the vacant chair.

How Elliot had managed to stay sleeping with the commotion and amount of people in the room was a mystery to

Minari.

"Maybe we can think up a plan in case anything happens," Elliot said. He looked up at Minari. "If they ask us questions or try to do something, then at least we'll be prepared."

"And do you think they'll listen to us? Nothing is stopping them from flat-out not believing anything we say."

Chloé propped her cheek against her hand. "It's going to happen, which is why Elliot's idea is probably the best thing we can do for now."

"You want us to devise a plan in a few hours?" Minari asked.

"Do you have any better ideas?"

Minari placed his hands on his hips, pacing back and forth. Elliot and Chloé were right. Their hand was being forced, and going into the assembly ready for any outcome was the only thing they could do. Best-case scenario: they would return to the inn in one piece. Worst-case scenario . . . Minari didn't want to think about it.

They might ask where he and Elliot had come from and what their purpose was in the lower lands. Those were all logical questions, and answering them would be simple enough. But if they were fishing for a specific response to paint them in a negative light, then they would need to change up their game plan. They would need to shift gears and adapt to their field. They would be mere pieces in the council's board game, and they would need to do everything they could to reach the final square before the others.

"You're going to dig a hole in the floor if you keep that up," Chloé said.

Minari's feet halted. "I was thinking of ideas."

"For tonight?" Elliot asked.

Minari nodded. "We'll have to form a counterattack of sorts."

"The council isn't going to actually attack you." Chloé frowned. "They'll just ask questions."

"You don't know that."

"I know—"

"You threw us into the *dungeon* the first day you met us, not to mention you threatened us with your pistols."

Chloé snapped her lips shut, sinking down into her chair, her red eyes downcast.

"Why did she throw you two in the dungeon?" Sage asked.

"It's a long story." Elliot smiled sheepishly.

"I don't feel confident entering the council assembly without my daggers, but I know I won't be allowed in with them." Minari shifted his attention to Elliot. "Do you think you'll be able to use your magic if they get offensive?"

Elliot's eyes widened, and his eyebrows rose. "Magic?"

"Like what you did with the scorpion. You created something like a barrier."

"I-I'm not sure if I can." Elliot rubbed his arm and shifted his gaze down to the table. "I don't remember how I did it . . . I don't think I can do it again." He shook his head. "No . . . I can't use magic."

"Elliot?" Minari placed a hand on the younger elf's shoulder.

Elliot jerked, yelping at the sudden contact. Minari quickly pulled his hand away. He stared at Elliot, mouth agape.

Had Elliot just flinched?

Elliot curled in on himself, holding his arms and bouncing his foot. He began mumbling incoherent words.

Luka rushed to Elliot's side, kneeling beside him. He placed a pale hand on Elliot's forehead. His fingertips glowed. "Elliot, calm down."

Elliot's pinched expression relaxed against Luka's touch. His body swayed, falling into Luka's chest. Luka moved his hand from Elliot's forehead to his chest. His brow furrowed, his lips pressing into a thin line.

"What is it?" Minari asked.

"I had a suspicion about what may have been causing Elliot's distress, and it seems my suspicion was correct."

Minari tensed. A possible answer to Elliot's recent agitated behavior.

Luka removed his hand. "Back in Oasis's hideout, Namir embedded a piece of her dark matter in Elliot's core, and it can, at times, alter his perception of reality. It is highly likely that he thinks he is back in Namir's grasp."

"Is that why Elliot doesn't think he can use magic?" Minari sighed. "Because of what happened back then . . . ?"

"It is not my place to say what happened to him, but let's just say Charlotte was not kind to him."

A weight seemed to have been dropped over Minari's chest, and it crushed his breath. His stomach tightened and twisted. He pressed his palm against his mouth and swallowed slowly, urging the queasiness to settle.

"Are you all right? You look like you're about to faint," Mimi said.

Minari took a breath through his nose. He gave a small

nod before bolting out of the room and running down the stairs.

He paid no heed to the shoulders he bumped into. He ignored the angry shouts directed toward him for not paying attention to where he was going.

His mind spiraled in different directions, clouding over in a fog. He couldn't think, yet he was thinking too much.

Minari suddenly found himself inside the inn's stables at Xander's stall. The ovis detected his owner's presence and made his way to the open window. Xander nudged Minari's cheek with his snout.

With trembling hands, Minari stroked Xander's head.

Minari wanted to scream. He wanted to yell. He wanted to shout. But his throat had seized up, locking away his voice instead. His vision started to blur, and he let out a shaky breath. Warm tears flowed down his chin.

It had not taken much for Minari to realize what Luka had said, and he probably hadn't realized it before because there was no physical proof of what had happened. Luka and Mimi had the ability to heal, so there was no evidence of what had transpired.

But Minari knew.

The reason for Elliot's agitation.

The reason for Elliot's withdrawal.

The reason for Elliot's change in behavior.

And Minari didn't want to imagine what Elliot had had to bear at the hands of *humans*.

9
TRIAL

"Are they armed?"

"No, there are no weapons on them," Chloé answered.

The guarding officer raised a skeptical brow, eyeing the two elves—especially Minari—up and down. "You sure?"

Minari narrowed his eyes at the questioning officer. His hair was black and slicked back in oil. Minari's nose scrunched at the officer's sour breath. He deeply wanted to shove the officer out of the way and tell him he had come unarmed, but if he hadn't come empty-handed, the officer should have thought twice before questioning them again.

Chloé pressed her foot against Minari's, and he relaxed his eyes. He looked away, bringing his eyes to the ground.

The officer sneered. "If anything happens, you know the consequences, Miss Gemme."

"We'll be late to the council assembly if you keep us any

longer, so if you don't mind . . ." Chloé smiled.

The officer rolled his eyes. He pulled the doors open, allowing the three of them through.

"There are a few things you two need to know," Chloé started, taking the lead down the hall. "You're not allowed to speak unless given permission. They use candles to show when you can talk. If you utter even the smallest noise when it's not your turn, they can deem you guilty. In this case, assume you are a threat." She stopped in her tracks. "Just keep your head low, and don't make eye contact with anyone."

"So, just act like we did before," Minari said. "Shouldn't you have told us that before we got here?"

"I would have, but you disappeared." Chloé frowned. "Or did you forget you ran out?"

Minari bit the inside of his cheek, turning away.

He had returned to the inn mere minutes before he, Elliot, and Chloé had to leave for the assembly hall. He hadn't meant to be gone for that long. He just wanted a space to clear his head, and he had somehow fallen asleep by Xander's side. By the time he woke up, the sun had already started to set, and, unsurprisingly, there was still no food or water in Xander's stall. He'd had to gather some himself and feed his ovis.

Minari peered at Elliot. He hadn't had a chance to see what Namir's dark matter had done to the younger elf.

Elliot was looking at Chloé, but he shifted his pale blue eyes to Minari. He tilted his head and gave Minari a small smile.

Elliot was picking his fingers.

His hands were in front of him, the fingernail of his thumb pulling at the skin of his index finger. He was digging into the skin as if he didn't feel any pain.

"How are you feeling?" Minari asked.

"Fine."

Fine.

"Nervous?"

Elliot shook his head. He kept his eyes on Minari as he tugged a piece of skin off his finger. The surrounding area began to seep a small flow of blood. "I'm fine."

Minari internally grimaced, but he forced his lips upward. "Y-yeah? I'm a little nervous."

"As long as we follow what Chloé told us, we should be fine."

Fine.

"Are you two ready?" Chloé asked. "It's about time."

"Ready," Elliot said, moving his hands to rest at his sides.

"Yeah, let's get this over with. I haven't eaten anything, so I could use some food as soon as we get back."

Chloé led them to the large double doors. Unlike the doors leading inside the building, these were unguarded. It was odd considering how many officers patrolled the streets of Valquent; they'd bumped into one almost every ten steps they took. Considering the council was behind these double doors, they should've had at least one officer acting as a guard.

Minari's entire body chilled as soon as the doors opened. It was like a gust of frigid air had blown past them. The intense stares were in unison as they gazed upon them. Not only was the room filled with council members, but with officer guards as well.

"Chloé, thank you for bringing in the two elves," a human woman said. "For this assembly, you will be allowed back in your seat. The two elves must stand in the center."

"Thank you, Sasha." Chloé ushered Elliot and Minari inside the circle of candles before she took her seat next to another nix with maroon hair. If Minari's memory was right, the nix's name was Licht. Licht Azure.

Chloé cleared her throat, tilting her head slightly down. She crossed her legs.

Minari mentally cursed and quickly tucked his chin in.

There was a snap of fingers, and the light dimmed while the candles around their feet were set ablaze.

"On your knees," Sasha said.

Minari's body jerked at the sudden order. A foreign weight suddenly fell on his shoulders, and his legs moved on their own, forcing him down onto his knees. It was as if invisible wires were attached to his limbs and controlling him like a puppet.

"Sasha—"

"Chloé, you may be in your seat, but remember your position is in a delicate place right now," Sasha interrupted. "It would be wise if you let us ask the questions and let *them* answer."

"I'd like to ask the first question," a man said. "We received notes from the late Oasis officer Charlotte. They talked about an oracle. They also said that the elf with green hair here is the oracle."

Minari's blood ran cold. He tried to turn to look at Elliot, but whatever was holding him prevented him from moving his head.

"We have the leader of the savages here?" It was a woman's voice. "Allen, you've got to be kidding me."

"That is what Charlotte's notes said," Allen said.

"Having the oracle in front of us, it's almost as if Chloé is giving us a chance to vanquish the threat," said another man.

"I like how you think, William," the woman said.

"Gwenevere, are you really flirting with my brother?" Allen asked.

"I'm simply agreeing with him."

Minari tried to force his body up, to speak, but no matter how much he struggled, the hold on him seemed to grow stronger. He opened his mouth to speak, but he suddenly felt a grip around his neck. It squeezed around his throat, and tears prickled the corners of his eyes. He couldn't breathe.

"Oh? I think the one with purple hair is trying to talk," Allen mocked.

"Do we even want to hear anything he says?" Gwenevere asked. "The other one is the oracle, right? I say we get rid of this one and interrogate the other one."

"As amusing as this all is, the whole reason we brought them here was to prove they aren't a threat," a deep voice said.

"Baron is right. We should at least give them a chance to defend themselves," Licht said.

"Release your magic," Baron said.

"Right now? But it's so fun watching him struggle."

Him? Was Minari the only one fighting the invisible hold? What was Elliot doing? His chest burned, and darkness danced around his vision.

"Well, depending on what happens here, your fun may continue later," Sasha said.

"Fine."

There was a snap of fingers.

Minari gasped for air. He fell forward, his body suddenly light as it was released from Licht's hold, and stopped his fall with his hands. The candle flames flickered from the movement.

"I'm surprised by how calm the green-haired one is," Allen said. "Even as his friend here was choking, he didn't try to move an inch."

Catching his breath, Minari turned to face Elliot.

He was still kneeling. His eyes were still staring at the ground, and his body was completely still.

Elliot clasped his hands together in his lap.

And tilted his chin up.

10
MIRAGE

Oracle. Oracle. *Oracle.*

The word echoed in his head.

Elliot was the oracle. He was the oracle tasked with fulfilling the prophecy. He had to gather warriors—*his* warriors. The oracle's four warriors were vital in succeeding. He needed them to be able to put a stop to the Necromancers. To Mykronos.

To the Dark God.

Elliot's breath caught in his throat as he saw a sway of gold in his peripheral vision. Suddenly, everything around him stilled. He lifted his head. Chloé was to his right, almost at the end of the table. Her face was filled with worry as she looked down at him and Minari. But she was frozen. Her bottom lip was stuck between her teeth, and her hand was clenched on the desk.

There was an empty seat to her left, but on her other side was a nix Elliot remembered as Licht. Licht had paid him and Minari a visit in the dungeons in Blanc Grotto. He wore a small smile on his face, and his eyes sparkled with excitement.

Next to him was another nix, though Elliot didn't recognize her. Her hair was a deep, rich shade of red, and she had sharp turquoise eyes that seemed to pierce through the darkness.

Elliot turned his body, taking in the surrounding members of the council. There were five other members, all human. Two of them were older than the rest. Creases of experience lined their faces, and streaks of knowledge were tangled in their hair. The female was seated in the center, right in front of Elliot, while the male was to her right.

They were all frozen as well, and the looks they wore sent shivers down Elliot's spine.

Elliot checked on Minari to his left, and he, too, was frozen in time. He was on his knees, head bowed, showing submission.

A flash of gold appeared again, behind Minari this time.

Elliot jerked in that direction.

And came face-to-face with a familiar grin.

"Hello, my little oracle."

Namir.

Elliot scrambled to his feet, backing away from the chimera. How did she get in here?

"Ah, not happy to see me?" Namir tilted her head, tapping her cheek with a finger. "And here I thought we could be friends."

"What—How—When—" Elliot had a million things he

wanted to say, but they were stuck in his throat.

"You and I are one, you could say."

What?

"Back in Oasis—"

Elliot flinched.

Namir's eyes flashed. "A sensitive word?" She circled around Elliot, her strides long and graceful. "Hmm, I guess it's to be expected, considering what happened to you." She stopped behind Elliot. Her hands crept around his waist and up his chest. Her warm body pressed against his back.

"I didn't mean to startle you, Oracle," Namir whispered in his ear. "I want to help . . . ease your pain."

Elliot held his breath. Namir's fingers glided up, her claws caressing his neck.

"It hurts, doesn't it? Needing to be someone you aren't. Needing to live up to expectations. The darkness that swallows your mind . . . I can help you, if you wish."

It was true that Elliot's future had been predetermined, and there were parts of him that didn't like it. Disliked it. *Hated* it. He wasn't allowed to follow the path *he* wanted because of some prophecy.

The future he deeply wanted had been stripped from him. It didn't matter if he wanted the role he'd been given; he'd been *forced* to take it. He'd been kicked out of Mistfall because he had to fulfill the prophecy.

Why had he been chosen? Why couldn't someone else have done it? Minari would have been a perfect match. He had the knowledge of a leader and the skills of a scout. He wouldn't have gotten captured by the Outlawers and then held captive by Oasis. No. He would've outsmarted them.

"Well, Oracle? I'm waiting. I could make everything disappear for you." Namir released him and crouched beside Minari. She ran her fingers through his purple hair. "You want him to be the oracle? I could easily make it happen."

"What?"

Namir chuckled. "Like I said before, we are one. I can hear your thoughts."

"No!" Elliot reached for Namir's wrist, pulling her hand away. "No. I am the oracle. It's my responsibility, no one else's."

Namir hummed. "Is that what you truly desire?" She placed her free hand on top of Elliot's, sliding her fingers across his. "You think you can do anything with these hands? The same ones you purposely mangled? Are you sure?"

Elliot pulled away, glaring at Namir.

"A fickle one, but no matter. I know how to get what I want."

Elliot blinked, and he was suddenly back on his knees. He watched the candlelight in front of him flicker ever so slightly.

"I'm surprised how calm the green-haired one is," a voice said. "Even as his friend here was choking, he didn't try to move an inch."

Elliot moved his hands from beside him to his lap. He intertwined his fingers and took a deep breath. His fingers were battered, but he wouldn't let that stop him. He was the oracle. He had a purpose, a role to fulfill.

He wouldn't hide anymore.

He wouldn't run anymore.

He was the oracle.

And it was time he acted like one.

Elliot tilted his chin up and smiled.

11
CHANCE

Elliot scanned the room, and he didn't falter. His gaze landed on everyone around him, their eyes meeting momentarily before he moved on to another member.

"This one is more annoying than the other one," the younger woman sneered. She tucked a caramel curl behind her ear and crossed her arms.

The older male pushed his candle forward. "Elf, we would like to confirm that what Allen said is true. Are you the oracle?"

Whispers to the left caught Elliot's attention. He peered over, and the two younger males were whispering to each other. One of them must have been Allen.

"Yes," Elliot said.

Tension flooded the room. The officers that were around the room gripped the hilts of their swords, ready to move on order.

Elliot could feel Minari's stare on him, but he didn't let that sway him. He kept his face forward, his attention focused.

The woman beside one of the males raised her hand. The officers relaxed but kept their suspicion on Elliot. "What would you like to do with him after hearing that?" she asked. "He confessed it himself."

"Sasha, you know what the oracle is! Why are you asking Baron that?" the woman sitting at the other end of the table asked.

"Gwenevere, if I may," Licht said.

"Tch."

"Let us not get too hasty. He did say he was the oracle, but nothing has happened to us yet," Licht said. "So let us say we are safe for now."

"What do you have in mind?" the man beside Gwenevere asked.

"Nothing yet. I just want to ask my share of questions before we set down the hammer. Unless you're thinking otherwise, William?"

"Kill them. Plain and simple."

"I don't want to think what might happen if we continue to let them roam around," Gwenevere said, leaning back in her chair, a scowl spreading across her features.

"Afraid?" Licht smiled. "Our little Chloé here has been with them for, what, two months now? I'm sure there's nothing to be afraid of. If they wanted to do something, they would've already done so. I'm positive there is nothing to fear when it comes to these two."

"Carry on, Licht," Baron said. He pulled his candle back.

Licht pushed his forward. "Why did Charlotte write you were the oracle in her notes?"

"Because I told her."

"I find that information a little odd to be throwing around, especially when the oracle doesn't quite have a positive reputation around here."

"The oracle isn't what you may think."

Licht's eyes widened, lips curling. "Oh? Are you insinuating something?"

"I mean what I said; the oracle isn't what you think."

"The oracle is the leader of the savages," Gwenevere said. "There's nothing else to it. You're going to bring down all the beasts from the mountains and cause another war!"

"That's a lie." Elliot clenched his fists in his lap. "We aren't going to cause a war."

"Ha! The elf wants us to believe him," Gwenevere said. "Unbelievable."

"Chloé, I'd like to hear your opinion on this," Sasha said.

"Y-yes." Chloé straightened up in her seat.

"What made you determine these two weren't a threat when you found them?"

"I kept a close eye on them while we walked around Blanc Grotto. I made sure nothing happened."

"Hmm," Licht mused. "Are you sure nothing happened?"

"Nothing happened."

Licht looked at Chloé, smiling at her before continuing. "If you say so. Moving on, from what I have heard, you had your magic-binding chokers on them when you three left Blanc Grotto."

"That's correct."

"And right now, the chokers are no longer around their necks. Care to tell us why?"

"I feel the collars were inhuman and unnecessary, especially when they meant no harm when they traveled to the lower lands."

"So, you granted them autonomy based on merit?"

"I believe it was the right thing to do. And if I may, I believe elves and chimeras should be treated as equals. There is no reason for the unfair treatment."

"Little girl, did you forget what happened, or did the history lessons fly over your head?" William asked.

"If there is no reason for unfair treatment," Licht said, eyeing William before returning his attention to Chloé, "then have you ever visited their home?"

"I . . ."

The room waited for the nix's response. Elliot knew the question that was going to come after. It didn't matter what answer Chloé gave them. They wanted to know where Mistfall was, just like Charlotte.

"Have you or have you not?" Licht asked again.

"No." Chloé shook her head.

Licht smirked. "And do you think that is fair treatment from them? You graciously allowed them to wander the lower lands, yet they can't do the same for you?"

"I haven't asked to be shown the mountains."

"And why is that? You said you wanted to explore Etheria. The mountains count as being part of Etheria."

Chloé narrowed her eyes. "The mountains aren't considered part of the kingdom. King Leonard VI doesn't have jurisdiction there."

"The mountains aren't part of the kingdom, no, but they're still part of Etheria itself. You didn't specify if you wanted to explore the kingdom or Etheria itself."

"It sounds like the oracle cast a spell on Chloé. He planted a worm in her mind, making her think these things," William said.

Panic welled up in Elliot's chest. He held his breath.

"And what better way to overthrow a kingdom than to plant yourself within the inner walls?" Sasha said.

Elliot gripped his pant leg. This wasn't how it was supposed to play out. He needed to figure out a way to turn the narrative around. Licht's candle was still at the edge of the table.

"That's—"

"Actually," Allen started, interrupting Elliot, "in Charlotte's notes, it's written that the oracle plans to start a war."

"That's a lie!" Chloé exclaimed. She stood from her seat, slamming the table. "Everything Charlotte wrote was a lie!"

"What makes you think so?" Allen cocked a brow. "What reason does Charlotte have to lie about this?"

Chloé glared at Allen. Her shoulders shook.

"Be seated, Chloé," Sasha said. "Getting agitated over this will not end well for either you or these two. Remember the reason that brought you three here."

Chloé bit her lip as she resumed her position.

"Charlotte forced me to confess certain things, whether it was the truth or not," Elliot blurted. "When I was captured by Oasis, she tortured me."

"Elliot . . ." Minari whispered.

Elliot had never told Minari what had happened because

he didn't want to remember and didn't want Minari to worry. He knew the older elf would've sulked for weeks if he'd learned the truth.

Elliot flashed Minari a comforting smile.

"There's no information about being tortured in her notes," Allen deadpanned.

"Do you have any proof she tortured you?" Sasha asked.

Elliot shook his head. "No. I was lucky enough to heal from the wounds."

"So, we have nothing to go on but your word," Baron said. "On what premise should we take your word over a captain's?"

Elliot held his tongue. He couldn't think of anything in response. He understood that they were going to always trust one of their own over an outsider. Because Chloé had associated with them, even she was under suspicion. Was there nothing he could do to persuade them?

"Not even worth our time," Gwenevere said.

Suddenly, the temperature dropped, and the candles blew out, submerging the room into complete darkness. There were murmurs amongst the officers, yet the council members remained silent. Footsteps echoed behind the double doors, moving closer and closer.

Until they stopped right outside.

The doors burst open, spilling light from the outside.

"Ragnar," Sasha said, "it's wonderful for you to finally join us."

12
PLAY

Ragnar held his head up, turning his chin as his gray eyes scanned the room. His long straight lilac hair was pulled back in a half updo. The castle robe draped off his shoulders gracefully. It was indigo, and gold ornaments decorated the sides. A single gold diamond earring hung off his left ear.

"Sasha, it has been too long," Ragnar said.

"Why're you here?" Gwenevere asked. "You never come to council assemblies."

Ragnar smiled at Gwenevere like a parent would at their child if they were to give them the least bit of acknowledgement. He ignored her, waltzing straight to Elliot and Minari. "Finally, a council assembly worth attending."

"Ragnar, one of these elves confessed to being the oracle," Baron said. "We were deciding what to do with him."

Chloé leaned forward in her seat. If anyone within the

council could help her, it would be Ragnar. Luka had mentioned that ethereals had a totally different set of records in their libraries—records that hadn't been altered by the hands of power. Ragnar should know what the oracle truly was.

"Oh?" Ragnar's eyes lit up. "This one?" He placed his hand on top of Elliot's head.

"Yes, that one," Baron said.

"So, you're the great leader of the savages."

What? Chloé blinked. What had Ragnar just said? Did he not know about the prophecy? But Ragnar had to be older than both Luka and Owen. Why wouldn't he know?

Ragnar's slim fingers glided through Elliot's pale green hair before resting behind his neck. "I can feel you tensing. You should relax, else I would feel threatened by you. I could easily snap your neck, you know."

In the blink of an eye, Minari had moved from his position, unsheathing a dagger. But Ragnar caught Minari's wrist. He gave the elf a smirk.

Chloé's blood drained from her face. Her mouth felt dry, and her throat tightened.

Minari had brought in a weapon even after she had repeatedly warned him not to. She'd even told the officer outside that they hadn't brought any weapons with them, and now her word was no longer valid. There was no reason the council would trust her.

Minari had ruined any sliver of hope they'd had at gaining the council's trust.

"Ragnar," Chloé started, standing up. "Please don't do anything to Elliot."

Ragnar turned his smile to Chloé. He squeezed Minari's

wrist, causing him to drop his dagger. It clattered against the hard floor. "So, you know their names? Who is this one then?"

"Minari."

His gray orbs scanned downward. "Feisty one, aren't you, *Minari?*"

"If you hurt even a single strand on his head, I will kill you," Minari sneered. His eyes were full of rage and hate.

Ragnar chuckled. "You are much too young to think about killing me." He shoved Minari to the ground, then grabbed the fallen weapon and examined it. "So, this is an elven blade, hmm? Dull. Probably wouldn't even put a scratch on me."

"What did—"

Ragnar swung his boot into Minari's gut. The elf doubled over, crumpling onto the ground. He gagged as he tried to catch his breath.

"He is also loud." Ragnar tucked the dagger into his robe.

"Ragnar, please," Chloé said. "They aren't a threat. You should know about the prophecy."

Ragnar tilted his head. He walked over to Chloé and leaned against the table. "Prophecy?"

Chloé gulped. She would do what she could to at least get the two out of here unharmed. It didn't matter what would happen to her. "Yes, the prophecy. He is Vylantra's chosen oracle, and Minari was tasked with protecting him. Please understand why he did what he did."

Ragnar's eyes flashed. He gave Chloé the slightest curl of the lips. He moved forward, his lips inches away from her ear. "The prophecy is of no concern to me."

Chloé backed away, pressing her palm against her ear. A

78

chill ran down her spine as she stared at the ethereal before her. Panic seized her chest as her heart raced.

"The matters of the elves are of no concern to me or the king. You should know better than this, Chloé," Ragnar said. He placed his hands behind his back and circled around Elliot and Minari. "Our god is Mykronos, not Vylantra. Anyone who thinks otherwise is not welcome in the kingdom and certainly not within the council." Ragnar paused in front of Elliot. "Yes, I am aware of the true role of the oracle, the prophecy, and the warriors he will need to find. But all of this is to stop Mykronos—*our* god. After seeing your behavior, it seems to me that you are a warrior of Elliot's."

Chloé froze. She opened her mouth to speak, but her voice was stuck.

"I'll take that as a confirmation."

"That explains everything," Licht said. "From her hiatus to her wanting to travel Etheria. It was all for the prophecy."

"No! I—" Chloé's stomach twisted into knots, and she pressed the back of her hand against her lips to suppress a wave of nausea.

"That explains everything," Sasha said. "You being a warrior and behaving like this. If you weren't one, this would never have happened."

"It's unfortunate it had to come to this," Baron said.

"Look at her. She's like a broken child who found out their favorite toy was taken from them," Gwenevere said. "I like it."

It took everything Chloé had to not collapse. The strength in her legs disappeared. She used the table as support, shaking her head. She needed to do something, but was there anything left for her to do? There was too much evidence against her.

How was it that the entire council knew about the truth of the oracle and the prophecy? Why had this information been kept from her? Had they doubted her from the beginning? Was it because she was too young? Was it because they'd known she was a warrior all along?

"Gerald would've been disappointed in you, Chloé," Emilee said.

Chloé's chest tightened painfully as she tried to bite back tears.

"It's a pity to see her like this," Ragnar said. "She had so much potential, and it's unfortunate fate dealt her with this hand."

"What do you suggest we do with the three of them?" Licht asked.

"Chloé," Ragnar said. His voice was soft, almost comforting.

Chloé took a breath through her nose, her hand still against her mouth. She looked at Ragnar. Her vision was beginning to blur from her welled eyes.

"If you want to live, I suggest you run."

Checkmate.

13
FAITH

Minari stared at the food in front of him, rubbing the base of his neck. The savory aroma of the vegetable soup filled his nose, but he couldn't focus on the dish. His neck ached, and he could still feel the constricting hold on him. Thinking back to the sensation of not being in control of his own body made Minari's skin crawl.

He'd hated it.

It had made him feel weak.

The council had been gracious enough to allow Elliot and Minari to leave, but they'd forced Chloé to stay behind. They'd been given one night to leave Valquent. Warrants for their arrest would be released in the morning. Ragnar was dead set on playing the game of chase. He didn't care how long it took the kingdom to find them, as long as they did.

Minari rubbed his hands against his face, suppressing a

groan. The aura around Ragnar had been the complete opposite from the one around Luka and Owen. He'd been full of menace. It was eerie how Minari hadn't *sensed* him. He was usually able to feel another's presence, but with Ragnar, he could only rely on sound.

Minari had never been disarmed by anyone other than a scout captain. Ragnar had done it so fast that the elf hadn't even had time to blink or breathe. His movements had been sluggish in comparison to the ethereal's.

It only agitated him more.

Minari gripped his hair before slamming his fist down against the table, causing the mugs to rattle.

"You should eat something to regain your strength," Luka said. His voice was cool, and it helped soothe Minari's inner turmoil. "If we need to leave by dawn, then this will be the last comfortable meal in a long time."

"To think we played right into their trap," Sage said. "Humans are despicable."

It was lucky they were confined in the elves' room. Though it was cramped, they were free of listening ears. If anyone had heard Sage, it would've ended up in another fight.

But honestly, Minari wouldn't have minded punching a human or two.

Minari wasn't much into fistfighting, but there was something satisfying about the thought of feeling the crack of cheekbones under his fist. Plus, it didn't matter what he did; Chloé's attempt at trying to give elves and chimeras equal treatment had been crushed. Everything was for naught. The council had known the game they were playing, and they'd played right into their trap.

"We need to find the last warrior," Elliot said. "And they're not here."

"Are you sure?" Mimi asked.

Elliot nodded. He placed his hand against his chest. "I don't feel anything here. It's empty."

Sage raised a brow. "This city is huge."

"I'm certain."

"But where would we go?" Mimi asked.

"If I may make a suggestion," Luka started. "The library in the Snowy Hills is filled with valuable information. It may be useful on our journey."

"You think the last warrior may be there?" Minari asked.

"It's a possibility. Remember, the warrior could be anywhere, even outside the kingdom."

"How far is it?" Elliot asked.

"Solime is about a four-week walk north. Afterward, we would need to travel by boat, though there's a high chance captains won't allow wanted fugitives on their ships. Luckily, humans can be easily persuaded with enough coin. You may leave transportation to the hills to us."

"What about Chloé?" Mimi asked. "Are we just going to leave her?"

"Ragnar's words are an extension of the king's," Luka said. "For now, it's best to abide by them."

"I believe and trust in Chloé," Elliot said. "She's a warrior."

Minari watched as Elliot did his best to keep his face straight, and he saw the slight tremors in the corners of his lips and the tiny crease in his brow.

Minari reached over the table and grabbed Elliot's bread.

His friend's mouth dropped as his eyes widened. Minari took a bite. "You didn't touch it, so I assumed you didn't want it," he said through chewing.

"I was going to eat it," Elliot said. He stood from his seat and attempted to grab the half-eaten bread from Minari's grasp, but Minari pulled his hand back.

"I didn't get to eat all day, and I'm hungry."

Elliot frowned. "It isn't my fault you ran away pouting."

Minari smirked before placing the bread back on Elliot's plate. "You're right. I'm sorry. By the way, the bread is pretty good."

Elliot took a bite from his stolen food, glaring at Minari.

Suddenly, tapping on the window caught their attention.

Everyone's head snapped toward the sound. They were on the third floor, and unless someone was scaling the walls, nothing should've been there.

There was a ginger owl perched on the windowsill. There was a rolled-up parchment attached to its right leg. It tapped its beak against the glass once again.

Elliot quickly unlatched the window and lifted it, allowing the feathered animal through.

It landed on the back of Elliot's seat.

"Is this . . . ?" Minari remember seeing an owl similar to this one back when he was with Chloé and Bunnie, searching for Elliot.

The younger elf untied the rope holding the small parchment to the owl. He unraveled it, eyes scanning it.

The corner of Elliot's lips tugged upward, and his eyes lit up the closer he got to the end of the letter.

"Well?" Minari asked.

Elliot grinned. "Chloé's fine. She's safe."

"That letter. Is it from Bunnie?"

"Not exactly," Elliot said, shaking his head. He showed the letter to Minari. "It's signed by one of the Nighthawk members."

Do not worry. The opal is safe. We will take care of her. Keep soaring on your mission. You two will be reunited when the time is right. Nighthawk.

Minari reread the letter a few times before shifting his attention back to Elliot. This was what they needed. "And you said you're confident the last warrior isn't here?"

"Yep."

Minari folded the letter and tucked it inside his coat. "Then let's get out of here. Xander's probably eager to get out of this shithole anyway."

14
HUNT

The moon had crossed the halfway point, nearly calling the sun to rise. The night breeze was cool and quiet, and the streets were empty.

Elliot hadn't been able to rest much the night before. His mind had kept him anxiously tossing and turning in his bed. He'd moved around so much it surprised him that Minari was able to stay asleep. He knew Minari was a light sleeper and could wake up from any sudden movement, but his light snores hadn't stopped.

They turned the corner to the back of the Twin Seasons Inn, and a floral fragrance filled the air. It was faint but potent enough to smell. The scent tickled Elliot's nose, and he scrunched it up. He pressed the back of his hand against his face, hoping to resist the urge to sneeze.

Minari mirrored him, covering the bottom half of his

face. "What is that awful smell? It's almost like burning flowers." Minari gasped, darting away from the group and to the stables. He swung the doors open and disappeared.

The aroma grew stronger the closer they got. A throb started to grow at the base of Elliot's skull.

"I don't feel good," Mimi said. He leaned against Sage, hands covering his mouth. "I think I'm going to be sick."

"This scent . . . It would be dangerous for anyone without a magic core to enter," Luka said. He had his sleeve covering his nose, and Owen was doing the same.

Elliot's breath hitched, heart racing. Minari didn't have a magic core. He ran inside the stables, hoping Minari was all right.

Elliot's eyes shot wide. His feet suddenly weren't his own. His legs forced him to stop, freezing him at the entrance. All the warmth in his blood disappeared. He knew this feeling. He slowly scanned down the aisle, hoping he was wrong.

A choked sob escaped his throat.

Minari was hunched over, knees and elbows pressing against the ground. Strangled gagging sounds came from his mouth. He was clawing at his throat as if attempting to pull at whatever was choking him, but there was nothing there.

Licht smiled down at the struggling elf. He was leaning against one of the stall doors, arms crossed with a pistol in his hand. The blue gemstones were glowing, emitting a soft aura as if absorbing energy from the moonlight.

Something rammed into Elliot's body, slamming him against wood. He yelped, pain shooting up his shoulder.

Mimi knelt beside him, but the illusion spell was no longer on him. His eyes were shining gold. The smaller boy staggered up. His head cocked to the side, and he looked straight at the other two before he lunged forward, drawing his rapiers.

Licht peered up and immediately swayed out of the way, dodging Mimi's attack. The tip of the blade cleanly sliced through the wood.

Minari gasped and coughed, taking in large gulps of air.

"It seems my presence isn't welcome," Licht sang. He tucked his pistol into his breast pocket.

"You . . ." Minari breathed. "What did you do to Xander?"

"Xander? Whatever do you mean? I do not know a Xander."

"You *bastard*. My ovis! Where is he?" Minari exclaimed, getting back to his feet. He gripped the front of his coat, chest still heaving.

"Oh, that enormous animal you had with you?" Licht chuckled. "Since Chloé never gave me the chance to test my experiments on you, I decided to test them on the animal instead. I figured it was the next best thing. That is, until I catch you myself."

In the blink of an eye, Licht had disappeared and reappeared right in front of Elliot. He pressed a cold hand against Elliot's chest. "Keep your core safe until we meet again."

And then he was gone.

The floral aroma dissipated, and the aura around the stables seemed to warm. It was almost as if Licht had stopped time and everything had resumed once he left. The sun was beginning to crack its way through the sky.

The thawing of time didn't seem to affect Elliot. He was

frozen in his spot. Licht had known where they were staying. He must have waited for them at the stables. It was too much of a coincidence to have run into him, and he had seen Mimi's true form. Licht was now aware of who Elliot and Minari were traveling with.

And he had just set his targets on them.

They were his prey.

Mimi's body morphed back to the human illusion Luka had cast on him. His brown orbs scanned the room. "What am I doing here?"

Elliot forced himself off the ground, his hand still gripping his aching right shoulder. "You don't remember?" He joined the two.

Mimi shook his head. "I just remember feeling sick to my stomach, and now I'm here."

Minari pushed by Mimi, entering what Elliot assumed to be Xander's stall.

But there was no ovis; it was empty. There was no hay, no food, and no water.

There was no Xander.

Minari stood in the center before collapsing on his knees. "I saw him," he whispered. "I saw him. I saw him—" Minari sucked in a shaky breath. He punched the ground. "Xander." Another punch. "Xander." And another punch. Sobs shook Minari's shoulders as he cried into the vacant space. His knuckles bore his emotions. They were marred with cuts, blood oozing from the open wounds.

Elliot knelt in front of Minari, placing a hand against the lamenting elf's shoulder. He could feel the tremors in the older elf's body as he wept.

89

Elliot's heart burned in his chest. His lungs tightened, and his throat closed up. He bit his lip as tears welled up in his eyes. But he refused to let them spill.

He pulled Minari down to his chest, rubbing circles against his back. Minari pushed his weight against Elliot.

Elliot tightened his hold on Minari, embracing him. He laid his forehead against Minari's shoulder, finally letting the heartache fall.

15
LIGHT

Three days. It had been three days since their departure from Valquent. Three days of avoiding the main roads. Three days of wandering around countless trees. Three days of listening to the quiet crackling of burning wood.

Minari was a hollow shell of himself. His body moved, but it had no direction. His eyes looked, but they didn't see. His lips moved, but he didn't speak.

His movements were sluggish, and his cheeks were sunken in. Dark shadows spread under his eyes.

Elliot listened to the soft buzzing of conversation around him. He watched as Minari nodded and smiled whenever his name was called out, watched him give short answers, shrugging as he did so.

"Minari," Elliot said, cutting the conversation Minari was having with Luka short.

Minari glanced up at him.

"I'm hungry."

"I have some more berries," Minari said. "Do you want some of mine?"

"Could you hunt me something to eat?"

"Sure." Minari stood. "I'll be back—"

Elliot grabbed Minari's wrist. "Did you hear what I just said?"

"You're hungry."

"Yes. What else?"

"You wanted me to hunt."

Elliot squeezed Minari's wrist. "Minari, you and I . . . don't eat meat."

Purple and gray orbs stared blankly at Elliot. Minari's brow furrowed, and he frowned. "No, we don't." He sat back down with a huff, rubbing his hands against his face.

Minari's attention had wavered since the incident with Licht. Though Elliot didn't know what had happened with Xander, he knew how much it tore Minari's soul to be separated from his most trusted companion. Elliot knew the feeling too, but he knew Xeno was safe back at home with his parents.

Elliot didn't want to fathom Xander's fate.

He knew the burden was heavy, and he knew sharing it would ease some of Minari's pain. But would Minari be open to share, or was the wound still too fresh?

Luka stood. "I am going to scout around the area and make sure we are going in the right direction." He turned to Owen, who stood up alongside him.

"We'll be back," Owen said.

Mimi shot to his feet. "Sage and I will do the same. We'll go in the opposite direction."

"Be careful you're not seen by anyone. It's especially dangerous since you two aren't under our illusion spell," Luka said.

"Understood."

The four of them disappeared into the darkness.

Minari still had his hands pressed against his face, his back hunched over.

The two of them stayed in silence. Elliot watched as the campfire danced and flickered, the light casting moving shadows.

The sky was clear of clouds, allowing the stars to shine. He wondered how his life would have been if he weren't the oracle, what life could have been if he'd become a keeper, how life would have been if he could go back to the same carefree life he'd had before all of this started.

Minari finally slid his hands off his face.

Elliot nudged Minari's shoulder with his own. "Hey."

"Mm."

"I didn't mean to trick you."

"No. It's good you did. I need to get myself together."

"Do you want to talk about it?"

Minari pressed his lips into a thin line, his gaze locked on the fire. His entire body tensed.

"When you're ready, I'm here." Elliot picked up a twig and tossed it into the flames. "I may not be able to do much, but I can listen."

"You've done so much, Elliot. Don't think otherwise," Minari said. He heaved out a breath. "It's *me* who hasn't done much of anything." He ran his fingers through his hair. "I'm useless. Useless keeper. Useless scribe. Useless scout. Useless son. *Useless.*"

Elliot blinked. "What?"

"You've gone through a lot and have already accomplished so much, while I . . . What have I done?" Minari gripped a handful of dirt and threw it into the fire.

The flames swayed but stayed lit.

"See?" Minari chuckled, eyes filled with disdain. "Can't do anything right." His lips quivered as he took in a sharp breath. He squeezed his eyes shut, head hanging low.

Elliot pushed his knees up to his chest. He crossed his arms over them and rested his chin. "Meeting you was the best thing that happened to me. You're my best friend and always will be."

Minari didn't respond, but Elliot knew he was listening.

"Remember when we first met? Your dad had me help find you since you'd disappeared. I found you at the bottom of a ledge. You tripped and fell, twisting your ankle." Elliot chuckled. "I remember your puffy face from crying so much. You thought you were going to die." Elliot smiled at the memory. It had happened before the accident with Melvin, so both of Minari's eyes had been purple. "Though I still wasn't sure what you were doing so far away from Mistfall."

Minari straightened his back, gaze still focused forward. "It was my first training session as a scout. I remember wanting to show my father what I could do." He let out a small chortle. "Ended up getting lost, twisting my ankle, and getting found by you."

Elliot nudged Minari's shoulder. "It was the start of a

beautiful friendship!"

Minari smiled at Elliot, the emotion finally reaching his eyes. "You were there for me, even on day one."

"I can say the same for you! Remember when Lily first tried to talk to me?"

Minari's eye twitched, but his lips remained curled. "You were so shy that your face turned the same shade as her hair. I had to tell her that you were sick and weren't feeling well."

"It was weird, okay? I didn't talk to anyone else besides your family." Elliot pouted.

Minari hummed. "Sure."

They continued to sit together in a comfortable silence. Elliot's chest felt light, and he couldn't stop himself from smiling. Even if it had only been for a slight moment, the light in Minari's eyes had returned.

And he would do his best to keep it shining.

16
CHASE

With a single swoosh of his sword, Luka cleanly cut a branch
full of apples. It was hefty in weight and had apples varying in
size, though most were juicy. The sun had passed the mid-
point, and it was probably around two in the afternoon. Sum-
mer was nearing its end, and autumn was already peeking
through. The sun would set in about two to three hours.
Though traveling at night made it easier for them to avoid any
patrolling officers, it didn't play well in their favor when it
came to the Hunters.

Luka and Owen had discovered them four nights ago
when they had left Elliot and Minari alone.

Luka knew the young oracle wanted time alone with his
friend. Understanding this, he took Owen around the
premises to survey the area.

He didn't count on actually finding something.

A man in his early adult years was following them. He had black hair greased back in a stubby ponytail. His shirt and trousers were covered in dirt and mud. His face was chiseled and grimy. He was alone, but Luka knew he didn't act as a single unit.

Luka silenced him with ease, gracefully disarming the human and pressing his own blade against his neck.

That was when he noticed a tattoo on the man's collarbone.

It was a horizontal sword, blade thin and bare. It lay under his left collarbone, pointing toward the right. There was an outline of a semicircle on top of the blade.

He was part of the mercenary guild called the Hunters.

They'd take on any job, no matter the difficulty or immorality, as long as the pay was right.

The officers worked under the jurisdiction of the kingdom, so these mercenaries must have been hired by the council. But which member hired them? The council didn't advocate for guild activities unless approved by them first. As far as he knew, Oasis was the only council-approved guild.

Luka debated whether he should interrogate the member.

It was when the man spat on Luka's sword that Luka chose otherwise.

The ethereal plunged his blade into the mercenary's neck.

The man's eyes bulged, jaw slacking as blood gurgled up his throat and ran down his lips.

Luka retracted his sword, flicking the blood onto the ground before sheathing it. The man thudded onto the ground, lifeless and quickly drowning in a pool of crimson.

"Why did you decide against interrogating him?" Owen asked.

"It would have been a waste." Luka rolled the limp Hunter onto his back with his boot.

"That tattoo . . ."

"He is a Hunter. Knowing his identity is enough information for me."

Owen didn't say anything after that. He must have figured it out as well.

They were being hunted.

And this man would not be the only one they'd run into.

Pushing the memory aside, Luka took another swing of his sword, cutting off another branch.

Minari jumped down, landing silently in the grass with a bundle of bright red apples in his arms.

The elf had improved after spending time alone with Elliot. It was soothing to see Minari more animated and back to his usual self.

"Ready to head back?" Minari grabbed one of the apples and took a bite.

Luka raised a brow. "You are going to eat now?"

Minari shrugged. "I found these, so I should be the first to eat."

Luka smirked. A few days ago, Minari would have said the opposite. He would have wanted everyone to take their share before he did.

Suddenly, a sharp tug in Luka's chest shocked his body. His eyes widened, and he stood completely still.

There was an additional thudding in his chest that wasn't

his heart. He pulled at his senses, which urged him to follow. Luka swung his head around, dropping the branches.

Elliot.

Minari seemed to sense the urgency. He dropped the apples he had gathered without a single word and grabbed Luka's arm.

Luka tapped into his core and teleported them to Elliot.

Trees whirled around him. The sky became the ground, and the ground became the sky. There was a spiraling feeling of floating for a moment before his feet touched solid dirt.

Luka expected to see the Hunters or officers. He was ready to fend them off to protect his oracle.

But his expectation differed from reality.

Chimeras were growling as they crouched on the ground, their eyes bloodshot. There must've been about thirty or so scattered around the trees: roosters, oxen, cats, dogs, snakes. They had them surrounded.

Mimi, Sage, and Owen were standing by Elliot, creating a three-pointed formation, guarding him from the chimeras.

"Elliot!" Minari yelled.

Elliot's head snapped up. He was breathing hard, his complexion nearly white. His hands were outstretched, glowing with a golden aura. His magic was binding them in place.

"They came out of nowhere," Sage said.

"We tried talking to them, but they wouldn't listen," Mimi said.

The number of chimeras was too much for Elliot's untrained core to handle, and his strength was quickly fading.

Luka rushed to Elliot's side and pressed his palm against the elf's chest.

"What—?"

Luka pushed stamina from his core through his energy stream. It traveled from his chest to his shoulder, down his arm, through his fingertips, and into Elliot's core. Luka had to be careful with how much and how fast his stamina was being transferred. He needed it to flow delicately into Elliot, or else he would face repercussions.

If he pushed in too little, Elliot's core would burn out.

If he pushed in too much, Elliot's core would break.

Luka could not risk harming the oracle's core. He knew it was possible to mend it, but he did not have that ability.

"Owen," Luka said sharply, "take everyone fifty miles north." Fifty miles would be enough distance away from the chimeras and close enough for Owen to teleport the other three.

"What about you?" Owen asked.

"I'll be behind you."

Owen looked at Luka momentarily before nodding. Mimi and Sage took hold of Owen's arm.

Minari was about to place a hand on Owen's shoulder before pausing. His orbs met Luka's. "I trust you."

Luka smiled. "Do not worry."

The elf's hand landed on Owen's shoulder, and they vanished.

Luka gasped as he felt a sharp snap in his palm. Elliot's hands fell to his sides, and his knees buckled. Luka caught Elliot, holding him up. His eyes were closed, and sweat beaded down his temple.

Free from their binds, the chimeras lunged, claws ready to tear into their flesh.

Luka reached into his core once more, urging his magic to bring him and Elliot to safety.

The world spiraled around him, knocking the wind out of his chest. He couldn't tell up from down. He hadn't felt this since he had first started learning to teleport. He held Elliot's limp body close, not wanting to lose him.

Luka collided with the hard ground, pain radiating across his back and the base of his skull. The weight on top of him was quickly removed. He felt arms wrap around his shoulders, propping him up. He cracked his eyes open, but his vision was blurry.

"Luka, are you all right?" Owen asked.

"I am fine. Do not worry about me." Luka pressed a hand against his temple. He must have put a little too much stamina into Elliot. He felt drained and fatigued.

Elliot groaned, his eyes opening. He quickly pushed Minari away, hunching over to the side before he started retching.

Relief washed over Luka. Nausea was a common side effect of stamina transferring. As long as Elliot was conscious, his core wasn't harmed.

They were safe—for now.

17
SHATTER

Chloé's hands were dry and cracked. She ran fingers through her locks. They snagged against her curls, but she did her best to work through the tangles. Her dress was full of crinkles and dirt splotches. No matter how many times she tried to brush the dirt off, it only stained the fabric further.

Chloé tucked her knees together, resting her chin against them.

The dungeons were underground, below Nexus Hall. They were windowless and warm. Even on the cusp of autumn, the stagnant air was comfortable . . . for the most part.

The cell she was in was smaller than the ones in Blanc Grotto. Her movements were limited to a small square. If she were to stand in the center and stretch out her arms, her fingertips could almost reach the walls. If she were any taller, she might have felt claustrophobic.

She looked at the small orange glow in the corner beyond the cell bars. She watched the shadows dance, moving back and forth, swaying and flickering across the stone walls. It was lonely company, but she welcomed the comfort of the small fire. Without it, she would have been in complete darkness.

Chloé reached into the top of her dress. Cold metal pressed against her fingertips.

When she was separated from the others and escorted down the dungeon stairwell by two officers, she found a coin in the corner of the cell. She would have missed it if one of the officers hadn't had a lamp in his hand. That brief moment of light was enough for her to see it shining in the corner. She had waited for them to leave before reaching for it.

Without proper lighting, she couldn't see what it was, but as she ran her fingers across it, she could make out the outline of a bird's head.

But not any bird.

An owl.

Chloé's chest tightened as she gripped the coin. The Nighthawks knew she was down here. Did that mean they would help her get out? But if she escaped, there was no turning back. The council and kingdom would have her head. If she stayed in the dungeons and kept her head down, she would at least have the chance of freedom, though she would be stripped of her status and power. Prim and Rose had been confiscated, so she didn't have a way to escape on her own.

She tucked the coin into the top of her dress, slipping it through the ruffles. She didn't know what the best choice was, but she knew she had to get back to Elliot and the others.

Chloé didn't know how many days it had been since she'd found the small metal piece. The meals they gave her didn't seem to fit a particular schedule. Sometimes they came a few hours apart, and some felt like even more. There was a chance she could have been given two meals in a day and sometimes four meals. She tried to regulate her internal clock by sleeping, but the cold, hard ground left much to be desired when it came to comfort.

The officers that delivered her meals were the same, like they had a rotating schedule between several officers, but the pattern never lined up with Chloé's prediction.

The tapping of footsteps and rattling of silverware echoed down the stairwell. Chloé peered up, keeping her knees close to her chest. Her eyes widened at the sight of two figures before her. Ragnar stood next to the officer, his hands behind his back and a smile on his lips.

"My, you look quite lovely," Ragnar said.

Chloé's hands twitched. She hadn't bathed in days, maybe weeks, and he had the audacity to comment on her appearance?

"Fallen from grace. A grungy and dirty look. Eyes full of defiance. It suits you."

Chloé pressed her lips together. She took in a breath before letting it out through her nose.

Ragnar tilted his head. "No response, hmm? No matter." He lifted the cup off the food tray the officer was holding. He tilted the cup, pouring the water onto the ground. "I have some questions for you."

Chloé swallowed, her body tensing.

Ragnar tapped the cup, ensuring every last drop of water

had been emptied out before he placed it back onto the tray. "The two elves you were with, they were the same ones who climbed down the mountains around two months ago, correct?"

Chloé remained silent. Her eyes followed Ragnar's hand as he reached for the dish of soup and flung it against the wall. The ceramic shattered, spilling the contents against the wall and ground.

Chloé flinched at the sudden loud noise. She clenched her hands, fingernails scratching her skin. Her heart thudded against her chest. Hunger spread down her limbs.

"How long have you known about the oracle?" Ragnar asked. "Was it when you abandoned your duties? Or perhaps later?"

Chloé wasn't going to feed into Ragnar's sick amusement. She refused to. She trusted her comrades, and in return, they trusted her. Elliot. Minari. Mimi. Sage. Luka. Owen.

Bunnie.

They'd been there for her, and she would be there for them.

Chloé smirked. "I seem to have forgotten. I've been down here for so long that all sense of time seems to have disappeared."

Ragnar's eyes flickered upward. "Oh? Is that so?" He shoved the bread into the officer's mouth. The officer jerked and dropped the tray, trying to take hold of the bread. "I seem to have forgotten that Vylantra fraternizers are supposed to have a public execution. This can all be arranged, of course." Ragnar unsheathed his sword in one swift movement and pierced the officer through his stomach.

The officer froze, eyes wide as he finally dropped the bread from his mouth. He looked down, body trembling. "R-Ragnar, sir . . . W-why?"

"Hmm? Oh, I suppose my hand slipped." He pulled his blade out, flicking the blood off before sheathing it. The officer fell to the ground, hands pressing against his gaping wound.

Chloé pushed herself off the ground, flinging herself to the bars. "What are you doing? Help him!" She glanced at the officer. His complexion was paling. Fast. Deep red was forming under him, and if he didn't receive help now, he wouldn't make it.

Ragnar tilted his head. "Whatever do you mean? Did you not hear what I said?" Ragnar leaned in, his long hair brushing against Chloé's ear. "Followers of Vylantra will be killed." He pulled away, smiling. He reached for the officer's hat, stripping it off him before placing it on his head. "I think I will keep this as a souvenir. Until next time." Ragnar disappeared up the stairwell.

Chloé couldn't move. Her mind disconnected from her body as she stared at the fading officer. His unfocused eyes looked at her, almost as if he had something to say.

The nix fell to her knees, but her gaze never left his.

It was then she recognized his hair. Recognized his eyes. Yuan Gale.

The officer who'd informed her about the impromptu council assembly. The officer who'd escorted her. The officer who'd wished her good luck.

He was the one who'd left the coin in her cell.

"Gale? Yuan Gale?" Chloé whispered. Her voice trembled as she forced herself to speak.

Yuan's lips curled ever so slightly. He nodded. Barely.

Chloé sucked in a shaky breath. Her vision blurred as tears welled up in her eyes. Her chest tightened and ached. "Why? Why? *Why?*" Chloé's mind fogged over as she begged. She begged and begged, hoping, praying anyone would come down and save Yuan.

The nix reached out, pushing herself so hard against the bars she could feel the metal imprint against her cheek and chest. Chloé's hand brushed against his, and she held on.

Their eyes never left each other, and Chloé kept her gaze on him even after the spark of light had left him. She kept her hold on his hand even after his had gone limp.

Warm tears ran down her chin. The strength in her arm weakened. When she finally pulled away, she let herself go. She buried her palms in her eyes, screaming.

Bunnie had trusted Yuan to keep an eye on Chloé, to keep communication between her and Nighthawk open.

Yuan had been her key to getting out of the dungeons. But he had *died* for *her* sake, and it tore Chloé apart. She couldn't rely on others—not anymore. It was up to her to get out of the dungeons. There was no other choice.

Chloé reached into her dress, pulling out the coin. Another sob escaped her throat as her eyes landed on the outline of the owl. She pressed it against her chest. "I'm sorry."

18
PROTECT

"What was that?" Mimi whispered. His whole body was still shaking, mind whirling. He'd never seen anything like that before.

"They looked almost feral," Sage said.

"That's—" Mimi shook his head. No. They couldn't have been feral. He wouldn't believe it.

"It's the most accurate description of what we just experienced," Owen said. "Salivating mouths, bloodshot eyes, unresponsive to words."

"There's no way!" Mimi clenched his hands. His father wouldn't have let anything happen to the tribe.

"Do you think something happened to Lyeokee?" Sage asked, changing to chimeran tongue.

"I don't believe it."

"Then how do you explain what happened?"

Mimi didn't want to admit that something dire had happened back home, but it was hard to prove otherwise. He just didn't want to *know* what had happened.

Chimeras only became feral when they were placed in extreme situations, usually under high levels of stress. There were so many questions about how it could have happened. His father was a powerful leader, so what could have possibly happened?

A small gust of wind suddenly blew next to them. Luka and Elliot appeared out of thin air, falling onto the ground with a thud.

Minari pulled Elliot off Luka's body, helping him sit up. Owen mimicked the gesture with Luka.

Elliot's eyes opened, revealing his cloudy blue eyes. He quickly pushed Minari away, turning to the side and emptying out the contents of his stomach.

Mimi turned away, attempting to tune out the nauseating noise.

"Are you okay?" Minari asked.

Elliot coughed, taking in a few deep breaths. "Just . . . dizzy," he mumbled. He wiped the corner of his mouth with the back of his hand.

"You exerted quite a bit of magic there," Luka said, rising up. "How is your chest feeling?"

"Heavy. Like there's a boulder on top of me."

"You may want to refrain from exerting any more stamina. You performed quite a feat, especially with your current ability level."

Elliot nodded. "Even if I wanted to, I don't think I could." He pressed a hand against his chest. "It feels heavy and hollow at the same time."

"I had to transfer some of my stamina into you, or else you would have burned out much faster. What you're feeling is the aftermath of using too much."

Elliot tried to stand and faltered. Minari caught his arms, easing him to his feet.

"It would be wise to set up camp here," Luka started. "Night is closing in, and Elliot is in no shape to travel." The ethereal looked around before heaving a sigh. "I was afraid of this."

"What is it?" Minari asked.

"Unfortunately, this area of land is barren."

"We're close to home," Sage said.

"This is where Sage and I first set up camp when we left the tribe," Mimi whispered. He turned around, his sandals kicking up dust. There were patches of grass, though sparse. There were trees, though few.

Mimi and Sage had left home in hopes of finding unclaimed territory to call home. The cramped tribe had been suffering from food and water shortages.

Could that have been why there were feral chimeras?

Had the situation at home become so dire that the chimeras had lost all sense of themselves and gone on a rampage?

But that didn't add up. The chimeras who'd ambushed them had almost acted out of command, like they were under orders. But his father wouldn't have issued an order like that.

"It doesn't look like there's much for us to make a fire," Minari said.

Sage scoffed. "This is what we have to live with. We're

given freedom, but this is no way to live."

"Chloé wanted to," Elliot said. He pressed a hand against his forehead, closing his eyes. "She will."

Minari steadied Elliot's shoulders.

"I can gather some twigs to make a fire," Mimi said.

He was a few feet out when he heard footsteps behind him.

Sage jogged up, slowing down as he walked beside the smaller chimera. Mimi felt Sage's hand brushing against his, and he welcomed it, intertwining their fingers.

The two of them walked in silence. They passed by numerous dry bushes without collecting any for a campfire.

"Are you going to ask?" Sage said in their language, finally breaking the silence.

"I shouldn't," Mimi said.

"But aren't you worried about the Lyeokee?"

Mimi's feet halted. Sage walked another step before pausing and turning. Mimi squeezed Sage's hand. *"I'm scared. Scared of what I might find if I return home."*

Sage cupped Mimi's cheek with his other hand, tilting his chin up. His brown eyes were soft as their gazes connected. *"I'll be there with you."*

Mimi leaned into his lover's touch, closing his eyes. *"I know. I don't know what I'd do without you. I'd be lost."*

Sage pressed their foreheads together. *"Whatever we find, we're in it together. I'll be by your side. Always."*

Mimi breathed in Sage's scent. His woodsy, musky scent had always helped calm his nerves, and this time was no different.

Mimi pushed himself onto his toes. His lips landed

against Sage's in a warm, tender kiss.

Mimi pulled away and leaned into Sage's chest, sighing as the older chimera wrapped his strong arms around his body. *"Do you think I should ask?"*

"Ask them?"

"If we should detour. I know how important it is for Elliot to find the last warrior."

"Do you think he wouldn't understand?"

"Elliot has a kind heart. I don't want to take advantage of it."

"You won't know unless you ask, just like how we wouldn't know what was beyond our territory if we hadn't left home."

Mimi gripped Sage's shirt. *"You don't think it's selfish?"*

Sage chortled. *"You're worried about your family. I don't think so."*

"But the prophecy . . . If it doesn't get fulfilled, then the entire world is doomed."

Sage hummed. *"I'll leave you to decide what's right: the immediate now or the later."*

Mimi knew finding the last warrior was vital to the survival of the entire world. If they failed, there would be no one left. Everyone would be gone. Yet, at the same time, how could Mimi hope to succeed in his role as a warrior if he couldn't even protect those who were dear to him? Protect those who needed his help? Not only did his father need him, but the tribe did as well. He was the Lykrine, the prince of the tribe. He needed to protect his people.

Mimi placed his hands on Sage's chest, pushing them apart. He looked up at Sage and smiled.

The taller chimera smirked. *"Figured it out?"*

Mimi nodded. *"Yes."*

19
PAIN

Putting on a strong front was something Minari should have perfected by now. When he was a child, Mayleen would scold him if he showed any bit of emotion, whether it be happiness, sadness, or worry. As someone who was next in line as Mistfall's leader, it was crucial for him to always remain strong in front of others. Though he'd allowed himself to be free around Elliot and Lily, Minari knew he shouldn't be free now.

The image of Xander's lifeless body replayed in his mind. He tried to push it out, but the more he tried, the more vivid it became.

Licht had been there, hovering over his ovis's body. Xander would never have allowed a stranger that close to him.

When Minari tried to unsheathe his daggers, his muscles tightened under an invisible hold. It was the same one that had taken ahold of him during the assembly. The same foreign grip wrapped around his neck and began suffocating him.

The pungent aroma he had smelled earlier was getting stronger, making his head spin. His knees hit the ground. The heavy scent overpowered his senses, making his vision fog and his hearing muddled. His stomach churned, and he let out a gag.

Suddenly, the hold around his neck tightened, as if punishing him for making a sound. Minari scratched at his neck, attempting to pry whatever was clutching him off.

The next thing Minari knew, the binds disappeared, and he filled his lungs with air. Peering up, he could make out through his blurry vision that Mimi was by Licht, his rapiers in hand. Licht had his pistol out, but he quickly tucked it back into his breast pocket. Words left the nix's lips, but Minari couldn't make them out. It sounded jumbled and muted, as if he were underwater.

And then everything came rushing back.

His vision sharpened. His hearing became clear.

But Xander was no longer around.

"You . . ." Minari breathed. "What did you do to Xander?"

"Xander? Whatever do you mean? I do not know a Xander."

"You *bastard*. My ovis! Where is he?" Minari exclaimed, getting back to his feet. He clutched the front of his coat. The scent hadn't disappeared, making his chest heavy.

"Oh, that enormous animal you had with you?" Licht chuckled. "Since Chloé never gave me the chance to test my experiments on you, I decided to test them on the animal instead. I figured it was the next best thing. That is, until I catch you myself."

Licht vanished, taking the aroma with him.

Minari stared at the empty space in front of him. His heart thudded against his chest. His breaths were shallow and quick.

Xander was missing.

Xander was gone.

Xander was—

Minari swallowed the lump in his throat.

He willed himself forward, pushing past Mimi and Elliot. When he stood in the spot where Xander should have been, he collapsed. Minari couldn't think. He just couldn't move. He couldn't breathe. His heart felt like it had been ripped in two. He didn't know why, but losing his father, Melvin, hadn't devastated him as much as losing Xander.

Minari didn't even want to know if Xander was . . . gone. If he was dead. There'd been no blood around the ovis, so Minari wasn't sure. But the way his body had lain on the ground, so still. Lifeless. It was hard for Minari to think otherwise.

Minari wasn't himself in the days that followed. It was difficult for him to wrap his mind around anything that wasn't related to Xander.

He wondered what his companion would think of the new scenery, the unknown places they'd ventured to, the different foods they had eaten. Even his scribe duties had suffered. Countless days were missing just because Minari couldn't get himself to think.

It was when Elliot tried to console Minari that he knew he had to slap on a mask. His pitiful behavior was unacceptable. He had no right to feel this way.

Especially given what had happened to Elliot.

Elliot had been kidnapped and tortured, and he, too, was without his ovis, yet he was still going.

Minari had to keep on moving forward too, and if that required him to wear a mask, then so be it. He knew it would ease the worries of the others. He couldn't bring the others down.

A sudden noise snapped Minari out of his thoughts. The pattern of the movements was unfamiliar, and it put him on edge. He reached for his daggers, staring in the direction of the noise.

"Something here?" Luka asked, his voice low.

"It's not Mimi or Sage."

Luka pressed a hand against his chest. "I do not have any stamina to spare. If we are getting ambushed . . ."

"I won't be of much assistance either," Owen said.

Elliot was still in a daze, and Luka and Owen were in no condition to fight. Mimi and Sage still hadn't returned, so it was up to Minari to defend them.

But there was no way for Minari to defend them if the enemy closed in on them. He had to take them out before they got any closer.

"Watch Elliot." Minari didn't wait for a response. He dashed, aiming straight for his target.

Whoever was near them wasn't close enough for the others to hear but was loud enough for Minari.

The sun was barely peeking over the horizon, casting a sharp orange light over the barren land. Without much to hide behind, whoever was around them should've been out in the open.

Yet Minari didn't see anyone.

He slowed down to a stop. Minari was about sixty-five yards out from the group. His breath was steady and quiet. He focused on any movement, any noise. But he was met with silence.

Minari furrowed his brows. He was certain he heard something. But now that he was here, they were gone.

Maybe whoever was here heard him approaching and left. But that would be impossible. The way his body moved was nearly silent. Only the scout commanders would have been able to hear him.

Minari's eyes scanned the area. He turned, keeping his feet light against the ground. Careful not to make any sound. Night was quickly closing in and the orange light transformed into darkness.

A chill ran up Minari's back. He twirled, his daggers unsheathed.

The ground rumbled, shifting the small pebbles by Minari's boots. The dirt near him erupted as something broke free. Minari didn't get a good look at it before it wrapped around his ankle, pulling him down. He bit his lip as his back collided with the ground.

Warm pain shot up Minari's leg as he began sliding across the dirt. Whatever had grabbed him was pulling him toward it. He leaned up, dagger in hand, ready to strike whatever was holding him.

It was a long slender black form with sharp edges that dug into his ankle. It pierced through his boot, cutting into his skin. Blood seeped from the wound, and the edges of his vision darkened. His body tingled with coldness.

"Dammit," Minari whispered. He needed to act fast. There was a good chance that whatever had him had also poisoned him. Squinting his eyes, he flung his dagger. It pierced what he assumed was a leg of whatever was underground.

A loud shriek echoed from underneath him, and Minari's blood ran cold. He knew he had heard that noise before.

It was the same sound from when he and Elliot had first left Mistfall.

20
PREY

Minari wiggled his left ankle free from the monster's grasp. He pushed to his feet and backed away from the twitching leg. Searing pain shot up from his wound to his knee and thigh. Wobbling, he held back a wince and forced himself to remain standing.

Minari wasn't in any shape to fight, but there was no question that he needed to lure whatever monster was underground away from the others. It was close—too close—and the only option he had was to run in the opposite direction and hope he could act as bait.

His head throbbed, and the world spun as he ran. He ignored the pain radiating through his leg, using adrenaline to propel himself forward. The ground rumbled; the monster was following.

Good.

But the more he ran, the more his vision swam. The more he breathed, the more he inhaled shattered glass. The more he moved, the more he saw shadows filling his eyes.

Minari wasn't far enough. He wasn't sure just how far he had already gone, but he was still too close to Elliot and the others.

A sudden thought of possibly *dying* filled his mind. It should have frightened him, but the thought of leaving the world was oddly soothing. It didn't bring the same debilitating sensations as when Xander had disappeared, and the more he thought about it, the more he welcomed it. If he was destined to live the last moments of his life alone in the middle of nowhere, then who was he to try to fight destiny?

Minari stopped, his injured ankle no longer supporting him. He lay on his side on the ground, taking shallow breaths. With his ear pressed against the dirt, he heard how the monster moved, how its body curved and circled around him, its multiple legs creating a tunnel, allowing it to slither through.

Minari shivered. It was growing more difficult to focus. The frigid night air bit into his cold skin. The sound of his breathing pulsated through his ears. The tingling that had started in his leg had spread up to his torso, chest, arms, and fingertips.

His vision was nearly gone. He could barely make out the cracks in the ground or the dried shrubs.

But his hearing never left. It was almost as if it was heightened.

Minari could hear the monster's joints crack and pop as it continued to slither. He could hear the stretching of its skin, the pushing of the dirt. Whatever it was, it was long—

extremely long. Minari guessed the monster was about twenty yards long and had over a hundred legs.

The air became silent. The ground beneath him stilled. Minari was certain the monster had moved to be right underneath him before stopping. Was it waiting for him to fall into unconsciousness? To draw his last breath? The elf's vision had completely left him, plunging him into complete darkness.

Minari pushed himself up with shaky arms. His entire body ached with fever, but he was still alive. The poison hadn't taken ahold of him yet, and the monster was biding its time. Even after Minari moved, the monster stayed quiet.

And then the monster came to life. The ground to Minari's left rumbled before breaking. He tilted his head down, attempting to shy away from the debris that blew in his face.

The air near him moved, and Minari heard the crackling of what he assumed were pincers. He reached for a dagger in his belt, but he couldn't find the strength to pull it out.

A cold, smooth surface pressed against his cheek. He gasped at the touch and pulled away. The contact sent painful tremors down his body.

Was the monster toying with him? Was it common for these things to play with their prey before killing it? Thinking back to the scorpion-like monster he and Elliot had faced before, he decided it wouldn't make sense. The monster they'd fought before had fully intended to kill them.

The cold surface returned, pressing against his cheek with more force, pushing him to the ground. A warm, wet sensation hit his face, and it slithered down his neck.

Minari's heart raced against his chest. His stomach clenched as the monster's tongue wrapped around his neck and brushed against his collarbone. Bile threatened to rise up his throat.

A voice broke through the darkness, and the tongue left his skin.

"Minari!" It was Mimi's voice.

Minari heard the thumping of Mimi's rushed footsteps against the ground.

A piercing screech tore through the air and straight into Minari's skull.

Everything went silent.

Minari smacked his lips. His mouth was dry, and his throat was raw. There was the crackling of a fire, and his head was against something warm and soft. He opened his eyes and was met by orange flames.

What happened?

He sat up. His body was light, and his vision had returned. He was at camp. Mimi and Sage were sleeping, huddled together. Luka and Sage were sitting with their arms crossed, but their eyes were closed.

"Hey."

Minari flinched. He turned his head and was met with worried blue eyes. Elliot tilted his head, smiling. "How are you feeling?"

"How am I feeling?" Minari stared at Elliot. Was everything that had just happened a dream? He snapped his head toward his foot. No, it wasn't a dream. His boot had been sliced, showing the pale skin of his ankle.

"Sage carried you back. I don't know the details since the

others don't either," Elliot said. "Mimi said he saw a giant centipede-like monster by you, but then it burrowed into the ground and disappeared. He used his blood to cleanse the toxins from you."

"How long was I out for?"

"A few hours." Elliot placed a hand on his shoulder and rolled his neck. "I told the others I'd keep watch over you."

"But are you okay?"

"I'm still a little tired, but it's nothing I can't handle." Elliot clenched his fists a few times. "I probably can't use any magic. My fingers still feel numb."

Minari wasn't sure if it had been pure luck or if there were outside factors that had brought him back from the brink of death. He'd been so sure he wouldn't have been able to escape the monster without help, yet just having the chimeras appear had chased it away.

Did that mean . . . they couldn't be trusted?

They already had to worry about the entire kingdom; did they have to worry about the chimeras too?

No. That didn't make sense. They'd been attacked back when he and Elliot were separated. But could that have been a part of their plan? Were they working together to gain Elliot's trust?

Minari shook his head. He couldn't think that way. Mimi was a warrior. There was no reason for him to do something like this.

But did it make any sense otherwise?

21
CALL

Bunnie pulled her coat off the back of her wooden chair. She slipped her arms through and fixed it so it lay smoothly against her shoulders. It was still early morning, and the sun hadn't risen yet, but there was no time to waste.

Yuan had been reported dead, and the report had reached her four days after his death. A delay that long was unheard of; it was a delay that could cost them.

Bunnie and Yuan had known each other for a few years. He was already a Valquent officer when they first met, and only when he was off duty at a pub had he shown his colors.

The young male hadn't been particularly fond of King Leonard VI's opinions. The king had special treatment when it came to the higher class, even though the working and lower classes were the ones paying their whole livelihoods away in taxes. Though Bunnie was fortunate to have a good amount of coin, she agreed with Yuan. She was not one for unjust treatment based on class.

Nighthawk, or Minerva to outsiders, was young in establishment. She hadn't expected anyone in Valquent to catch wind of the traveling band.

But to her surprise, Yuan had approached her and asked if she was part of Minerva. He had recognized her from her performance two nights prior. There were a few people who'd attended the performance, and Bunnie did not recall seeing the young man there. Bunnie knew at that moment she wanted him to join Nighthawk. Someone who was a part of the Valquent officers, had similar views, and could hide in plain sight would be a valuable member.

She had slipped him one of her bronze coins and asked him to meet her at the central fountain in two nights time. And two nights later, Yuan showed himself. Only she and the twins, Deveran and Oliver, had been part of Nighthawk at the time. Yuan, without hesitation, became the fourth member.

Bunnie knew her line of work wasn't perfect. Casualties were to be expected. It wasn't the first time death had happened within the Nighthawk guild, but it never got easier.

Bunnie slipped her boots on, grabbed her crossbow, and left her house. The damp air hit her face, water splashed against her boots, and the soft pitter-patter of rain landed on her coat. But that didn't stop her.

Lonin city folk bustled beside her, umbrellas in hand. Some ignored her. Some eyed her with confusion. But she paid no mind to them.

Bunnie swung the doors open to the Purple Pub. Her clothes clung to her skin, dripping water onto the wooden floors as she entered.

"Bunnie," Lavender said in greeting. She placed an empty glass underneath the counter. "You're drenched."

"I didn't have time," Bunnie said.

"To find an umbrella?" Lavender cocked a brow.

"You know what happened." Bunnie looked around. It was still too early for the pub to open, but sometimes Lavender's usual customers would take the liberty of waltzing in before opening hours. Luckily, they weren't around. Bunnie locked the doors. "I like the new cut," Bunnie said, taking a seat at the counter.

"Yeah?" Lavender flipped her bangs. Her long wavy brown hair had been replaced with a lilac pixie cut. The color complemented her hazel eyes. "I needed a change."

"It suits you."

"Thank you."

Bunnie took a closer look at the pub. On the surface, anyone who had been to the Purple Pub wouldn't notice the changes. They would still see the same circle tables, worn-out seats, scratches on the floor, and yellow hanging lights.

But Bunnie noticed the slight change in decorations.

All the potted bellflowers Lavender loved to place around the pub were gone.

It was a minor detail any drunk patron wouldn't be able to recall.

Lavender let out a loud sigh before grabbing a bottle from behind her and pouring a glass. She slid it toward Bunnie before making herself one.

Bunnie swooshed the amber liquid, inhaling the sharp scent of whiskey.

She took a sip before placing the glass back down on the counter. "I'm sorry."

Lavender flinched. She took a sip of her own drink before gulping it down and slamming her glass against the wood. "I can't believe it."

"I didn't mean for this to happen."

"I know you didn't." Lavender took a deep breath. She rested her elbows on the counter, pressing her forehead against her balled-up hands. "I just wish he were still here."

Bunnie took another sip, relishing the bitter liquid. It traveled down her throat and warmed her belly. "I tasked Yuan with watching over Miss Gemme."

Lavender scoffed. "And? How is she? Last I heard, she was locked up in the dungeons."

"Unfortunately, she's still there."

Lavender shook her head, still hunched over.

"Your identity hasn't been revealed. You should be safe."

Lavender shot up, eyes wide. "Safe? *Safe?* Just how long will I be safe for? We were *engaged.* How in the name of Mykronos would the council or the king not know I have ties with him? With you?" Lavender's shoulders shook, tears welling up in her red-rimmed eyes. Her cheeks flushed.

"Yes, you were engaged, but as far as being official . . . there was no marriage. The kingdom hadn't recognized you two as a couple." Bunnie took another sip.

"We would have been . . . We had a wedding planned out. It was supposed to happen in three months."

"I know."

"Well then, what now? What comes after? You still need me, right?"

127

Bunnie stood up, the legs of the stool scraping against the scuffed floor. She reached into her coat and pulled out a black cloth, then held it out to Lavender. "We need to get Miss Gemme out of there, and you're the only one who can do it."

Lavender stared at the cloth. Smirking, she placed her hands on her hips and tilted her head. "You want me to infiltrate the dungeons and free Miss Gemme?"

Bunnie nodded.

"After what happened to Yuan, you think I'll accept?"

"I know you will. Living a peaceful life as a pub owner has never been your calling, Lav."

The woman chortled. She untied her apron and threw it to the floor. She swiped the cloth out of Bunnie's hand. "I wouldn't be a Nighthawk member otherwise."

22
DISCORD

The bright morning light seeped through Elliot's eyelids. He tucked his head into his chest, hiding away from the offending sun. He had just fallen asleep and wasn't ready to continue on their journey. His body was weak, and his chest was heavy. Staying awake with Minari may not have been the smartest decision, but he'd wanted to make sure the older elf was all right.

The pressure against Elliot's back disappeared. He blinked his eyes, peering behind him.

Minari sat up, shoulders hunched. He placed a hand on his shoulder before rolling his arm. There were dark shadows underneath his different-colored orbs. "We should get moving."

Elliot stayed silent.

"I know you're awake." Minari peeked over his shoulder.

"How are you feeling?"

"Mm," Elliot moaned. "Still tired."

Minari sighed. "Next time, don't stay on watch duty."

"Mm." Elliot knew it had to be him. Luka and Owen had been in no condition to stay awake. The two ethereals had probably exerted more stamina than he had. Mimi and Sage might have been able to keep watch, but he hadn't wanted them to. They had left a second time to search for resources to build a fire. If not for them, they would've slept without any warmth.

They were also lucky the monster hadn't returned. Elliot shuddered at the thought.

"There is still time to rest if Elliot wishes," Luka said. Though his skin was already fair to begin with, his complexion had warmed since yesterday.

"What if that monster comes back?" Minari asked.

"Then we fight it," Sage said, punching a fist into his palm. "Thing ran away scared when it saw us."

"Allowing Elliot to fully rest would benefit us," Owen said. "If he's tired, it will only slow us down. If he's well, then we can expect smooth travel."

Minari narrowed his eyes before shrugging. "Fine."

Elliot pushed himself up into a sitting position, crossing his legs. "I'm fine to keep going."

"You just said you were still tired," Minari said.

"Yeah, but Solime isn't going to get any closer if we stay here." Elliot stood, patting the dirt and dust from his pants

"Actually," Mimi started, "I have a request." His hands were clasped, fingers fidgeting.

"Hmm?"

130

Mimi looked at Sage, who nodded, before turning his attention back to Elliot. "The chimeras from yesterday. I'm worried about my tribe. I . . . I recognized them, and I find it hard to believe that they're . . . feral."

"You want us to take a detour," Minari deadpanned.

Elliot blinked. He hadn't heard Minari use that tone since meeting Chloé.

"The proph—"

"We can," Elliot said, interrupting Minari. Minari looked at Elliot with wide eyes. Elliot raised a brow. "Mimi's family could be in danger."

Minari's mouth opened and closed, sputtering words.

"Do you have a problem with that?" Sage asked, crossing his arms.

"The prophecy. Did we forget we need to fulfill it?"

"It's not that," Elliot said.

"Then what is it? Chloé is stuck in Valquent, and we need to find the last warrior, but you want to wander around to find chimeras?"

Elliot gaped. He was at a loss for words. It wasn't that he had forgotten about Chloé. He knew she was still in Valquent, but he had trusted Nighthawk to take care of her. It was true that he hadn't heard from them since they'd been in the capital, but he trusted in them. He knew they would be reunited again.

Ever since being in Ruglow, Elliot hadn't felt the presence of another warrior. When it came to Chloé, Mimi, and Luka, he'd recognized their presence and auras. Their souls sang in harmony with his, like a chorus that meshed with his verse.

131

But ever since their departure, he had not felt anything. No pull. No tug. No calling. When Elliot closed his eyes and focused, he still only saw Mimi's golden string and Luka's light blue string connected to his pale green string. Their souls were still intertwined. The thin black string was still connected to him, but even now, it didn't lead to anywhere. It didn't pull his soul to anyone. Elliot assumed it would lead to the last warrior, but it stayed severed.

"There is no reason to be agitated," Luka said.

"I am not agitated," Minari said.

"Annoyed."

"Not annoyed."

"Displeased."

Minari glared at Luka, his lips pressed into a thin line. He threw his arms in the air, shaking his head. "Fine. Let's put our entire journey on hold and waltz right into chimera territory. I'm sure we'll find the last warrior there. Then we can forget our trip to Solime and the records in their library. If we're lucky, maybe we'll also run into the hero. Oh, and then we can make our way back to get Chloé since the Nighthawk guild isn't doing anything about it."

"Minari, *what* has gotten into you?" Elliot asked.

"Nothing. Someone has to remind you what we're doing this far away from home."

"I didn't forget."

"I'm sure you didn't. Just wanted to take a vacation."

"A vacation? How do you expect us to fulfill the prophecy to save Etheria when we can't even protect those in front of us?"

"By looking at the bigger picture. We fulfill the

prophecy, we save the entire world. If we fail it, there won't be anyone left."

Elliot was fuming. He clenched his fists, trying to keep his hands from shaking. He shook his head. "Something has gotten into you."

"No, Elliot." Minari stared into Elliot's eyes. "I was tasked with protecting you so you could fulfill the prophecy. I am your keeper, a scribe, and the future leader of Mistfall. We have other priorities, and we should keep to them."

"What's Mistfall? Is that a place near Rainwell?" Sage asked.

Elliot's eyes widened. He mentally cursed. He'd never told Mimi and Sage about Mistfall.

Minari put his hands on his hips. "Rainwell?" He pursed his lips. "I guess you could say that."

"How far is the chimeran tribe from here?" Luka asked. Elliot's shoulders sagged. He was thankful Luka had changed the topic.

"A day's walk," Mimi said. "But maybe three days with all of us together."

"Do you think we can spare three days or so, Elliot?" Luka asked.

Elliot nodded. "If it'll give Mimi and Sage peace of mind, then it doesn't matter how many days it will take us." His eyes shifted to Minari.

The older elf's expression darkened. His brows were pinched, and the corners of his lips sank. His posture was stiff.

Maybe Minari was anxious. Stressed. He had just lost Xander and had been attacked by a monster the night before. Maybe this was a lingering side effect of the poison.

Elliot hoped this was just a phase.

23
RIFT

They were two and a half days into the travel to the chimeran tribe, and Minari hadn't said a word to Elliot. It was like the two were walking side by side on the edge of a cliff. A single whisper could send either of them over the edge.

The dry soil had turned into soft dirt the farther they followed Mimi and Sage. The golden bushes transformed into those filled with green leaves. Though they were moving on from the barren land, parts of it were still evident.

Elliot peeked over his shoulder. Minari had been trailing behind them, keeping a distance from the rest of the group. It was only Luka who was able to break Minari's hard shell, just enough for him to say a few words. But other than the brief interaction, Minari would not try to speak with anyone else. If Mimi or Sage tried to talk to him, he would only stare and maybe give a one-word response if they were lucky.

Minari's eyes had lost any compassion and were filled with skepticism and doubt. His nights were filled with his nose in his scribe duties, his pen in constant movement throughout the night. Sometimes the scratching of the scroll was all Elliot heard from the older elf.

"It looks like we've kept on track," Sage said, breaking Elliot out of his thoughts. Sage pointed to the upcoming dense trees. Elliot squinted. The forest was about three miles out.

"We should make camp in the forest before entering the tribe," Mimi said. "We aren't welcoming of strangers, especially when they come too close. In the morning, I will seek my father."

"I'll stay behind in case anything happens," Sage said. "Don't want any roosters coming around shanking you guys."

It hadn't struck Elliot that there could be other kinds of chimeras. He knew Namir was a different chimera than Mimi and Sage, but he hadn't noticed any others. The events that had happened within Oasis were a blur to Elliot.

Elliot peered over his shoulder again.

He hadn't thought Minari's expression could darken even further.

"I need to talk to you," Minari said.

Elliot blinked. His hand paused, still holding a berry. "Okay."

"Privately."

Elliot looked over at the others. Luka and Owen were quiet, eyes closed, enjoying the warmth of the campfire. Mimi and Sage were talking to each other, enjoying their meal from their recent hunt.

"Now," Minari said.

Elliot popped the last berry into his mouth before standing. The others shifted their attention to him.

"Going somewhere?" Sage asked.

"A stroll," Minari said.

"It's not safe to wander." Sage's eyes narrowed. "Mimi mentioned it earlier."

"He'll be safe with me." Minari's voice was sharp. He took Elliot's wrist and pulled him away.

The older elf kept away from the open area, weaving through the dense layer of trees and moss. They finally stopped, standing at the edge of the forest.

Minari let go of Elliot's wrist. "I don't trust them."

"Huh?" Elliot stared at the back of Minari's head. What did he mean he didn't trust them? Them as in the others?

"The two chimeras."

Elliot frowned. "They have names."

"I don't think venturing farther into their territory is a good idea."

"Why?"

"I don't trust them."

"What do you mean you don't trust them?" Elliot couldn't believe Minari. He had no idea why he wouldn't trust them. Mimi was a warrior, and Sage was his lover. So, on what premise did Minari have the audacity to distrust them?

Minari turned around, his face scrunched into a scowl. "Have you noticed how convenient things are when it comes to them?"

"What?" Elliot furrowed his brow. "Convenient?"

"Back in Venin, when you were 'kidnapped,' they found you, right? Back in Oasis's hideout, they were the ones who stopped Namir, right? Back when I was attacked by the monster, it stopped because of them, right?"

"*What?*" Elliot shook his head. "No, that's not right. You know the warriors are drawn to me, like Chloé and Luka."

Minari scoffed. He pressed his index finger against Elliot's chest. "Have you even recovered from the attack? How tired are you?"

Elliot bit his lip. He knew he shouldn't answer Minari's question. It would only solidify his doubts, and Elliot truly believed there was nothing suspicious between Mimi and Sage. He couldn't bring himself to believe that the two of them would be behind the feral chimera attack.

Elliot's core had been recovering each day, but he noticed it was slow. His chest still felt heavy, and the hollowness in his core was still there. Throughout their travel, he would get hit with brief dizzy spells, but it wasn't anything he couldn't handle.

Minari pushed Elliot's shoulder, and he staggered backward. "I know you know I'm right."

No. No. No. No. No. Elliot wouldn't believe it. He couldn't. Mimi and Sage didn't deserve to be doubted by Minari. He just wished he knew where this was all coming from. "We're going to the chimeran tribe whether you agree with me—*us*—or not."

Minari let out an exasperated sigh. "You know I don't have a choice otherwise."

"You do have a choice: return to Mistfall or stay with us." Elliot turned, making his way back to camp. "I don't care which one you choose."

Elliot took long strides, this time not caring to avoid the open areas like Minari had. He didn't see why he should. As long as Mimi or Sage were with them, the other chimeras wouldn't hurt them.

Elliot didn't hear Minari's footsteps behind him. Only his own breath and hasty movement reached his ears. The loud crunch of the grass underneath his boots echoed throughout the deserted forest.

He inhaled deeply before letting out a shaky breath. His chest tightened, and his stomach twisted. Had Minari really decided to return to Mistfall? Elliot slowed down, peeking over his shoulder, hoping to see the familiar purple-haired elf, but he was greeted only with the darkness of the leaves.

He was alone, away from the others and away from Minari. His thoughts raced back to Mimi's warning about how chimeras were wary of strangers. Surely Minari wouldn't have left Elliot alone, knowing this could happen, right?

Or was Minari trying to prove a point?

Elliot's legs picked up the pace. He needed to get back to the others.

Suddenly, the familiar glow of the campfire came into view, and Elliot released a sigh. His shoulders sagged as he slowed to a walk. But the closer he got to the camp, the more he sensed something wasn't quite . . . right.

Instead of four people in the camp, there was only one, and Elliot did not recognize him. Was it a chimera out on watch?

Elliot's foot snapped a twig, and his heart jumped.

The figure twitched, aware of Elliot's presence. He stood,

body turning slowly.

Elliot held his breath, keeping completely still.

24
SPRING

Chloé stared at the flickering shadows through the cell bars. She sat on the ground, her legs crossed and wrists against her knees.

Every day, she would wake up from a dreamless sleep. Every passing week, she'd see the same three walls of the cell. Smell the same stale, muddy air. Hear the crackling of burning wood from the torch. Feel the same cold, hard ground beneath her. Ignore the aching pains that traveled from her shoulders, back, and hips.

It was almost like a ritual.

Without seeing herself in a mirror, Chloé knew her once bright pink hair was a dull matted mess. Her fingers would get caught in the thick knots.

Time blended together for Chloé. Day after day, it got harder for her to tell how long she had stayed in the dungeons.

How long it had been since Yuan had been killed right in front of her. How long it had been since she'd promised to free herself from the dungeons.

Ragnar hadn't returned to the dungeons after the incident with Yuan. The ethereal was the only one who had the jurisdiction to release Chloé, but no matter how much she demanded to meet with Ragnar, the officers shrugged her off.

After numerous failures, Chloé knew she would need to force herself out. Using brute physical force was out of the picture, but she could figure out how to manifest her magic without the use of Prim and Rose.

She had seen Licht use magic without his pistol multiple times, so she knew it was possible.

She just didn't know how.

Chloé knew Elliot was able to cast his magic through his hands and Licht was able to cast his magic through the snap of his fingers. She looked at her hands. Examined how dry her skin had gotten. Examined how brittle her nails had become. Examined the grime and dirt beneath her nails. Could something so ugly cast something as divine as magic?

She shook her head. Whether or not her hands were unsightly shouldn't hold her back. She *had* to do this. Elliot and the others were waiting for her.

Chloé took a deep breath and closed her eyes. She focused on her core, feeling the flow of stamina course through her. When she used Prim and Rose, it was like they connected to her core through her palms. The two guns were able to pull her stamina from her core and release magic. She just needed to do that with her hands.

Chloé turned her hands, allowing her palms to face up–

ward.

All she needed to do was create a connection from her core to her palms, create an exit, an out for it to become magic.

But the more she focused on her core, the more she felt her stamina just . . . sitting there. It was stagnant in her chest, as if her will to have it leave her palms wasn't enough.

Chloé let out a huff. It had been easy for her to use Prim and Rose with little training, but trying to use magic without weapons didn't seem to be a natural talent she had.

How long would it take for her to learn to manifest magic without weapons? Would Elliot and the others already be in the Snowy Hills?

Would they have forgotten about her?

No. That wasn't possible. Elliot was the oracle, and she was a warrior. There was no way they would forget. But if she was gone for too long, would they come to her rescue?

Chloé groaned. She couldn't rely on them to get her out. The last time that had happened . . .

Chloé pressed her lips together. She needed to do this.

Chloé walked through the familiar empty hallway. The walls were painted a brilliant white, and the wine-colored carpet was plush against her bare feet.

She was home, back when life was simpler. Her father would be busy with his studies in his office, and her mother would be downstairs with the maids preparing dinner.

Chloé was . . . happy.

Everyone she knew and loved was alive and safe. There

weren't council duties she needed to tend to. There wasn't a general public population she needed to impress. She was the happy little nix who adored wearing frilly pink dresses and wore her pink hair in pigtails with red ribbons.

Chloé stood in front of Gerald's study. The double wooden doors were closed. She'd been told to always knock before entering, so she did. Curling her small fist, she knocked twice.

"Come in," a muffled voice said.

Chloé smiled, reaching for the golden handle and pulling it down.

Gerald was sitting behind a large mahogany desk. Scrolls and parchment littered the surface. He had a pen in hand, eyes glued to the parchment.

"Daddy!" Chloé said.

Gerald's pen paused, and he looked up, his lips perking. "Chloé! What brings you here?"

"Nothing, just missed you."

Gerald laughed. "You just saw me." He patted his thigh. "Come sit."

Chloé's eyes widened, and she grinned. She raced up, planting herself on her father's lap. "What are you writing?"

"Oh, just a letter to Uncle Licht. You remember him, right?"

"Hmm . . ." Chloé pursed her lips. "He had dark red hair."

Gerald chuckled. "That's him." He wrapped an arm around Chloé's middle and continued writing.

"What's the letter about?"

"Just council duties. Nothing too exciting."

Chloé hummed, swinging her legs back and forth. She peered at the letter and furrowed her brow. For some reason, whenever she looked at it, the words blurred together, making it impossible for her to read. She didn't remember Gerald having terrible handwriting where it wasn't legible.

Suddenly, the scene around her shifted. The walls began to seep thick blood, the carpet began to crack, and Gerald's body shook. The hand holding the paper was twitching, moving the pen back and forth.

Chloé looked up. Her eyes bulged as she saw the whites of Gerald's eyes turn black. His mouth was agape, drool dripping down his chin. His skin was ashen.

She pushed herself off his lap and ran toward the door.

"Chloé . . ."

She stopped, her small hands on the door handle. She slowly looked over her shoulder.

Gerald was reaching out to her, but his fingers had grown black claws, and his arm bent backward.

Chloé didn't know what was happening to her father, but she knew she had to get herself out.

She pulled the door open and took a step out.

It was too late when she realized she was falling.

She screamed, body twisting and turning as it fell into oblivion. Darkness spiraled around her.

Her heart pounded against her chest, and she felt her core resonate.

A tingling feeling moved from her chest to her legs and then down to her feet. It was electrifying, urging her to move her legs.

Chloé pushed her chest forward and her legs down, changing into a crouching position. Her body had shifted from being a small girl to her present self.

She focused on the flow of stamina from her core to her feet.

And let go.

Chloé collided with the ground as a burst of magic exploded from her feet.

Chloé's eyes shot open, and she gasped for air. She leaned forward, clutching her chest. She was drenched in cold sweat, and her body was shaking. Her lips trembled as her eyes drifted to her feet.

Her socks were filthy, and her pink heels were scuffed.

But underneath it all was her key to freedom.

25
BOUNCE

Chloé gripped the bars that separated her from the outside world. She leaned against them, looking toward the spiral staircase.

There hadn't been an officer in a while, which either meant there would be one coming down soon or there wouldn't be one for a few more hours. She could wait and make her move after food got delivered, but there was an un-known factor of when that would happen. She could break her way through now, but there could be a risk of running into an officer. And if she ran into an officer, what was she going to do? It wasn't likely they were going to just let her go. But she wouldn't be able to bring herself to harm them either.

Chloé tapped her forehead against the bars.

Now.

Later.

Now.

Later.

Now.

Chloé took a few steps back. If she ran into an officer, she would deal with that problem when the time came. But for right now, she needed to get out. She needed to escape this dungeon and Valquent and find her way back to Elliot and the others. She would worry about the consequences later.

She tapped into her core and felt it radiate stamina. It spiraled around her chest, waiting for her to will it out. Chloé closed her eyes, imaging the flow down her body and to her feet. The same tingling sensation she'd felt in her dream was more prominent. She felt the surge of stamina travel past her hips and knees, wanting to be free.

"Chloé."

The nix snapped her eyes open, startled at the sudden voice. It broke her out of her concentration, reversing her stamina into her core.

"Bunnie?" Chloé blinked. Was she seeing who she thought she was?

Bunnie nodded. "We're here to get you out."

"We?"

A woman clad in black stepped from behind Bunnie. Chloé couldn't see any of her features besides her piercing eyes. They were a mixture of green and brown, olive-like. Her outfit was fitted, as if her clothing were a part of her skin.

The woman reached behind her, pulling out two thin metal sticks. She bent onto one knee and inserted them inside the keyhole.

"I'm sorry it took us so long to get here," Bunnie said, her voice hushed into a whisper.

Chloé bit her lip. It wouldn't have surprised her if Bunnie hadn't wanted anything to do with her after what had happened to Yuan.

"Did you run into any officers?"

Bunnie shook her head. "It was quiet. No one was around."

Did Ragnar think Chloé wouldn't try to escape herself, or that murdering Yuan was enough of a message to prevent anyone else from coming to Chloé's aid?

The lock clicked, and the bars squeaked open.

"A simple lock," the woman said, tucking her pins back into her hip pouch. "The security here isn't that great, it seems."

Bunnie crossed her arms. "Let's hope it stays that way. I don't want to deal with any trouble on the way out."

Chloé stepped out of the cell. Her legs wobbled, but she forced herself to stand. She was finally free.

"We need to hurry," Bunnie said. "Even though there weren't many people around, I still have the Nighthawks stationed around the city to make sure we don't run into anyone. The quicker we get out, the better."

Chloé nodded, following the two up the stairwell.

Their movements were quick, and Chloé tripped over her toes a few times. Being confined in a small cell hadn't contributed much to her mobile abilities.

The dungeons in Valquent were underground, beneath Nexus Hall. Chloé had never imagined she would be rushing through the empty halls as an escapee, but she'd also never imaged she would be put in the position of a prisoner. Granted, she was still technically part of the council; she'd just been put under "observation."

The wooden doors of Nexus Hall swung open, and the cool night air hit Chloé's cheeks. The dark sky was free of clouds, and the moon glowed, as if welcoming her back to the surface.

True to Bunnie's word, there weren't any guards patrolling the area. What exactly were the other Nighthawk members doing to keep them away?

Bunnie looked around the area before turning to the nix and the other woman. "Five minutes."

The woman peered over at Chloé. "I'm not sure if our young nix here can do five minutes."

"If push comes to shove, we'll have to make do. But for now, we have five minutes."

"Five minutes for what?" Chloé asked.

"Five minutes to get you out of here," the woman said.

Nexus Hall was right near the middle of Valquent. Though it was secluded, it wasn't going to be easy to get from the center to the outer walls in five minutes. Even when running, it would take anyone ten minutes or more.

The woman smirked. "Worried? You've been staring at me like I'm crazy."

Chloé's mouth opened and closed. She shook her head. "No."

"That's the spirit."

"The southern gate is the closet and a straight shot from here," Bunnie said. "There aren't many patrolling officers in that direction."

The three darted, staying close to the buildings and hiding away from streetlamps.

The unnamed woman moved with stealth. Her body moved quickly and silently through the night. She reminded Chloé of Minari. The nix wondered why the woman hid her face while Bunnie didn't wear a cloth over her face. Her coat flapped in the wind, a stark opposite of the other woman's inaudible clothes.

Chloé was certain they had been running for over five minutes. Her legs ached, and her lungs burned. Her breathing echoed in her ears. Her pace had slowed, and she knew the other two were slowing down to match her speed. Luckily, there was no run-in with any of the patrolling officers.

Chloé wondered how long they could stretch this luck.

The southern gate came into view. Chloé held her breath. She was almost there.

"The horses are right outside," Bunnie said, her voice rushed. "We managed to get Windfall for you."

Chloé nodded. She had nearly forgotten all about her mare. She would need to thank Bunnie properly once they made it out.

Suddenly, Bunnie took off her coat and threw it over Chloé's head. Her wrist was then grabbed, and she was urged forward quicker. Chloé heard grunts. Grunts from her side.

Officers.

They had found them.

"Don't stop," Bunnie said. The grip around Chloé's wrist tightened.

Chloé couldn't see where she was going. She didn't have a choice but to keep moving forward. The hard cobblestone ground turned into soft grass. The coat was ripped off her head.

"Get on," Bunnie ordered.

Chloé looked behind her. The woman wasn't with them. "Where's—"

"Lavender can take care of herself. We need to focus on getting you out and away from Valquent. I'd be surprised if Ragnar doesn't know you're missing."

Chloé took a breath, pulling herself up into the saddle. Bunnie did the same, now riding Lightning. Bunnie kicked her mare's sides, and they bolted.

26
SEEK

"Where's Elliot?" Minari asked, emerging from the darkness of the forest.

"He's not with you?" Luka asked.

"No. We got separated." Minari turned away, eyes downcast.

Luka narrowed his eyes at the elf. Minari leaving Elliot alone was out of character for the elf. Something was amiss. "Separated, you say?"

"He headed back ahead of me. I figured he would've arrived back by now."

"Are you insane?" Mimi said, standing up. "Why did you leave Elliot alone? Didn't you hear what I said about the other chimeras?"

Minari clenched his fists, glaring daggers at Mimi. "I *know* what you said."

"Then why?"

Minari clicked his tongue and mumbled incoherent words.

"You got something to say?" Sage asked, stepping forward to meet the elf face-to-face. "I don't like how you're talking to Mimi."

"It doesn't concern you."

"Anything that concerns Mimi concerns me."

Minari pressed his knuckles against Sage's chest. "You're invading my space."

Sage cocked a brow. "Oh, am I now?" He took a step closer, and Minari's body stiffened.

Luka quickly went over, placing an arm between them. "That is enough. We should not be wasting our energy on one another."

"Luka is right. We should spend our time and energy in search of Elliot," Owen said.

"Tcht," Sage sneered. "Keep your attitude in check."

Minari stayed silent, expression darkening as he watched the ox turn away and reunite with Mimi.

Luka placed a hand on Minari's shoulder. The elf flinched, but his eyes lightened up. "Where did you last see him?"

"By the entrance of the forest."

"You *what*?" Mimi's eyes widened. "You last saw him at the entrance? Do you have any idea how far in we are right now?"

"Not that far," Minari deadpanned.

Mimi pulled at his hair.

Luka's eye twitched. He pressed his fingers against his

154

chest. The commotion between Minari and Sage had distracted him, but now that they had calmed down, Luka realized why Mimi was so distraught.

The connection with Elliot had been severed.

But what was odd was that it hadn't been sudden. No. The feeling must have been gradual. The connection had been there until recently.

"We need to find him," Mimi said.

"I can look for him," Minari said.

"We should all look for him," Sage said.

"I don't need your help," Minari said.

"What did you say?"

Mimi grabbed Sage's elbow, pulling him back. "We can form groups and look for him."

"Two groups," Luka said. "It's vital we have at least one of you with us, correct?"

Minari shrugged Luka's hand off his shoulder and began marching off.

Luka shook his head. "Sage, will you come with us?"

"Seriously?"

"Mimi should go with Owen—a chimera and warrior in each group."

Sage looked at Mimi. He said a few words to the smaller chimera in their native tongue, and Mimi nodded in response. They gave each other a squeeze of the hands before separating.

"We should circle back here in thirty minutes," Mimi said. "I don't want to wander away for too long . . ."

"All right. Let us hope Elliot is with one of us within that time."

155

Minari led the way. He would occasionally pause before shifting direction, as if he'd heard something. Luka followed with Sage behind him.

The three of them had not spoken a word since embarking on their search, and based on how many twists and turns they'd taken in the forest, they were about halfway into their allotted time limit.

Minari suddenly stopped, his fist colliding into a nearby tree. They were by the entrance, meaning the last place Minari had seen Elliot.

And Elliot was nowhere to be found.

"Well, find any clues?" Sage asked, crossing his arms.

Minari removed his fist. Bark stuck out from his red flesh. He shook his head. "He's not here. He's not here." Minari paced back and forth, fingers running through his purple hair. "He's *not here*."

Sage grabbed the front of Minari's coat, pulling him up so their faces were mere inches away. "Pull yourself together."

Minari smacked Sage's hand away, stepping back. "I don't need the likes of you to tell me what to do!"

Sage's brow furrowed, and he frowned. "What did you say? The likes of me?"

"I don't have to answer you." Minari rolled his eyes. He continued to walk along the outer line of the trees, head turning back and forth.

Sage clenched his fists. His shoulders shook.

Luka put his hands on his hips and shook his head. Whatever had wrapped itself around Minari's mind, it was affecting his behavior is the worst possible way. Luka thought back to

156

when the elf had first started to display erratic behavior.

The incident with his ovis and Licht.

The incident with the mysterious monster.

Luka tapped his chin. It was quite possible Minari's pride had been hurt when Mimi and Sage had come to his aid. He was already emotionally damaged from the loss of his companion, and needing to be rescued would've been like putting salt on his wound. The elf's ability to fight was surely something he was proud of, and returning from battle wounded and unconscious . . .

But that had happened to him before, back in Oasis's hideout. Minari had been at death's door, and if it hadn't been for Mimi and Luka, he would've died.

Luka paused.

Twice now, Mimi had saved Minari.

Luka chuckled.

The young elf's pride must have been delicate to have him behave in such a way. With time, it would pass. Minari would learn to rely on others without the cost of his pride.

Suddenly, a burst of energy exploded inside Luka. He staggered, pressing a firm hand against his chest.

It was warm. Welcoming. Knowing. Longing.

Elliot was nearby, and he was willing his warriors to him like a beacon. Luka had never experienced this sensation before, and it left his entire body tingling, from his fingertips to his toes. The force was urging him to return to his oracle.

Walking back would take too long. He would teleport them back to Elliot's side.

"Take my hand," Luka ordered. He outstretched his hand.

"What?" Sage raised a brow.

"I sense Elliot. We need to return now. Minari!" Luka called out once the ox had placed his hand in Luka's. Luckily, the elf hadn't wandered too far. "I sense Elliot. I will teleport us back."

Minari's eyes widened as he pivoted. He ran back, reaching for Luka's free hand.

Once their fingers touched, the air was ripped out of Luka's lungs as they ported.

27
PIECE

Mimi clutched the hilts of his rapiers so tightly that his knuckles turned white. Owen was beside him, sword ready.

Elliot stood in front of a human, arms outstretched, protecting him. But why? Why was Elliot with him? And what was he doing here? They were still within chimeran territory. There was no reason why any human would be near.

Unless they were poachers.

But the man behind Elliot didn't seem like one.

The man was unusually tall for someone who wasn't an elf. The top of his head barely passed Elliot's. His black hair poked out from underneath his hat, and his eyes were brown like dirt. Based on his clothes, he must've been one of those officers who pranced around Valquent like they owned the place.

"Mimi, Owen, calm down," Elliot said.

"Not until he explains himself." Mimi raised his blade, pointing the tip at the human. "Can't you see what he's wearing? How could I possibly trust him?"

The man placed a hand on Elliot's shoulder, and Mimi tensed. He was too familiar with Elliot, and Mimi did not appreciate it.

"Let me explain," the man said, his voice gentle.

"No, I should," Elliot said. He took a deep breath. "He helped me find my way back. I got lost earlier."

Mimi's eyes narrowed. "How did he find you? How did you get lost?"

"When Minari and I got separated, I must've taken a wrong turn."

"The way to us would have been a straight shot from the edge of the forest."

Elliot's eyes widened. "How did . . . ?"

"Minari came back before you. We separated to look for you. And to think you were here all along with a *human*."

"He's not as bad as you think."

"Elliot, if I may," Owen said. His voice was calm in comparison to Mimi's. "The man before you is unknown to us. He wears an officer's uniform. And Luka and I haven't gotten the chance to inform you of this, but there is a mercenary guild known as the Hunters. They wish to apprehend us on the council's behalf."

The man shifted behind Elliot, and Mimi moved. He launched himself from his position, rapiers in hand, ready to attack.

Suddenly, a gust exploded in front of Mimi. He squinted but kept moving forward until he collided with a solid mass.

160

Pain erupted from his chest, and he lost his grip on his blades. He let out a yelp as he collapsed onto his back.

"Shit. That hurt." It was Sage's voice.

Mimi sat up, groaning as fiery agony burned across the front of his body. He pressed an arm against his midriff. He gave out a hiss as he tried to control his breathing, but every breath sent a shock of pain through him. He must have run full force right into Sage and either bruised his ribs or fractured them.

"Mimi, are you okay?" Sage crouched in front of him, gentle hands landing on his shoulders.

Mimi bit his lip, shaking his head. "Running into you is like running into a wall."

"Sorry. Luka said he felt Elliot and wanted to teleport back. I didn't mean to have you run right into me. Did you miss me that much?"

"Shut up," Mimi hissed. He felt his cheeks warm slightly. If he weren't sitting with so much pain, he would have smacked Sage for insinuating such a thing at such a crucial moment.

"Minari!" Elliot yelled.

The man behind Elliot had one of Minari's daggers between his fingers. He dropped it to the ground.

"Who are you?" Minari seethed.

The man smiled. "First throwing a dagger at me and then asking questions? Your friends are quite the bunch."

Minari lunged, another dagger already in hand.

The man stepped in front of Elliot, pushing him to the side before drawing his blade. Metal clashed as the two struck. He swept his sword up and swung a leg into Minari's side. The

161

impact sent the elf crashing into a nearby tree.

Everything happened so fast that Mimi didn't even have time to blink. He stared, mouth agape. It was like a blur that moved and paused only ever so slightly. He had never seen anyone who was well matched against Minari's speed, let alone someone who was *faster*.

Minari moved to stand but paused, wincing as he placed a hand over his side. His fists shook as he gripped his daggers. His glare was directed at the human.

"You didn't have to do that," Elliot mumbled.

Mimi held a breath. Why wasn't Elliot going to Minari's aid? Why did he stay with the human?

Luka drew his sword and pointed it at the human. "State your identity."

The man sheathed his sword. "I am no one important."

"Important or not, state your purpose."

The man looked at Elliot. The elf's eyes shifted between him and everyone else before landing back on the unknown man. Elliot nodded.

"All right then," he said. "My name is Hiro. Family name is not important, as I do not have one." Hiro paused, as if waiting for someone to interrupt him. "As you can tell from my uniform, I am an officer, but I am not like the ones you see patrolling Valquent." He removed his hat and unlatched his scabbard from his hip. He knelt on one knee, placing his weapon in front of him.

"Showing us this only proves our suspicion about you," Luka said. "What is one of the first officers doing in the chimeran forest?"

Hiro smirked. "Out of everyone here, it is no surprise the

ethereal is the one to recognize this sigil."

"The gold laurel etched into your scabbard is well-known to anyone who isn't a chimera or an elf."

Hiro stood, but instead of putting his hat back on, he placed it on top of Elliot's head. Elliot furrowed his brow before taking it off. Hiro smiled at Elliot before tying his sword back onto his hip.

"Tell us the reason you are here," Luka said.

"Though I am a first officer, I can assure you I came here disregarding my duties." Hiro took his hat from Elliot and placed it back onto his own head. "I'm one of the missing pieces of the puzzle."

Mimi's heart skipped a beat. Missing piece of the puzzle? Did that mean he was a warrior? But he didn't feel anything from him. It wasn't the same connection he had with Chloé or Luka. There was no pull of companionship like with the other warriors.

Hiro felt like a complete stranger.

28
DARKNESS

Lily tapped her fingers against the wooden table, foot swinging as she sat cross-legged. The hut she was in was void of any light, but the darkness didn't bother her. She could see everything clearly, as if it were midday, except everything was monochrome. She had lost her ability to see color when her Necromancer powers had awakened.

She had tracked down the location of the chimeran tribe in hopes of finding other Necromancers. There was no solid indicator when one was near; it was only obvious when they exchanged eye contact. Their eyes would radiate red, reaching out to each other. But looking at people in the eyes was bothersome for her. Troublesome. To think centuries had passed and the other races still segregated against elves.

Pitiful. Truly.

It made it difficult for her to wander anywhere in the

lower lands.

Lily released a sigh before standing. She circled around the unmoving chimera. Based on information, he was supposedly the leader of the bunch. Pale skin. White hair. A bronze snake cuff on his left ear. He was physically smaller than the others though. Lily had assumed a leader would have a . . . stronger appearance, would be taller, bulkier.

And have the ability to put up a fight.

The leader had fallen without even lifting a finger. When Lily had infiltrated the hut, the only thing he could do was look at her in disbelief before his throat was slit. It had been four nights since then, and nothing had changed. It typically took two nights after death for a Necromancer to manifest. If this leader was one, he would have awakened by now.

"Still waiting?" Aiden asked, pushing aside the grungy fabric that was supposed to act as a door.

Lily stopped, placing her hands on her hips. "Unfortunately. I was hoping he was a late bloomer."

Aiden took a seat on the chair, moving his feathered cloak to the side. The wood creaked under his weight. "Maybe he isn't one. It's not like there's a way for us to know for sure."

"Namir seemed to know you were one."

Aiden shrugged. "Maybe she was hopeful."

"Hopeful enough to drag your dead body out before the entire hideout was cleaned out?"

"Or maybe she couldn't resist my charming appearance."

Lily scoffed. "I think not. You're too full of yourself."

Aiden was tall, at least for a human. He was slender, but with a muscular build. His shoulders were broad, evidence of his swordsmanship. His hair was pitch-black, and his eyes shone a brilliant crimson red.

Aiden smirked. "You don't have to lie to me, dearest."

Lily rolled her eyes. "Charlotte is probably rolling in her grave as you openly flirt with me."

Aiden's face darkened. His smile flattened into a thin line. "That filthy chimera will pay for what he did to her."

Lily didn't respond, her attention shifting to the open window. She went to it, her eyes wandering to the night sky. The stars greeted her, sparkling against the sea of black, and the moon was large, as if it were laughing at her.

Lily frowned. The moon. The symbol of the oracle. The symbol of Vylantra. The mere thought of living so close to the oracle made her want to puke. She'd had countless opportunities to kill him, to end his life before he even had a chance to fulfill the prophecy.

But it was too late.

That night . . .

Lily crouched down next to the unmoving body. It hadn't been five seconds since she'd mentioned the loss of her handkerchief before Lily had slit her throat. There was no doubt in the elf's mind that the person before her was the one who'd been breaching Mistfall's security.

The intruder's eyes were open wide, staring blanking. Blood dripped from the corner of her lips. At least her death had been quick. It was something Lily was sure to always achieve. She wasn't fond of prolonging someone's demise.

Lily sighed. "If you'd just stayed in the lower lands, this wouldn't have happened to you," she muttered. She reached out, placing her hand over the intruder's dark red eyes. "Good night."

Suddenly, the intruder grabbed Lily's wrist.

Lily yelped, yanking her arm away. She stood, backing away. Her heart raced, her breaths coming in quick bursts.

The intruder sat up, her head tilting as she grinned at Lily.

Lily's eyes widened. The gash she'd inflicted . . . was gone. It had healed. But how?

"That's quite the greeting," she said. "As expected."

Lily's body tensed. "What do you mean?"

The intruder stood, dusting the dirt off her dress. "I suppose I shouldn't be surprised. Someone like you would be skilled in killing."

Lily reached for her dagger.

"Ah-ha!" She raised her finger, wagging it. "You can try to kill me again, but you won't succeed."

Lily narrowed her eyes. She didn't doubt the words the other had said. There was something else at work, and she wasn't sure if she would be able to handle it herself. Should she retreat? It would be wise to inform Captain Errol and Commander Silas of her finding.

"I'll make this quick," the intruder said. "I can't promise I'll be as quick and clean as you, but if your friends are anything like you in combat, then we have nothing to worry about."

Lily tried to make sense of what she'd said, but she decided it would be better to spend her energy elsewhere. She needed to inform the others about this intruder, and she needed to do it now. She turned, pivoting on her heel before darting off.

Lily jumped into the trees, leaping across the branches, and she made her way back. She felt a presence behind her, as if someone was following her. It wasn't the intruder. No. The way the other moved was very similar to how she moved. It was another scout. But she wasn't overlapping with anyone else's rounds. Commander Silas was diligent with the distribution. He made sure no one landed on the same route twice.

So, who was it?

A body suddenly collided with Lily. "Agh!" She fell, landing on her back. She hissed as pain spread across her body.

Rowen landed beside her. "Are you all right?" He offered her his hand.

What was Rowen doing here? Lily was sure his route was the opposite of hers. There was no chance they would've had even the slightest overlap.

Lily hesitated, but she eventually accepted the help. Rowen pulled her onto her feet.

"I'm sorry about that," Rowen said. "I didn't see you there."

"What do you mean you didn't see me?" Scouts were trained to have sharp hearing and vision and quick reflexes. "And what are you doing here?"

"I'm making my rounds." Rowen cocked a brow. "That's what you're doing too, right? What brings you all the way to my side?"

Lily froze. His side?

"What's wrong? You look pale," Rowen said.

Lily grabbed Rowen's biceps. "Rowen, we need to return to Captain Errol and Commander Silas!"

Rowen blinked. "What—"

"I ran into the intruder. She's not like anyone we've seen. She can—"

The intruder peeked from behind Rowen, a smile spreading across her lips. "I can what?"

Lily pulled Rowen away. What was she doing here? How had she followed her so fast?

"How did you . . . ?" Lily had to keep herself from shaking. She forced her breathing to remain steady. She couldn't show weakness.

"I just followed." The intruder nodded toward Rowen. "Your friend helped."

Lily's blood ran cold. She slowly turned to Rowen, eyes wide. Rowen looked back at her, his expression now blank.

"Ro—" Lily's words were cut short. Gargled noises came from her mouth. The last thing she saw was Rowen holding a bloodstained dagger.

Lily didn't feel herself fall.

When Lily regained consciousness, she was in Valquent. Aiden was by her bedside, but he said nothing upon her waking up. Flashes of memories from her previous life as a Necromancer told her everything she needed to know. Told her the reason she'd been targeted. Told her the reason she'd had to die that night.

Lily had needed to die in order to awaken as a Necromancer.

But she had awakened to her true self too late. Reminiscing about it made anger bubble in her chest. But at the same time, she knew there wasn't anything she could have done to change it. The events had happened because they were meant to be.

Just like how Elliot was meant to die by her hands.

Fate could be cruel sometimes, yet she welcomed it.

Lily would've been lying if she said she didn't have any sort of feelings left from her past life. She had memories of enjoying Elliot's company. Memories of enjoying Minari's company. Memories of enjoying her everyday normal life.

But those memories only brought feelings of pure disgust.

There was a stark contrast between her and Aiden. Her fellow Necromancer companion still harbored feelings for his dead sister. It had been strange to learn about it at first until he mentioned they weren't blood related. That made it a little bit more acceptable, though still strange.

"You're doing it again."

Lily blinked, stepping away from the window. "What?"

"Staring out into nothing. Letting your mind wander." Aiden propped his elbow on the table, resting his cheek against his knuckles. "You have this expression of longing when you do that."

Lily cocked a brow. "Really now?"

"Miss your old life?"

"Only missed my chance at killing the oracle."

"You'll get your chance. Everything that happens now happens for a reason. Father is playing his tune, and we just need to dance to it, never moving too fast, never moving too slow."

"Unless it comes to the topic of revenge. The reason we came here was to find that ox who killed your sister."

Aiden slammed his fist against the wall. "And he isn't here. I ransacked every hut and murdered every chimera that hadn't already gone feral. He isn't here." His eyes moved to the dead chimera. "And we're still here in hopes this one is a Necromancer."

"Chances are slim."

"But . . ."

"But?"

"I heard from a little birdy that my prey and your friends are nearby. Maybe they will come this way. Care to wait?" Aiden wiggled his eyebrows, giving Lily a crooked smile.

"Oh?" Lily licked her lips as they curled upward. "You don't say?"

"It could be our chance to play around with them a bit. What do you say?"

"As long as we're playing within Father's tune."

"As long as we play within Father's tune," Aiden repeated, enunciating every syllable.

A chill ran across Lily's back. She shivered. She couldn't stop herself from grinning. "It would be rude to give them a cold welcome otherwise, especially since your prey will be paying his home a visit."

29
MIRTH

The air was so still that any movement could've caused a shock wave.

"The last piece of the puzzle?" Minari asked. He was still leaning against the same tree he had collided with, a hand pressed against his shoulder. "You're telling me you know what Elliot is? What we're all here for?"

"That's correct," Hiro said.

"You expect us to believe that?" Minari seethed. "Expect *me* to believe that?"

"Whatever you are, that alone won't alleviate us of our suspicion," Luka said. "Not after knowing that the entire council knows of the prophecy. You being aware of the prophecy doesn't surprise me."

Minari stood, hand still gripping his shoulder. "I don't trust you."

"And neither do I," Luka said, his sword still drawn. He took a step forward. "Based on your actions, I find it very difficult to believe you are a warrior."

"I feel nothing from him," Mimi said. "He is empty."

Hiro chortled. "All right, fine. You got me. I am not a warrior. But I am a Nighthawk member. I am sure you all know of our leader."

"Bunnie? Did she send you?" Minari asked.

"Yes. After taking care of Miss Gemme, I made my way over to you. Think of me as a connector between you two." Hiro lifted his right hand and snapped his fingers.

The surrounding trees moved, morphing into a blur as they raced past, yet the ground stayed solid. The stars and clouds above spun like a whirlpool, connecting to a single point. It was as if time had sped forward and stopped at the same time.

And then everything snapped into place. The trees were crisp, and the sky was open.

Mimi scrunched his face. "What is that?" He patted his chest. "I don't feel any pain."

"Just a little trick I learned."

"That was a barrier. A magical barrier. Humans cannot learn magic, let alone create something so sophisticated," Luka said.

"Once you've lived as long as I have, there are things you pick up along the way." Hiro reached into his coat, pulling out a bronze coin. "Recognize this?"

Luka sheathed his sword. "A hero and a member of Nighthawk, hmm?"

"*Hero?* You think he's the hero?" Minari seethed.

173

"A human who has the ability to use magic. Someone who has lived a long time. What else could he be?" Luka raised a brow.

Minari released the hand that was on his shoulder. He clicked his tongue, eyes downcast.

"Upset that the human got the better of you?" Sage asked, helping Mimi up.

Minari didn't answer. He turned his back and disappeared into the forest.

"Minari, wait!" Elliot quickly followed, not wanting to lose the other elf.

He'd known the confrontation wouldn't end well. They had separated on the wrong foot, and he hadn't wanted to provoke Minari further. But Hiro had insisted Minari needed rough treatment to snap back. Elliot had been reluctant at first, but he'd eventually agreed.

A familiar head of purple hair came into view. Elliot sped up. "Minari!"

Minari didn't stop, but he slowed down just enough for Elliot to catch up.

"Are you upset?"

Minari paused. "You're asking me if I am upset?" He furrowed his brow, frowning.

Elliot bit the inside of his cheek. "I didn't mean to upset you."

"You're not the one I'm upset over," Minari mumbled. He took a seat, leaning his back against a tree. He propped his knees up, resting his elbows on them.

Elliot joined him, letting his legs stretch out in front of him.

The two of them stayed in silence, simply enjoying each other's company. Elliot listened to the leaves rustling in the wind. He felt the chilly breeze against his cheeks and neck and inhaled the warm scent of the woods.

"So," Minari said.

Elliot hummed. "So?"

"How'd you run into Hiro?"

"I . . . I just ran into him."

"Heroes don't just pop out of nowhere."

Elliot crossed his legs. "After you and I separated, I headed back to camp. I got lost along the way and ran into Hiro."

Minari leaned forward, eyes locking with Elliot's. "You got lost. Walking in a straight line."

"Maybe 'lost' isn't the right word."

"Clearly. I was starting to worry our oracle was terrible with directions."

Elliot elbowed Minari. "I am not terrible with directions."

"Sure. We'll leave it at that."

Elliot leaned back, lacing his fingers together and propping his hands on his knee. "He is what he says he is." When Minari didn't comment, Elliot continued. "He had a barrier up, and since I'm the oracle, I was able to walk right through it."

Earlier that night . . .

Elliot felt like an ovis that had gotten caught eating an apple it shouldn't have. His eyes were wide, and his body was unmoving as the man laid his gaze on him. Elliot recognized his clothes immediately: navy with gold embellishments and a one-shoulder cape.

An officer.

The warmth in his blood drained. Had they found them? Was that why he couldn't find the others? Had they already been taken away? Should he run? But he couldn't abandon them.

The man's jaw went slack, orbs scanning up and down. "You're an elf."

Elliot blinked. The man's voice wasn't full of disgust or malice. It was soft. Curious. He nodded slowly.

"And you're . . . the oracle, right?"

Elliot didn't know how to respond. He knew he should respond with a no, but part of him wanted to trust the unknown man and say yes. The conflict only made him blurt out a response that wasn't exactly a word; it was a spew of a noise.

"Don't worry. I'm not here to hurt you," the man said. "I was sent by Bunnie to find you and your friends."

Elliot's body unlocked itself upon the mention of a familiar name. His arms and legs felt light, and it was easier to breathe. "You know Bunnie?" Elliot asked, finding his voice.

The man nodded. "Yes. I'm part of Nighthawk. My name is Hiro, and you're Elliot, right?"

"Yes."

Hiro smiled. "I came here after assuring Miss Gemme's safety in Valquent."

"Chloé?" Elliot's heart skipped a beat.

"Yes. She is safe now, probably together with Bunnie."

"Is she coming here?"

"Here, as in the forest?"

Elliot nodded furiously. When was the last time he'd seen her?

"The plan is for you two to rendezvous, yes. And since I've found you, I'll be sure to send a message to Boss."

"Thank Vylantra," Elliot whispered.

"Will you join me?" Hiro asked. He gestured to the fire.

"Sure." Elliot took a step forward. *Wait.* He paused. He was supposed to find the others. Minari had probably already made it back and would be worried that Elliot hadn't returned.

Or had he actually returned to Mistfall?

Their argument played in Elliot's head. He honestly didn't know why Minari was acting the way he was. Now more than ever, they needed to stick together, especially with the council on their tracks.

"Something on your mind?"

"Ah, no. Just . . ." Elliot couldn't sit here and wait for the others to look for him. He needed to find them.

"Thinking about your friends?"

Elliot stared at Hiro. Was he reading his mind?

Hiro chortled. "Sorry. You were thinking so hard it was showing on your face." He tapped his temple. "Your eyes wander off into the distance when you're deep in thought."

Elliot's cheeks heated up. He hadn't known it was obvious. And how could someone he'd just met read him so well?

"Sorry, didn't mean to embarrass you." The corner of Hiro's lips perked. "Your comrades are actually nearby. I saw them first but noticed you weren't around. I made a barrier just in case anything happened. For example, if you had a run-in with a chimera. Once you entered the barrier, you would essentially vanish from their radar. They wouldn't be able to smell, hear, or see you. But I noticed one was missing. I remember Boss mentioning there were two elves."

Minari.

Had he actually returned to Mistfall then?

"We had a fight," Elliot mumbled.

Hiro raised a brow. "About what?"

Elliot shook his head. "Nothing important."

"I doubt that. A fight over nothing important wouldn't bother you this much."

Elliot bit his lip. He didn't want to believe the older elf would abandon him. Minari wouldn't do that. Even if their friendship was rocky, Minari took pride in his duties.

"Look, I've never met him before, but maybe a good punch would help."

Elliot gaped. "What?"

"You know, like knocking sense back into him." Hiro smirked. "Based on Boss's info, he's skilled in fighting. But I am quite skilled myself, very likely more skilled than your friend. Having a little sparring match might help."

Elliot had never thought something like that could work. Then again, he and Minari didn't get into fights. It wasn't something he was accustomed to.

"Oh! I forgot to mention that I will create another barrier when this happens. Any injury would seem like it's real, but it's actually an illusion, so no need to worry if I accidentally let myself go."

"You really think it'll work?"

"Humans do it all the time. I'm sure elves are no different." Hiro smiled.

Minari's jaw dropped. How could he have possibly agreed to allow someone he'd just met to *punch* Minari? Though Hiro had kicked rather than punched, it had still hurt. A lot.

Minari remembered the sharp fire he'd felt when Hiro's boot met his side. How he'd felt an agonizing crack when his shoulder hit bark. How much it had hurt to move or breathe.

But what had hurt the most was when all that happened and Elliot didn't react. He'd stayed by Hiro's side. Minari had thought Elliot hated him after their argument. He'd thought maybe Elliot had replaced him, found someone he could confide in since Minari was out of the picture.

All of those thoughts had gone away when Elliot followed him through the forest. He hadn't stopped until Minari slowed down to let him catch up.

Minari ran his fingers through his hair. "So, you let someone you'd just met kick me around?"

"What else could I have done?" Elliot frowned.

"I don't know. Talk?"

"We tried that."

"Talk again?"

"Just admit Hiro got the better of you."

"He's unnaturally fast. It's weird to see that kind of movement from anyone who isn't a scout." Minari chewed on his thumbnail. "Even Commander Silas." Minari recalled the sparring sessions he'd had with Silas. He could see the way Silas's body moved. It was usually his own body that wasn't quick enough to respond. But with Silas, his entirety was a blur. He couldn't make out any part of his body.

When Minari had lunged for an attack, he hadn't seen Hiro draw his sword or move his leg. He hadn't been able to decipher anything, and that alone made Minari's skin crawl. If Hiro was who he said he was, then there was nothing for Minari to worry about. But if he wasn't, then . . .

No.

He shouldn't doubt Hiro. Doubting the chimeras was what had gotten him and Elliot into the mess in the first place. He needed to trust Hiro.

Even if his gut told him otherwise.

30
WANTED

Chloé let herself fall on top of the soft bed as soon as Bunnie opened the door to the spare room in Nighthawk's hideout. They had been traveling nonstop since escaping Valquent and had finally made it to Trox. A journey that normally should've taken about four days had been reduced to two. Exhaustion spread across every limb in her body. It was even tiring to breathe.

"I'm sorry, Chloé. You can't fall asleep yet," Bunnie said, closing the door behind her.

Chloé bit back the urge to groan. She knew Bunnie must've felt just as tired, if not more. She didn't have the right to be complaining.

Chloé pushed herself up into a sitting position. The room was dimly lit with a single candle held in Bunnie's hand. Bunnie walked over to the center circular table and set the candle on it. She reached into her pocket, pulling out a folded parchment and flattening it onto the wooden surface.

Chloé stood, the bed squeaking from the sudden shift in weight. "What is it?" she asked as she made her way over. Bunnie had laid out a map of Etheria.

"I know we just got her, but it's not safe to stay. I cannot jeopardize the members who are already stationed here."

"Is it . . . Ragnar?" Chloé bit her lip.

Bunnie nodded. "He's moving fast. I don't suppose he finds it flattering that we slipped you out right under his nose."

Chloé pressed her eyes shut. She didn't even want to imagine the casualties that might have happened during her escape. To think others like Yuan had died for her sake . . . It made her stomach churn.

"I received word that one of my members has a good idea where Elliot and the others are."

Chloé's eyes shot open. She slammed her hands onto the table. "Elliot? Do they know if he's okay?"

"Based on their tracks, they're avoiding any open areas. Travel is slow for them, but they've kept out of sight. But . . ." Bunnie paused.

"But?"

Bunnie clicked her tongue, her brows pinching. "The council had the nerve to hire the Hunters."

Chloé's blood ran cold, a chill crawling up her spine. The Hunters. Why did it not surprise her the council would stoop so low? Without any regard to law, the guild's services could be bought at the right price. And knowing the council, the Hunters were being paid a hefty amount of coin.

"It's been two days, and Ragnar already has the entire

kingdom looking for you." Bunnie pinched the bridge of her nose. "The Nighthawks who are working as officers are doing the best they can to slow down the search, but . . ." Bunnie took a breath. "I've ordered them to lie low. Ragnar is catching too many of my men, and I cannot lose any more."

The room fell silent. Chloé hadn't properly apologized to Bunnie for Yuan's death. There'd been no time while they were traveling. Maybe now was a good time.

"We'll need to stick together until things die down. As the leader of Nighthawk, I'm a wanted criminal now," Bunnie said. "We should leave in the morning."

"Where to?" Chloé mentally scolded herself. She hadn't meant for Bunnie to take the lead on the conversation again.

"The only place we can go is north." Bunnie tapped the map. "The others were heading to Solime, so that's where we should go, though I'm not too sure if the Snowy Hills will be out of Ragnar's reach."

Chloé frowned. "From what I understand, Ragnar doesn't have many ties there since he left to join the kingdom's inner circle and council."

Bunnie propped a hand on her hip. "That's the hope."

There was a pause. It was Chloé's chance. "Bunnie—"

"The Snowy Hills are technically still under King Leonard VI's rule, so we'd need to be careful."

"I agree."

Bunnie folded the map and tucked it into her pocket. "I'll leave you to rest then. There're only a few hours until the crack of dawn. We'll need to leave then. I will get my men to prep Lightning and Windfall." She turned to leave.

"Bunnie, wait!" Chloé outstretched her arm.

Bunnie looked over her shoulder. "Hmm?"

Chloé closed her hand into a fist, pressing it against her chest. She had the chance to apologize, but now her words were caught in her throat. Her heart raced, pounding against her hand.

Chloé cleared her throat. "Good night."

Bunnie's eyes softened, and she gave Chloé a small smile. "Good night, Chloé. Rest well." The door clicked behind her.

Chloé heaved a sigh, her knees sinking to the floor. Her head and arms rested against the table as she stared at the candle. She couldn't believe she hadn't done it. She'd had her chance to properly apologize, and based on the conversation, it wasn't just Yuan who had lost his life. So had other members she had never met, members she didn't know the names of. They'd been Bunnie's trusted companions. She wouldn't be able to see them. Talk to them. Laugh with them.

They were gone.

Forever.

Chloé dragged herself back to bed, not bothering to blow out the candle. She collapsed on her back, kicking off her heels. Her fingers glided across the sides of her thighs. Her holsters were empty, vacant of Prim and Rose. The nix wondered if she would ever have her twin pistols in her possession again. The chances were slim. She was a wanted criminal, and she'd dragged Bunnie into it.

Chloé groaned, turning onto her side and throwing the covers over herself.

She was still a Gemme, and she wouldn't let them take that away from her.

31
GO

"Have you ever thought about what you want to do when you grow up, Chloé?"

Chloé looked up at Gerald. Her father's expression sparkled as his burgundy eyes gazed at her. Gerald had just picked her up from school. Her hand was in his as they walked down the path leading to home.

"I'm going to be part of the council like you and Mommy!" Chloé grinned. She looked up to her parents and wanted to be a respected nix, just like them.

"You have a long time before you have to do that, love."

Chloé puffed her cheeks. "But you asked me what I wanted to do!"

"I did. But you're only seven."

"I'm not a little kid anymore."

"Sorry. Sorry." Gerald chuckled. "You're growing up so fast.

185

Sometimes I wish you were still smaller."

Chloé let go of Gerald's hand and ran in front of him, blocking his path. She placed her hand against her forehead and lined it up against his waist. She rose onto her tiptoes, hoping it would make her appear taller.

Gerald went down on one knee. "There, now we're the same height."

"That's cheating!"

Gerald patted the top of Chloé's head. "Have you ever wanted to travel outside?"

Chloé tilted her head. "Outside?"

"Outside Blanc Grotto. To travel Etheria."

Chloé hummed. She pushed her bottom lip out. "Only if Daddy and Mommy come with!"

Gerald laughed, giving Chloé one last pat before standing up and taking her small hand back in his. "I'm sure your mother and I can manage that. We can also visit your friend."

Chloé blinked, her gaze wandering back to Gerald. "My friend?" Chloé had never ventured outside of the grottos. It wasn't possible for her to have made a friend.

"Yes." Gerald tilted his chin down, but his face was a blur, the setting sun casting a harsh shadow against him. "Your friend—"

"Chloé." A hand pressed against her shoulder, giving Chloé a soft shake. "Chloé, it's time to wake up." The voice was stern, but it had a soft edge to it.

Chloé murmured, attempting to push back the waves of drowsiness.

"Chloé," the person said, giving her another push.

Chloé cracked open her eyes, finding it difficult to focus. A small orange light hovered above her. Her eyes tried to focus on the figure by her bedside, but colors just mushed together.

"Still sleepy?"

Chloé's body jerked up, and her heart raced, thudding heavily against her chest. She hadn't heard that voice in *years.* "Mommy?"

There was a pause.

"What?"

Chloé's vision adjusted to the low light, her chest heaving as she saw who was trying to wake her up.

No. Her mind was playing tricks after that dream. Chloé pressed her palms into her eyes. Elizabeth couldn't be here. Her mother wasn't even alive.

"I'm sorry, Chloé, but we need to go. Now," Bunnie said, her voice stern.

Chloé took one last breath before slipping her heels back on. "Okay. Sorry."

Bunnie shook her head. "I should be the one apologizing. If I could, I would make you a cup of tea to ease your worries away." She turned. "Come, the twins have the horses ready."

Chloé followed. They rushed through the dark halls of the hideout. It was still pitch black; the morning sun had yet to crack into the sky. As early as it was, there was movement. Members ran past her and Bunnie, only giving brief recognition before moving along. Bunnie pushed the front door open. Oliver and Deveran were waiting outside, already mounted on their horses. Black cloaks were wrapped around their shoulders. Windfall and Lightning were by their side.

"Morning, Boss."

"Morning, Deveran." Bunnie placed her foot into the stirrup, swinging over. Deveran held up a black cloak. "Thank you again for preparing on short notice. I'm glad the two of you will be joining us." Bunnie put the cloak on, pushing the hood over her head.

Chloé kept her head down as she mounted Windfall. She had traveled alone with Bunnie since escaping, so she was used to the older woman looking at her in her current state. But having others? Chloé quickly realized how improper she appeared. She hadn't bathed in who knew how long. Her hair was a matted mess, and the fabric of her dress had shifted color.

One of the twins trotted by her. "Here, put this on."

Chloé peered through her bangs. Oliver was holding a black cloak.

"Even though the entire guild is wanted for aiding your escape, as least this can hide your identity for the time being."

Chloé's eyes widened. That was right. She was on the run, hiding from the kingdom.

Chloé looked up, eyes meeting Oliver's.

He smiled. "Long time no see. You're looking lovely as ever."

Words choked up in Chloé's throat, her mouth opening and closing. Her cheeks warmed. She grabbed the cloak from Oliver's hand, wrapping it around her shoulders and putting the hood on. Luckily, it was large enough to hide her face.

"Are you flirting with Miss Gemme?" Deveran asked.

"Why would you accuse me of such a thing?"

Deveran didn't answer, but Chloé could imagine the expression the younger brother would be making.

"Boss!" a voice called out. Chloé recognized it as Lavender's. Relief washed over her. She'd survived the ordeal in Valquent.

"What is it?" Bunnie asked.

"Reports from the other members. The Hunters are dividing their forces. Some of them are after the guild. They know Miss Gemme is amongst us."

Bunnie clicked her tongue. "Of course Ragnar would do something like this."

The Hunters. That was why everyone in the hideout was bustling about. They were forming groups, and each would travel across Etheria to help hide her. But she wasn't worth the danger. Why would they risk themselves for her?

"Your worry is showing," Oliver said. "And you are much cuter when you're smiling, so turn that frown upside down! You're going to be with us and Boss. There is no better protection."

Chloé bit her lip. Protection wasn't what she was worried about. She couldn't let the other members do this for her. It didn't make sense. "No. No, you can't!"

Nearby members slowed to a stop, their attention on Chloé rather than the tasks at hand.

"Can't what?" Bunnie asked.

"Do this. Why do you need to do this? Is it to protect me?"

"Why else would we do this?" Lavender asked. She marched up to Chloé's horse, orbs blazing. "Why do you think we would do this for you?"

Chloé shook her head. Her chest tightened, and she felt

the burn of her eyes as tears formed. "I don't know. I'm not even a council member anymore. Not after the escape."

Lavender frowned. "No. No, you're not."

Chloé tightened her grip on Windfall's reins, attempting to hide her shaking hands.

"But," Lavender said, "you are the one who represented us. You are the one who believes what we believe. No other member can match up to your bright ideas and values. And that is what is important to us. You gave Nighthawk a voice."

"I . . . I what?" Chloé choked. When had she done all of that? It was only when Chloé met Elliot that she realized the unfair treatment between the races, so what were they talking about?

Lavender smirked. "It must have been hard pretending to agree with everyone." She shifted her attention to the paused members. "Keep moving, everyone. We need to get out of Trox by the crack of dawn. We have about an hour to spare until that happens."

The rush of motion began as quickly as it had stopped. Black cloaks rushed around, getting ready to depart.

Had Nighthawk been watching her ever since she began her council duties four years ago? Why had they decided to do that? Was it because she was young and essentially a new member?

Or was it something else?

32
OFFER

Mayleen laid several scrolls across the table. They were recordings of her son Minari's scribe duties. At least, up until Alder had decided to retract his familiar. Because of this, the reports Mayleen had were outdated.

"Are you worried?" Errol asked.

Mayleen tapped her finger against the wooden surface, not meeting Elliot's father's eyes. "No."

"We've known each other for a long time. There's no need to keep secrets from me."

Mayleen shot a glare at Errol before slouching into her seat. She propped her elbows against the desk and pressed her forehead against her intertwined fingers. Her hair had grown out, but it was unkept. The bun she usually had neatly on her head was lopsided. Stray strands cascaded down her cheeks and past her chin.

Errol stayed silent, waiting for her to answer.

Mayleen took a few deep breaths. "Alder informed me of some grave news."

"What is it?" Errol hoped it wasn't something to do with Elliot.

"His power is draining. The barrier he has up around the Moon Shrine is draining his power too fast."

"And if this keeps up, Alder is going to end up in a deep slumber for who knows how long until he can recover enough energy," Errol finished.

Mayleen nodded.

Errol knew this was not good news. If Alder were to fall into a slumber, they wouldn't be protected. The illusions up the mountain would disappear. The barrier around the Moon Shrine would vanish. The elves would be exposed to every possible danger.

Lily had not returned since escaping, and for the most part, it had been peaceful. There were only a few imps wandering around in close proximity to them, but they weren't as much of a threat as when Lily had been around, so the scouts had been able to take them out.

"How long has Alder been keeping the barrier up?"

Mayleen shook her head. "That . . . That I do not know."

Errol's eyes widened. Mayleen had always been able to keep track of time and details. "Is something wrong?"

The female elf leaned back into the chair. She lifted her chin to look at Errol.

"These past few days seem like a blur to me."

Errol scanned Mayleen's features. Her skin was ashen. Her vibrant amethyst orbs were dim. Her hair seemed to have

192

grayed.

And she had fine wrinkles near her eyes.

Mayleen looked like she was aging. Could it have been stress? Was Mayleen so severely stressed that even her mind and body were wavering?

Errol walked around the table. He lowered himself to his knee and placed a gentle hand on Mayleen's knee. "You don't need to carry this burden by yourself."

"There is no one left," Mayleen whispered.

Errol furrowed his brow. "What do you mean?" Was she missing her family? "You have Stella."

Mayleen let out a soft chuckle. "Stella . . . I hope she can forgive me one day. Assuming the role of the false oracle must have put a burden on her. To be secluded at a young age, with little interaction with Minari and Elliot . . ."

Errol stood. "What are you talking about, Mayleen?" His breath caught in his throat as Mayleen's eyes became unfocused. They stared forward, blank. He took ahold of her hand. It was cold. "Mayleen?"

"Hmm?"

"Why are you . . . ?" Errol swallowed. "You're fading."

A small smile crept across her cheeks. "For a while now. I was trying to hold on for as long as I could. But this is for the best." Mayleen squeezed Errol's hand. "You will need to take over when I'm gone."

"I can't!"

"Minari is not here, and Stella does not have the proper training." Mayleen turned her head toward Errol. "Watch over her for me."

Errol shook his head, holding Mayleen's hand with both

of his. Pain wrapped itself around his heart. He'd already lost Estelle, his love, and now he was about to lose his childhood friend, his confidant. He didn't know if his own heart and will would be strong enough to push him through the grief.

Errol's lips quivered as he nodded. "You know I would do anything for you." He took a deep breath. "My light," he whispered.

Mayleen closed her eyes. Her smile was still against her features. "Thank you, my sun." Her hand went slack in Errol's hold, but he held on. He held on so tight his knuckles turned white.

Errol collapsed to his knees. He pressed his forehead against her leg, his hands still intertwined with hers. He didn't fight. He didn't fight the tears that broke free, allowing them to flow down his cheeks. Each breath he took sent shards of glass into his lungs.

Everyone was gone. Elliot. Estelle. Lyla. Melvin.

Mayleen.

Errol bit his lip hard enough to break skin. The bitter blood seeped through the open wound and onto his tongue.

Mayleen had been his light, his first and original love. His love for her had never truly disappeared. He'd learned to love her from a distance. He'd learned to distract himself enough to love another. He'd learned to cope with the elder's decision for Mayleen to wed Melvin. There had been nothing Errol could do but respect their decision for her. They knew what was best, and Errol had believed it. Becoming a scout was the least he could do for her. He had devoted his life to protecting her and the village.

But now she was gone.

Minari and Stella were the only ones left of her. He had to protect them. He would be damned if he wasted his life away. He would not succumb to the dagger that dug deep into his chest, twisting anguish into his heart and pouring sorrow into his soul.

He would not allow the feelings of grief to take over. He would push through it as Mayleen's sun, as someone who had saved her from the darkness.

Errol would need to guide Stella away from the darkness as well. He would not allow Mayleen's daughter to follow the same fate.

"Errol."

Alder's voice broke Errol out of his trance. He leaned up, his muscles unhappy with the sudden movement from being in the same position for so long. He didn't know how long he'd been on his knees. It was still dark outside, so probably only a few hours.

"Mayleen has passed."

Errol closed his eyes, taking a deep breath. The way the demigod's words left his lips, it was as if he'd known this was going to happen.

The demigod's footsteps were light against the grass. It was as if the tiny blades swayed, moving away from the small figure. Alder placed a hand over Mayleen's eyes, and her body began to glow.

Errol stood, backing away. Her body was . . . fading. Disappearing. Sparkles of dust were emitted from her body. The light that outlined her shape grew brighter as she grew trans-

195

parent. And then, with a final flash, she disappeared. The speckles of light floated momentarily before being absorbed into Alder's palm.

"Did you just . . . ?" Errol stared at the demigod.

"She is one with me now."

"You . . ."

"Her spirit has returned to me." Alder pressed his palm against his chest. "She informed you about me, correct? About how my powers are weakening?"

"She did. But what do you mean her spirit *returned* to you?"

"Errol, you are a clever elf. I did not expect you to require an explanation, though I can imagine the shock you may have endured within the past few hours."

Errol shook his head. "No. No, I need to be alone right now."

"Very well. Please meet me in the Moon Shrine when the morning comes. We will need to discuss how to go on from here."

Alder vanished, leaving Errol completely alone. He put his hand over the empty seat. It was cold. He curled his hands into fists.

Mayleen wouldn't have a proper funeral. Then again, Errol couldn't remember if he had ever experienced one. He racked his brain for memories of when Melvin had passed away. Mayleen and the elders hadn't held a funeral. He thought back to the fallen scouts when Mistfall had been invaded by imps. There had been no time for a funeral. And, in all honesty, he'd simply forgotten.

Elves were Alder's creation.

They were born from him.

And fallen elves were to return from whence they'd come.

33
DISTURBANCE

Ragnar threw the parchment onto the wooden desk before leaning back into his chair. He ran his fingers through his long silky locks, puffing out a sigh. His men were making quick work, cleansing out the double agents within the officer unit, but they'd still failed to keep Chloé within Valquent.

Ragnar did not have time to micromanage them and had trusted them to at least keep the little nix within the capital's walls. But the order seemed to have been a much greater feat than what they could handle.

The Nighthawk double agents had gotten the better of them, making it easy for her to escape.

"If you want a task done correctly, best do it yourself," he mumbled. He peered at the parchment he had discarded earlier, his eyes scanning the words.

The Hunters he'd hired to track down the oracle had lost

sight of them, and the other group of Hunters hadn't been able to locate Chloé. It seemed their reputation was all talk. Typical human behavior. They liked to speak highly of themselves, but in reality, they were the weakest race.

The ethereal hoped to see the oracle fail the prophecy just so Mykronos could eradicate Etheria.

Perhaps Ragnar should have simply killed Chloé. Without her, there was no way for the elf to fulfill the prophecy, no way for Vylantra to have her way. But that would have been too easy. He wanted to see them suffer. He wanted to see all hope fade from them as they realized they'd failed their one purpose.

He'd almost had it when he'd silenced Yuan. The torment in the nix's eyes when she realized the double agent had died because of her had been priceless.

And Ragnar hungered for more.

He knew word had traveled about him terminating all double agents. He had hoped it would force the nix out of hiding, but it seemed she was still being elusive.

A punishment was in order.

He would show her where she stood in his plan.

"Sir Ragnar," a soft muffled voice said from the other side of his door.

Ragnar narrowed his eyes. Who could possibly be bothering him this late in the evening? "What is it?"

"Sir, there is a young . . . lady who would like to speak with you." His voice trembled.

There was only one "young lady" who would dare seek Ragnar when it was common knowledge that he did not like to be disturbed past eight. "Allow her in and see yourself out.

I do not want to be disturbed."

The door swung open, slamming against the wall. The guard flinched, and Namir strutted in.

Ragnar shook his head. "Close the door and leave."

"Y-yes, sir." The door clicked softly.

Namir looked around as she made her way to Ragnar's desk, her golden feline eyes analyzing the numerous books and scrolls that filled his shelves. She only stopped once she was right in front of him. She placed a hand on the desk, leaning forward. "Your people slaughtered the entire chimeran tribe."

Ragnar cocked a brow. He propped his elbows on the desk, intertwining his fingers. "And?" It wasn't the first time he'd heard the news. He'd first received reports of feral chimeras and the obliteration of the tribe that morning. He was surprised by how long it had taken Namir to make her appearance.

Namir narrowed her eyes. "Why?"

"Why what?"

"Why did you let them do that? I know it wasn't by your order."

"My men were tasked to fulfill their order. I do not care for the repercussions."

"What were they doing inside chimeran territory?"

Ragnar smirked. "Why are you concerned, Namir? Wasn't it you who wanted revenge on those who'd shunned you?"

Namir sneered. She straightened her back, crossing her arms. "We were supposed to be working together. The rise of Mykronos is our goal."

"Yes, and it still is."

"So why—"

"Namir, I must remind you that I do not have need of useless pawns. I'd advise you to return to your task."

She clicked her tongue and shot Ragnar a glare before leaving, slamming the door behind her.

Ragnar wondered if he was giving the female chimera too much freedom. Their agreement had been created because of her ill-willed nature. It was perfect to feed. With the creation of Oasis, it would have been easy for her to offer up souls to Mykronos. She had the power to take whatever chimera came her way and offer them to the Dark God.

It was not common knowledge that Mykronos fed off souls. Ragnar knew even the oldest scrolls hiding within the elven lair did not have this knowledge. The more souls that were offered to Mykronos during the prophecy's promised time, the harder it would be for the oracle to succeed. Ragnar needed Mykronos to break free.

With Namir's dark matter inside the oracle, it made it all the easier for him to succeed.

It was his mission, and he would fulfill it no matter the cost. He had made multiple plans, ensuring that if one were to fail, another would take its place.

Ragnar was destined to be Mykronos's host. That was his prophecy.

34
THRILL

"It's that easy, hmm?"

"What do you propose, Raven?" Ragnar didn't turn from his seat, but he knew the Necromancer was standing only inches behind him.

"She has the location of the oracle, and she went out of her way to confront you about your decisions. Don't you think you gave her a little too much freedom?"

Ragnar chortled at the fact that Raven had read his mind.

"Wouldn't it be better if you ordered her to corrupt his core?"

"I suppose you think a mere chimera could do enough damage to the oracle. Vylantra's powers aren't weak."

Ragnar shifted in his seat, his eyes now resting on Raven's red gaze. The Necromancer's soul was housed in a late teenaged human. His hair was a deep reddish brown and curled around his head, ending right at his chin. His body was enveloped in a thick black feathered cloak. His complexion was pale.

"Unfortunately," Raven said. "The demigods are able to feed her powers, but Father does not receive any from them. He relies on us to feed him souls."

"I would say we are more of his children than the demigods are," Ragnar said before facing the mess on his desk. He shuffled through the parchments, organizing them into a neat stack. A headache had started to creep through his temples from reading all the failed reports. Namir's disturbance had only fueled the growing pain. He would need to generate a plan to capture Chloé. He couldn't let her reunite with the oracle.

"Ah." Raven's voice interrupted his thoughts. "It seems we have a visitor." He outstretched his arm and flicked his wrist. The door swung open.

Gerald stood on the opposite side, a rolled-up parchment in his possession. He entered Ragnar's office without batting an eye. The nix placed the report on the desk.

Ragnar peered at the wax seal: a sword.

"Report from the Hunters."

"Again." Ragnar frowned. "I grow weary of failed reports. Tell them if they've made no progress, do not waste time writing nonsense to me."

"They have a lead on the whereabouts of Chloé Gemme."

Ragnar pressed his lips into a thin line as he observed Gerald's expression at the mention of his daughter's name. His deep rose eyes didn't waver. They remained sharp, locked on

Ragnar, waiting for him to read the report.

The ethereal let out a sharp sigh before reaching over. He destroyed the seal and opened the report.

Ragnar's eyes raced across the parchment, skipping over any detail that was unimportant. True to Gerald's words, the Hunters had found a lead on the runaway nix. She was headed toward Solime, and if she made it there, she would be out of his reach. Ragnar crumpled the report. He couldn't let her escape.

"Say," Raven started, "why not have Gerald pay Chloé a visit? It's been a while since they last saw each other."

"Go on," Ragnar said.

Raven circled around Gerald. The nix remained still. "The council now has an opening. One that Chloé left behind. Luckily, we have someone who could take her place: another Gemme."

Ragnar smirked. As young as Raven was in comparison to him, he admitted Raven had good ideas. "You want Gerald to tell Chloé she has been forcibly removed, perhaps even tell her how disappointed he is in her, how he raised her better than this."

Raven raised a hand, pointing his finger up. "Exactly. And why not top it off by having you pay her a visit as well?" He placed his hands behind his back, body now fully facing Ragnar. "We let her go, but we leave her with a parting gift, something that will destroy her even more." He placed a hand on his chest.

Ragnar's eyes widened, and he grinned. His heart thudded in his chest. He felt his fingertips tingle. This was the exact message he needed to send to make it crystal clear where she was in his plans, to show her just how minuscule she was in comparison to him. She could try for greatness, but she would be nothing before his feet. Her wings would be clipped, and her heels would be slashed.

"We teach her what it means to turn her back on her duties," Raven said. He leaned against Gerald's back, arms around his shoulders. He glided his fingertip across the nix's cheek. "What do you say? An enticing idea, isn't it?"

Ragnar stood. "We leave tonight."

35
HIT

A foreign voice shook Elliot awake. It was rushed and mingled together with Mimi's and Sage's. Both spoke in chimeran tongue.

Elliot sat up, groaning at the ache in his back. He pressed his hand against his shoulder, hoping the small massage would be enough to push back the growing pain.

Sleep had not been comfortable for him. After he and Minari had returned to the group, exhaustion had immediately taken over, and he'd fallen asleep on the first open spot on the ground he saw.

"Good morning," Hiro said. He smiled at Elliot before turning his attention back to the two chimeras. His arms were crossed over his chest, and he stood firmly in front of Elliot.

"Good morning," Elliot said. He peered in front of Hiro.

A woman stood by Sage and Mimi. She was taller than

Mimi but shorter than Sage. Her brown hair was pulled back, but it didn't hide the numerous tangles that wove together. Her clothing was a mirror image to the two familiar chimeras, yet hers were worn. Her slate cloak was torn with numerous holes and mud stains. Her top and bottom weren't spared from the distress, and her feet were bare.

The woman's mouth opened, and a rush of words gushed out. Her eyes glistened with unshed tears.

Mimi turned around, his attention now on Elliot. "You're awake!"

"What's going on? Who is she?" Elliot asked, finally standing up.

"This is Amelia, a female ox," Sage said. The woman grabbed Sage's arm and pressed herself against him. Her held tilted down, but her eyes stayed on Elliot. Sage whispered to Amelia. She shook her head.

Mimi narrowed his eyes at the two. "She's from the tribe," he started before bringing his gaze back to Elliot. "She said they were attacked and everyone was killed. It was a miracle that a few of them managed to escape."

Elliot's eyes widened. "Killed? Everyone? But how?"

Amelia sneered, yelling at Elliot before Sage hushed her.

"She started to freak out as soon as she saw me," Minari said. He was leaning on a tree, his shoulder resting against it, arms crossed. "She'll wail if I get any closer than this." He waved his hand.

"What is she saying?" Elliot asked. Tears had begun to spill from Amelia's bright brown eyes.

Sage pressed his lips into a thin line as he and Mimi looked at each other, as if they weren't sure what to say. They hesitated, their mouths opening at the same time, but nothing came out.

"What is it?" Elliot asked. He took a step forward, but Hiro raised an arm.

"It's best if you remain where you are," Hiro said. He nodded toward Minari. "As long as you two keep your distance, her reactions are pretty tame, at least in comparison to when Minari was only a few feet from her."

"She will not allow any of us near her besides Mimi and Sage," Luka said. "Is it possible she recognizes me and Owen from when we were part of Oasis?"

"But she mentioned the chimeras were killed? How could that be possible?" Elliot asked.

"She said she saw someone who looks like you and Minari slaughter the entire tribe," Sage said.

The air was completely still. Elliot couldn't feel himself breathe. He pressed his lips into a thin line, forcing himself to swallow without choking.

"She saw elves?" Minari asked, eyes widening. He shook his head. "That's not possible."

"I know what I saw!" Amelia said, bursting into common tongue.

Sage placed his hands on Amelia's shoulders. "Calm down."

Amelia shrugged Sage's hands off, shrieking as she spoke in rapid chimeran tongue.

Elliot's mind raced, trying to make sense of everything that was happening. Amelia claimed she'd seen someone who looked like an elf slaughter the entire tribe. That was not possible. There were no other elves in the lower lands besides him and Minari. There was no reason for anyone else to have come down.

Unless they thought Elliot was a mistake.

Had Vylantra sent a message to Stella indicating Elliot was not fit to be the oracle?

But that wouldn't explain someone coming down from Mistfall and slaughtering the chimeras.

"Where are the others?" Elliot asked, hoping his voice would break through the female ox's cries.

"You think I'd show you where my family is?" Amelia spat. She glared at Elliot. "I won't lead you to them. I'm surprised you haven't already killed these two, especially since your kin happily murdered our Lyeokee!"

Mimi's jaw dropped. "What . . . What did you say?" He stared at Amelia, eyes wide. "What did you just say?"

Amelia huffed before answering Mimi in chimeran tongue.

Mimi's eyes went out of focus as Amelia continued to talk. His body began to sway, and Sage caught the smaller figure before he fell. Sage snapped at Amelia, causing her to stop.

"Even the Lyeokee is gone, huh?" Hiro mumbled.

"Who is that?" Minari asked.

"Leader of the chimeran tribe," Hiro said. "Without him, it's like Etheria without a king."

"Mimi's father," Luka said.

"So, the reason she's like this is because . . . And Mimi . . ." Elliot trailed off. It was as if timed had slowed and reality had come crashing down. The *fear* in Amelia as she bared her fangs at Elliot, like an injured, frightened animal doing whatever it could to seem threatening. But Elliot knew Amelia could have easily overpowered him. If she was as strong and skilled as Sage, Elliot wouldn't stand a chance. He wouldn't tap into his magic. No. He couldn't do that to her, even if she was mistaking him and Minari for someone else. A traumatic event like that would surely have caused insanity in anyone.

The only thing he could do was try to get her to trust him and Minari. Elliot wanted to help Amelia, but he couldn't if she didn't trust him, if she didn't accept him as harmless. But how could he get her to believe he was a comrade?

"Amelia," Elliot said, trying to keep his voice gentle. "I understand what you're going through—"

"Lies!" Amelia yelled. "I do not want to hear anything you have to say! I know you're keeping Mimi and Sage captive! Let them go!"

Elliot bit the inside of his cheek. Amelia couldn't see Mimi and Sage were by no means staying with him against their will. They weren't captives; they were here because they wanted to be.

Elliot blinked.

Wait.

Were they here because they wanted to be?

He knew Sage would follow Mimi wherever he went, and Mimi was with him because he was a warrior. But they had originally left the chimeran tribe because they were searching for new land to expand their territory.

If the two of them had never joined Elliot, would this have happened? Was the attack on the chimeran tribe related to the prophecy? No, that couldn't be right. It could've been because Ragnar knew Mimi and Sage were chimeras and had sent an attack on the entire tribe. Ragnar was an ethereal, and the Hunters were human. Though both were vastly different from elves, it was possible Amelia could've simply made a mistake. But this just meant it was *his* fault this had happened. In the end, it was because of the prophecy that this had happened.

It was his fault.

All the casualties that had happened so far were because he was the oracle, because he had set off to fulfill the prophecy.

If not for me, none of this would've happened.

"Hey," Hiro said. His voice was clear and gentle, and it broke through the spiraling darkness that clouded Elliot's mind. He felt a warm hand grab his. Hiro pressed Elliot's hand against his chest. The soft thump of Hiro's heart thudded against Elliot's palm. The steady rhythm calmed Elliot. "You okay?"

"Mm." Elliot nodded.

"Amelia, Elliot isn't keeping us captive," Mimi said. He eased himself off Sage. "There is another reason we are with him."

Amelia furrowed her brow, frowning. She spoke a few words before Sage interrupted. Elliot dearly wished he knew what they were talking about, but he would need to wait patiently.

Mimi let out a sigh. "You deal with her," he said to Sage before walking off.

Amelia shouted, attempting to follow the smaller chimera, but Sage blocked her.

"He went to find the survivors," Sage said. "They aren't far." Amelia gaped at Sage. She slapped him across the cheek before backing away. Sage placed his hands on his hips. "You need to trust us, Amelia. These people aren't like the ones you saw."

Amelia pointed at Luka and Owen. "You mean you want me to trust them? You've lost your mind! Anyone associated with Oasis should not be trusted!"

"We are no longer part of Oasis," Luka said. "Owen and I were under Namir's powers, so we were not able to leave at the time." He lowered himself to one knee, and Owen did the same. The two of them bowed, and Amelia gasped. "Please accept our humble apology."

"W-why?" Amelia stammered. "Is this some kind of trick? I will not be tricked by your kind!"

"Amelia," Elliot started, "I want you to know that we wish to help. We were on our way to the tribe because Mimi and Sage were worried. They're important to us, so you and the others are important to us too."

"What kind of sick trick is this?" Amelia's voice quivered. She pointed a finger at Luka and Owen before pointing it at Elliot. "You think giving me an apology and saying we're important to you is enough for me to believe you?"

"Is there anything I can do? Please let me know."

Amelia only stared at Elliot. Their gazes locked; neither of them dared turn away.

"Kiss my feet."

"What?" Elliot was taken aback.

Amelia pointed down. "Kiss my feet. That was the last thing Lyeokee did to his murderer before she slit his throat."

"Amelia, don't—"

"Sage," she interrupted. "If I do not kill him, then that means I trust him. You will just have to see where he stands in all this."

Elliot took a few steps forward, waiting to see if anyone would stop him.

No one did.

He glanced at Minari. The other elf frowned, clearly on edge with Amelia's words, but he knew this was what Elliot wanted to do, what he *needed* to do. They needed Amelia's trust if they wanted to move forward. Mimi and Sage surely wouldn't rest well otherwise.

Elliot saw how Minari's body tensed as he took another step. His hands were ready to reach for his daggers at a moment's notice. It was reassuring knowing Minari wouldn't let anything happen to him. But he knew it wouldn't be necessary.

Sage moved away, allowing Elliot to stand in front of Amelia. They were standing at the same height, though there was a slight bend in her leg.

Elliot brought himself down to his knees. The cool soil seeped through his pants. He placed his hands against the dirt, lowering his chin.

He closed his eyes, lips meeting Amelia's foot.

36
UNITY

Minari's body relaxed as soon as he saw tears flowing down Amelia's cheeks. Her entire body slackened, and she staggered backward. Sage reached for her, but she put a hand up. She shook her head, whispering to Sage.

Minari bit down the frustration, forcing it back into his chest. He knew there wasn't much he could do, but he couldn't stop feeling like they were trying to hide something from them. No one could understand them.

Elliot stood, smiling. "Thank you."

"I should be thanking you," Sage said. "It hasn't been easy for her."

"I can imagine," Elliot said.

"It happened recently, so everything is still fresh in her mind."

"How recent?" Minari said, pushing off the tree and toward the group.

"About two or three nights ago," Sage said.

"How many survived?" Minari asked.

"Just Amelia and her family: father, mother, two younger brothers."

"So only the five of them," Elliot said.

Sage sighed, scratching the back of his head. "And it makes things difficult."

Amelia clenched the front of her shirt. Words left her lips, and Sage nodded.

"What's wrong?" Elliot asked.

Sage cleared his throat. "It's just . . . Amelia and the others don't have a place to stay. The tribe is in shambles, and there is no food. The forest is vacant, so they can't hunt."

A small blush crept across Amelia's cheeks, and she looked down. Minari frowned. That wasn't what they were talking about. What were they hiding? "Are you sure that's what you two said?"

Amelia's eyes shot up, and Elliot's eyes widened at Minari.

"They have no reason to lie," Elliot said.

"Based on her reaction, I'd say there was something else they said, maybe something they didn't want us to overhear."

"The matter doesn't concern you," Sage said. "Drop it."

Minari clenched his fist. "It concerns us if we are going to be helping them."

"This particular matter does not concern you. So. Drop. It." Sage glared.

"I'll drop it once you tell us what you really meant." Minari met Sage's narrowed eyes with his own.

Sage clicked his tongue. "It's a personal matter."

"Let it go, Minari," Elliot said. "I'm sure it's nothing."

Minari resisted the urge to continue. He didn't need to get into another argument with Elliot—not when they'd just mended their relationship. "Fine."

"Should we meet up with the others since Mimi went to search for them?"

"He knows where they are," Sage said. "They aren't too far from here. We'll probably be able to meet up with them by evening, but it takes us a day or two away from the tribe. I know Mimi is going to want to see things with his own eyes, but that would be up to you." He nodded at Elliot. "It's your call if we've detoured long enough or not. I'm sure Mimi will understand."

"No," Elliot said. "No. If Mimi needs to go, then we still go."

Sage smirked. "He'll be happy to hear it."

"Are you sure?" Minari asked. He mentally winced and regretted asking. He knew he should not have asked, but he wondered if Elliot knew how far they'd trod off their original path. Had he forgotten they needed to reach Solime?

"You don't have to question every decision I make," Elliot snapped back. He narrowed his eyes at Minari before shifting back to Sage and Amelia. "Lead the way?"

Sage turned to Amelia. "Are you well enough to go?"

"I am not weak," Amelia said.

"No, but you are starved. You're shaking."

Amelia bit her lip, turning away. "It's not concerning. We can go."

Evening fell upon the sky by the time they saw the light of a campfire come into view. Mimi was with four other chimeras. Their clothes were in a similar state as Amelia's: tattered and torn. They were huddled close to the fire, attempting to absorb any warmth the flames provided to fight against the chilly night.

Mimi's head snapped up as soon as he realized they were nearby. The other four chimeras followed his gaze. Their eyes widened, and as soon as their eyes landed on Minari, Elliot, Luka, and Owen, they tensed. They quickly stood, positioning themselves in front of Mimi. Mimi stood with them, quick words leaving his lips. They looked at one another, brows furrowed.

Sage paused, lifting a hand. "Mimi may not have told them about us yet, and they are protective of him. Could you all stay here until Amelia and I clear things up?"

Elliot nodded. "Take your time."

Sage and Amelia proceeded forward.

Words were exchanged, and mixed emotions emerged. The younger chimeras pointed at their own ears and then toward Elliot and Minari. Mimi shook his head. Amelia said a few words, but the two older chimeras didn't seem to budge. Their shoulders remained tense. They held their position close to Mimi, sparing glances at the two elves.

They didn't trust them. It wasn't surprising.

Minari thought about how easy it had been for Amelia to trust Elliot once she'd given him the chance. It was like all the stress and worries had been released from her bones the moment Elliot came into contact with her.

Could there have been a connection? Was Amelia a warrior? It could be a possibility.

"Elliot," Minari said. "Is Amelia a warrior?"

Elliot blinked. "No." He shook his head. "She isn't one."

"Then how did she trust you so easily when she asked you to kiss her feet?"

"You know how animals can sense if someone is threatening or not?"

"You think she sensed that in you?"

"Elliot's magic might have helped with that," Luka said. "Elliot's overall aura is peaceful. Perhaps Amelia sensed it. I would not be surprised if anyone without a core could feel it." He glanced at Minari. "Are you able to sense it?"

Minari pressed his lips together, looking forward. He had never been able to sense what kind of aura Elliot had. He just felt Elliot. It hadn't changed from before he'd awoken as the oracle to now.

But Elliot did have ways of calming him. Sometimes just being around Elliot would bring Minari down from his storm of emotions, easing his mind.

"I can," Minari said. "It's something that I've gotten so used to that I almost forgot it was there."

Elliot cocked a brow. "You've gotten so used to me that you forgot?"

"Our friendship." Minari smirked. "It feels so natural to me that you could say it's unconditional. It's the reason we are here now. Together." Minari recalled the memory of how he'd first met Elliot. He recalled how utterly distraught he'd been when he had fallen off a ledge and twisted his ankle. The amount of shame and embarrassment he would have to face

218

when he met up with his father again, but also the fear of *if* he was ever going to see Melvin again. The pain in his ankle had been so bad that Minari couldn't help but cry. Tears fell down his cheeks in combination of fear of being lost forever and the swelling injury.

When Elliot found him alone and drenched from the rain and covered in mud, Minari's nerves immediately relaxed, but he was also drawn to Elliot's calming aura. Even though the situation had been dire, the younger elf had been able to ease Minari's worries enough to leave him alone to fetch Errol and Melvin.

Minari would never forget Elliot's kindness.

37
PLACE

The rising sun burned Errol's back. His shoulders were hunched forward, and he slouched as he trudged toward the Moon Shrine. The skin on his face felt tight, and his eyes felt puffy. He knew he was in no shape to be showing his face in public, but he didn't care. The early-morning elves spared quick glances at him, but they said nothing. His scouts cast worried glances but left their captain alone.

Errol closed his eyes, letting his legs take him forward. He pictured Mayleen. Her smooth skin would glow whenever the morning sun shone against her features. Her sapphire eyes would glimmer and twinkle. Her expression would be stone, but Errol could tell what she was feeling based on the slightest twitch of her eyes.

Errol suddenly collided with something solid. He staggered backward, eyes shooting open. Silas stood in front of him with Stella right behind him.

"Errol," Silas said, disregarding formalities. "You look terrible."

Errol chortled. "You don't say."

"I heard what happened." Silas looked behind him. "Stella told me everything."

Errol's eyes widened. How did Stella already know? How was she holding up?

The skin around Stella's eyes was pink and puffy. Her skin was dull, and her hair was not in its usual ponytail. Her tousled indigo hair flowed past her shoulders, the ends reaching right above her waist.

"How . . . ?" Errol asked.

"How did I know?" Stella whispered. She clutched the front of her shirt. "How did I know mother had left?" Her voice quivered.

Errol didn't respond. He waited, wanting Stella to answer the question when she was ready. He wouldn't push it.

"She spoke to me in my dreams last night," Stella began. She took a deep breath. "She told me she was sorry and she loved me . . . and to be here when Minari returns." She paused, allowing the tears that were slowly welling in her eyes to fall. "When I woke up, I knew she was gone. I felt it in my chest. In my heart. In my soul. Similar to when father passed away . . ." Stella tucked her chin, her shoulders shaking. Soft sobs escaped her trembling lips. "B-but I know . . . she . . . can finally rest. She w-worked so hard . . ."

Errol pushed past Silas and pulled Stella into an embrace. Her cries grew louder, but they were muffled against Errol. He placed his chin over her head, running his fingers through her hair, careful not to snag on any of her tangles.

His chest ached, and he knew there wasn't much he could do for Stella other than to be there for her and to provide his company, though he wasn't sure how much comfort that alone could give.

"Where were you headed?" Silas asked.

"The Moon Shrine," Errol said.

"Why?"

"Alder wishes to speak."

Stella suddenly pushed Errol away. She looked at Errol with watery eyes before running off.

"Stella!" Errol reached out for her, but Silas lifted an arm.

"Leave her to me. It seems like you have a lot on your plate now."

Errol let out a heavy sigh. "Thank you, Silas. I know it's sudden, but she was entrusted to me. I can't lose her too." Errol had a hunch that Silas knew of his feelings for Mayleen and that both of her children held a special place in his heart.

Silas nodded. "I've got everything under control."

Errol nodded in return, giving Silas a smile before continuing on.

The stairs leading up to the Moon Shrine seemed large and vast. The white staircase was usually welcoming, but Errol's nerves were on edge. His stomach churned with each step he took. He kept glancing around, expecting to see someone looking at him, but there was no one around. Not a single soul. The inside of the shrine was also empty. Not a keeper in sight.

Errol narrowed his eyes. Even if there wasn't an oracle inside the shrine, he knew there were keepers around.

The sound of sloshing water caught his attention. Alder climbed out of one of the rivers. His brown hair clung to his cheeks and chin.

"What are you doing?" Errol asked.

"I was regenerating my powers."

Errol bit his lip. The demigod dared mention he was regenerating his powers when he'd already absorbed the spirits of the elders and Mayleen? Errol clenched his fists. "Why?"

"Ara has been sharing some of hers with me." Alder gestured to the river. "In order for her to transfer her powers to me, I must be inside the river."

Ara was the demigod of water, though Errol had never seen her himself. He hadn't known demigods were able to do something like this. Why couldn't Ara do this instead of Alder needing to absorb the spirits of the elves? Were their sacrifices not enough for the hungry demigod?

"She cannot keep sharing her powers with me," Alder said, as if he'd read Errol's mind. "It is not something we demigods do for one another, as it poses risks in our own territory. The seas would not bode well if she grew weak."

"Does it matter? Who travels by sea anyhow?"

"Depending on your decision, we may."

Errol blinked. Why would they need to travel by sea? He shook his head. "Why would we need to do that?"

"You must decide if you wish to stay here. I cannot provide protection for the elves indefinitely. Creating a barrier around the shrine takes a great amount of energy. There is a chance I will fall into a deep slumber if I exhaust everything. The choice you have is to return to Mistfall or seek new lands the Necromancers are unaware of."

Errol knew Mistfall was in shambles. If they were to re-turn to the village, they would need to rebuild it from the ground up. But they would have to do that while avoiding the imps that wandered outside the barrier. It was like there was a never-ending supply.

Seeking new lands would be the better option, but where would they go? Elves were not welcome in the lower lands, and they would need to outrun the imps. Had Alder men-tioned traveling by sea because he knew a place they could go?

"You mentioned we may travel by sea. Is this what you meant? If we search for new lands, we will need to travel by sea?"

"Correct. Staying on this continent would not be safe. Not until the oracle has fulfilled the prophecy."

"And you know where we can go?"

"There is a place that was founded by the elves long ago. I know it is still there, but it is vacant."

"If we left, how would Elliot and Minari know where to return?"

"That is a concern they would need to remedy when the time comes."

"So, if we leave, they return to nothing. If we stay, they may return to us being dead because the imps have overrun us."

"The choice is yours."

Errol ran his hands through his hair and gritted his teeth. The two options weren't options at all. He knew if Alder fell asleep, the land would be jeopardized. They could face a famine without Alder there to make the mountains habitable.

"How much time do I have?"

"One week. Return here by then."

Errol didn't want to make the decision alone, but he had a feeling he knew which one would be the better one. He wanted to ask Stella's opinion at least.

He believed she should have a say in the future of the elves.

38
DECISION

Silas and Stella looked up as soon as Errol entered his tent. The younger elf used her sleeve to wipe her stray tears. Silas stood from his seat.

"You're back," Stella said, standing up from the bed. Errol lifted his hand, gesturing for her to sit back down. Stella nodded, relaxing back onto the furniture.

"That didn't take long," Silas said. "What did Alder say?"

Errol walked over to his desk and leaned his hands against the surface. He shook his head. "Nothing good." Errol racked his brain, trying to figure out a way to convey the two options Alder had offered him. They weren't ideal, especially with how things were now. It was nearing noon, and everyone knew the elders were gone, as well as their leader. Errol was honestly surprised he hadn't been bombarded on the way back. He would have to thank Silas for that. The commander had probably taken measures to keep everyone calm.

Or as calm as they could be.

Errol straightened up, pinching the bridge of his nose. He could feel Silas's and Stella's gazes as they waited for him to answer. They were eager to know what awaited them, and rightfully so.

"Well?" Silas asked.

"Two options," Errol said. "Alder gave me—no, *us*—two options." He stood straight, his eyes now meeting theirs. "Alder is growing weaker the longer we stay here. He can't protect us for much longer."

"Then what should we do?" Stella asked.

"We can either return to Mistfall or seek new lands."

"What? What sort of options are those?" Silas asked. "There's nothing left in Mistfall, and we can't very well go to the lower lands."

"What would Mother do?" Stella mumbled. She cast her eyes down. "She would know what to do."

Errol pressed his lips into a thin line, closing his eyes. Mayleen would've confidently picked a choice she knew would be right, would be the best choice.

But she wasn't here anymore. They would need to make the choice now.

Errol opened his eyes. "Stella."

Stella's head snapped up. "Yes?"

"I apologize, for this is a heavy burden, and a sudden one at that."

Stella shook her head. "It is nothing. Please do not worry about me."

Errol gave her a soft smile. "You are practically a daughter to me, Stella. Of course I worry about you."

Stella's cheeks went pink, and she turned away. "It's not that I don't know you worry about me. It's just . . . I do not wish to be a bother to you."

"You are not. In fact, I would greatly appreciate your help in this decision. I cannot make it alone."

"Me? Are you sure?"

"Of course." Errol reached for the map of Etheria. He didn't know how outdated it was, but it was better than nothing. He unrolled it, flattening the edges. "Come, Stella."

Stella immediately stood, taking a spot by Silas.

"Alder mentioned there is land beyond the sea that we could seek refuge in," Errol said. He scanned the map, but he didn't spot any islands around Etheria.

"I don't see anything but the kingdom," Silas said.

"Perhaps it is hidden," Stella said. She pointed at the body of water next to the mountains, away from the lower lands. "It could be there."

"What brings you to think so?" Errol asked.

"Well, Alder mentioned it, so he must know of a place, right?"

"That is correct. He did say that to me."

"It can't be too far if he means for us to travel there, and I assume we will be under his protection while doing so."

Errol nodded. That did make sense. He hadn't considered it could be relatively close. They hadn't done it before, but they could get everyone down to the base of the mountain in about a week. How they would travel by sea was a different matter. Would they need to make boats? And how long would the journey be before they reached the island?

"But if we return to Mistfall, then we need to repair everything," Silas said. "When the ensnaring trap was activated, it destroyed everything. I can't imagine it's habitable."

"Everyone would need to work together to rebuild Mistfall," Stella said.

"And that will take some time. Time Alder does not have," Errol said.

Stella's shoulders sagged. "But if we leave, then what will Minari and Elliot do when they return? They would return to a ruined Mistfall."

"That's something that also concerns me." Errol frowned. "After a long journey, they deserve to have a delicious meal and a warm bed ready for them to sleep in."

No one spoke, their brains buzzing. Errol knew there would be pros and cons with either of the options. It was just a matter of picking the one with pros outweighing the cons.

There was a comfort with returning to Mistfall. He knew the terrain, and so did the others. When Elliot and Minari returned, they would be there, welcoming the heroes home.

If they moved, that meant the Necromancers wouldn't know where they'd gone.

The only reason they knew now was Lily.

The thought that Lily knew nearly everything about them sent shivers through Errol's body. What information had she already told the other Necromancers? How much time did they have until the Necromancers grew tired of using imps and sent other monsters? Errol didn't want to find out.

"We can leave a note for them," Stella said. "With Redd."

Errol stared at Stella, eyes wide. That would be perfect. Alder would be able to call upon his familiar once his energy returned. Minari was able to communicate with Alder through Redd. It was a foolproof plan.

His chest swelled, and his lips spread into a grin. "That's brilliant."

"Huh?" Silas looked between Errol and Stella. "Through the songbird?"

"Minari would be able to get the message clearly," Errol said.

"Minari can talk to birds?"

Stella chuckled. "No. Since Redd is Alder's familiar, he and Minari can communicate with each other."

"Oh! That's right. I didn't know Alder could speak to Minari through Redd."

Errol smirked. "Now you know."

"So, by the sound of it, this is the decision we're going with? Venturing into new lands?" Silas asked. "I kind of like the sound of that. It's exciting."

"We have a week until we decide. Alder wants an answer then, so we don't need to rush," Errol said.

"Since Lily knows our whereabouts, I think leaving would be our best bet at survival," Stella said. She pressed her hands against her chest. "And I believe this is what Mother would have decided. She would believe this was the best choice."

"I agree," Errol said.

The tips of Stella's ears turned pink as she smiled.

"I know it's something we all agree on, but I think it would be wise to sleep on it. Let's return to this topic in six days to see if we all feel the same way."

Silas and Stella nodded, and Errol returned the gesture.

He'd given them six days, but he knew neither of them would change their mind.

And he wouldn't either.

39
PAIR

"Miss Gemme, please wait!" Oliver called out. "You shouldn't be wandering alone!"

"It'll just be a moment," Chloé yelled back, not slowing down.

"Miss Gemme . . ."

Oliver's voice faded as Chloé wove through the dense trees. They'd been traveling for days now, and the three others were right on her heels. She couldn't do anything alone—not even bathe. She knew this was for her own protection, but it was suffocating. She hated feeling coddled.

Chloé needed to be alone. To hear her own thoughts. To breathe.

"I can handle myself," Chloé mumbled. "I don't need them following me everywhere. I can protect myself."

She stopped, feet planting firmly in the grass. She grazed

her thighs where Prim and Rose would've been. She hadn't held her pistols in what seemed like forever, but she could still feel the ghost sensation of them being with her, as if they were still with her even though she knew they were back in Valquent.

Chloé clenched her fists, wondering what Ragnar could've done with them. Were they being kept in a safe place? Had they been tossed in a pile of junk? The only person who could remotely use them was Licht, but Chloé wasn't sure if the other nix would find any use for them.

The weapons nixen used were crafted to match their cores. The gemstones embedded in the weapons resonated with the flow of their stamina, making it easy to command the weapons. Chloé had never tried using a weapon that hadn't been specially made for her, so she did not know how difficult it would be for someone else to use hers.

But knowing Licht, he could probably figure it out.

Chloé hated the fact that Prim and Rose weren't with her anymore. She remembered the day her mother had awoken her from her slumber.

Twelve years ago . . .

"Chloé, dear, it's time to wake up." Elizabeth's soft voice lured Chloé out of her dreams.

Chloé pulled her soft blanket against her face. She felt like it was too early to be woken up.

"Chloé." Elizabeth placed a hand on Chloé's shoulder,

nudging her softly. "Did you forget what today is?"

"Mm." Chloé didn't budge. Whatever today was, it could wait.

There was a knock against her door.

"Is she still sleeping?" Gerald asked.

"Afraid so," Elizabeth said. "At this rate, we'll be late for our appointment."

Chloé's brow twitched. Appointment? Were they leaving the house? Did they want Chloé to be awake so she could see them off and watch over the mansion? She peeked over her covers. "Are you two going somewhere?"

"We are," Elizabeth said, smiling.

"And we're going to be late if you don't get up, love," Gerald said. He crossed his arms and leaned his shoulder against the doorframe.

"Where are you two going?"

"Did you forget?" The corner of Gerald's lips perked up.

Elizabeth stroked Chloé's hair. "It's your birthday."

Chloé gasped. She threw the covers off and jumped out of bed. Her feet landed against the plush pink carpet. She jumped up and down. "It's my birthday! My eighth birthday!" She grabbed Elizabeth's hand, bringing her up from her seated position. "We have to hurry, Mommy!"

"Dear, you need to get ready first. You don't want to visit the Jaspers and Chromes while still in your nightgown." Elizabeth chuckled.

Chloé's cheeks warmed, and she pouted. "How much time do I have? You said we were going to be late!"

"Cecilia is already waiting for you in the bath. Don't worry. We have time," Gerald said. "We'll wait for you downstairs."

Everything from then until Chloé found herself in front of Chrome's Armory was a blur. She didn't remember getting into the bubble bath or Cecilia doing her hair. She didn't remember getting into her favorite pink silk dress or slipping on her small pink heels.

Chloé gripped Gerald's and Elizabeth's hands tightly. They were standing next to her, side by side.

Chrome's Armory was the soul of Blanc Grotto. Every nix got their weapons specially made by the skilled weaponsmith. Their skill was passed down through generations, their secrets kept safe within their lineage.

The walls of the building were painted black, and the roof was made of iridescent stone. The tall wooden door had a door handle that sparkled in the early-morning light.

"Dear, your grip is going to snap my hand," Elizabeth said.

Chloé shook her head. "No, it's not!"

"You're eight years old now. I can feel you getting stronger," Gerald said. "I can't feel my fingers."

Chloé squeezed tighter. "That means I get to have two pistols, right?" She grinned.

"We will have to see about that, love," Gerald said. "Reed and Lyle are the ones who will decide."

Chloé nodded, doing her best to keep her feet on the ground.

They entered, and two heads turned toward them. The two nixen stood, opening their arms, but they stayed behind the desk.

"Gerald, Elizabeth! Welcome!" The nix smiled. His wavy

reddish-brown hair was tucked behind one ear.

"It's good to see you, Reed," Gerald said.

"And this is Chloé?" the other nix said. His hair was similar in shade and style, but it was pulled back in a small ponytail.

Chloé let go of her mother's hand, hiding behind Gerald.

"Yes, this is Chloé," Gerald said. "What are you getting so shy for? Weren't you excited? They're going to help you get your pistols."

"I-I'm not shy!"

"Then why are you hiding?"

"I'm not hiding either."

Gerald chuckled. "Then what are you doing?"

"I'm not ready to say hi yet."

"Okay, we will wait," the nix with the ponytail said.

Chloé peeked around. Dark wooden tables displaying different gemstones were in every corner of the room, and there was a closed door behind the other two nixen. Chloé pointed at it. "What's in there?"

"That's where we make the weapons," Reed said. "Lyle here picks the gemstones, and I craft the weapons."

"Am I allowed to see?"

"Unfortunately, we can't do that," Lyle said. He placed an index finger over his lips, winking. "It's a secret!"

Chloé puffed out her cheeks. "How come?"

"Chloé, dear, it's not polite to ask," Elizabeth said. She knelt to Chloé's level. "Reed and Lyle have an important role, just like we do, and there are certain things that cannot be shared. Understood?"

Chloé pursed her lips, nodding. She didn't fully understand why, but not everyone in Blanc Grotto had access to the extensive library she often went to or the school she attended, and it was her responsibility to ensure no one who hadn't already been given that knowledge received it.

"Good girl." Elizabeth stroked the top of Chloé's head. "Are you ready?"

Chloé took another peek at Reed and Lyle. They smiled, patiently waiting for her to approach them. She nodded. "Yeah."

Gerald and Elizabeth followed Chloé forward.

Chloé's eyes widened at the array of gemstones that lay on the desk. They spread across the surface in a straight line. They were all opals, yet they shone and sparkled differently. Chloé was mesmerized by the gemstones.

"Aren't they beautiful?" Elizabeth asked.

Chloé nodded. "I like all of them!"

"You can't take all of them, love," Gerald said.

"Why not?" Chloé pushed out her lower lip.

"This is for your pistol, remember? So only one. You have to pick the one that resonates with you the strongest."

Chloé rested her chin against the desk, eyes scanning.

"My apologies. We should have thought of this before, but do you need a chair, Chloé?" Reed asked.

Chloé shook her head. "I'm tall enough!"

"Okay, okay. If you say so."

Chloé resumed gazing at the opals. The way they sparkled differently was distracting. She couldn't hear them speak to her—at least, not clearly. The voices of the gems were muddled together, as if they were all trying to speak at the same time.

The young nix closed her eyes. She tuned out the others around her, focusing on the opals in front of her.

She heard them hum. She heard them vibrate. She heard them sing.

Their voices were crystal clear. She could understand them perfectly. Some sang melodies of love, some sang melodies of happiness, and some sang melodies of adventure.

There were two that sang songs of a thrilling adventure, and they drew Chloé in. With her eyes still closed, she reached for the gemstones, clutching them with her hands.

And the song erupted in her ears.

You will travel far.

You will see it all.

Meet fellow friends.

Who are different from you.

But the bonds you share.

Will be true.

Chloé's eyes shot open. The gemstones in her hands were shaking and glowing. She released them, and they clattered onto the wooden desk.

No one spoke a word, mouths agape.

"I've never seen anyone have two gemstones," Lyle said. "No two gemstones are alike, so I am surprised two of them reacted so strongly with Chloé."

"I need to get to work straightaway," Reed said, taking the gemstones into his hands. "Please return in two weeks' time. I apologize for it taking so long, but I hope you understand."

Gerald nodded. "Of course. Please take your time."

Reed nodded at Lyle before taking his leave, disappearing

into the back room.

"That was a sight to see. I still can't believe what just happened," Lyle said. "Chloé, you must be special."

Chloé nodded, smiling. "It's because Mommy and Daddy are great!" The lyrics to the song still rang in her head. The voice was soft, but the words were clear.

"Chloé?"

Chloé's breath was caught in her throat. She snapped her head around, searching for the origin of the voice. Her eyes scanned the trees, looking for the familiar figure that belonged to the voice she had just heard.

Her mouth went dry, and her legs grew weak.

"Father?"

40
SACRIFICE

The campfire was warm, but it didn't affect the frigid air around the group.

Even after brief introductions, Mimi was separated from Elliot and the others. He watched as Amelia's family observed Elliot's and Minari's every move. Their careful gazes caught every slight movement. They watched how they interacted with Sage and Amelia, ensuring nothing happened. Even though Mimi had explained to them numerous times that Elliot and Minari meant no harm, they didn't believe him. It didn't help Mimi had forgotten to mention Luka and Owen. The ex–Oasis captains had them on edge.

"There is nothing to fear. They won't harm you," Mimi said in chimeran tongue.

"Let us decide, Lykrine," Anna, Amelia's mother, said.

"You did not tell us about them, but if you trust them, then we

can learn to as well," Nero said. *"Zale and Nolan look up to you."*

Mimi nodded. Amelia's two younger brothers were one year apart from each other but had a ten- and nine-year difference from Amelia.

The two brothers looked similar. They'd inherited their strong appearances from their father, while Amelia had inherited her appearance from her mother. Their skin and clothes were covered with dirt and grime, but it did not hide the fire in their eyes, their will to survive. They would do whatever it took. They'd escaped a massacre and broke free through the forest, unsure if whoever had committed the crime was following their tracks.

"Lykrine," Nero started, his face solemn, *"we are the only ones left. The chimeras you see here . . . That is all."*

"I will not believe it," Mimi said. *"There have to be other survivors."*

"We were there," Zale said. He had his knees tucked into his chest. *"We saw everything that happened."*

"Do you think we're lying to you?" Nolan asked.

Mimi shook his head. *"I do not. But I refuse to believe there isn't anyone left."* Mimi debated if he should mention the feral chimeras he'd seen earlier. Though he didn't know of a way to reverse their state, knowing there were other chimeras out there brought ease to his mind.

It helped him not feel so alone.

"It would help to speed up the engagement," Nero said. *"It would benefit the race."*

"What? How could you think of something like that right now?" Mimi couldn't believe what he had just heard. How could Nero be considering something like that when they

should've been focusing on finding a safe place to stay?

"Lykrine, you are young, but surely you understand it's for the future of our kind. If we all die here, then it's the end for us."

Mimi stood, clenching his fists. *"No."*

The others turned to him at his sudden outburst.

"Mimi?" Sage asked. *"Something wrong?"*

"It's nothing," Mimi said. He sat back down on the log with a huff. He shot a look at Sage, giving him a small nod. Sage nodded once in return before returning to his conversation with Elliot, Amelia, and the others. Mimi put his forearms against his knees, clasping his hands. *"I do not wish to talk about it."*

Anna clicked her tongue. *"They are strong, Lykrine. Capable of creating a powerful litter."*

Mimi bit his tongue, forcing his voice down and his lips closed. He knew of Sage and Amelia's engagement—his father had been the one to arrange it—yet he didn't like it. Not one bit.

Serzio had ruled with an iron fist and had been a Lyeokee every chimera respected. Mimi's mother had suffered from poor health and, as a result, had lost her life shortly after having Mimi. Her last words were her uttering the name she had given him. From that moment onward, Serzio believed only the strong should procreate. He'd been devasted when he'd learned Mimi was attracted to men.

"It's what he would've wanted," Anna said. *"You know it, Lykrine."*

Mimi took a deep breath. His chest was tight, and he wanted to scream. They were pushing his father's ideals onto him, but Mimi wanted to be his own person. He did not want to walk in the same footsteps as his father, to be a mirror image of him. Mimi was strong in his own way, and that shouldn't have been dictated by who he was attracted to.

"Though you are free to do what you wish, remember your role. Remember who you are and what you were meant to be," Nero said. *"And I am sure Sage is aware of his role."* Nero nudged his head. *"Just look at him and Amelia. A beautiful couple."*

Mimi balled his hands, his nails digging into the skin of his palms. The smile that was plastered on Sage's face as he spoke to Amelia . . .

Mimi knew it was just pleasantries. There were no romantic feelings between him and the female ox.

At least, Sage didn't feel anything.

Mimi was fully aware Amelia harbored unrequited romantic feelings.

The way she would playfully touch Sage's arm or place a hand on his leg made Mimi grit his teeth. He needed to force himself to calm down, and he repeatedly told himself Sage had chosen him and not her. But he knew it was . . . unnatural to be attracted to males. Part of him wondered if Sage truly did return his feelings or if he just felt sorry for him. Granted, with everything the two of them had been through, it was hard not to believe Sage loved him.

"Lykrine is staring at Sage, Mama," Zale said. *"He's looking at him like how you and Papa look at each other."*

"Is that normal?" Nolan asked. *"Aren't boys supposed to look at girls like that?"*

Mimi didn't want to listen anymore. He removed himself from Amelia's family.

He wanted to be alone, so he left.

Mimi ignored the questions of where he was going, letting his legs lead him wherever they took him.

For most of Mimi's life, he'd heard how strange or wrong it was for him to be attracted to men, how he should be ashamed as the Lykrine because it put shame in his father's name. Serzio had made sure Mimi was strong and desirable, yet his efforts had been in vain. When Mimi had confessed to his father, the relationship between them had spiraled downward.

41
ROLE

Two years ago . . .

Mimi crept up from behind the bushes. He crouched, his posture low as he stepped closer to his prey. The plump brown boar in front of him would be enough to feed him, his father, and another family. He knew Serzio would be proud of him if he was able to kill the boar and haul it back before sunset.

The boar was larger than Mimi, but he couldn't fail.

This was his second try at the coming-of-age ceremony. He had failed last year. He hadn't been fast or skilled enough to hunt down his prey. It had outrun him, and by then, the other chimeras had already finished their tasks. With the constantly shrinking amount of food, there wasn't any prey left for Mimi.

He'd had to return home empty-handed.

245

Serzio had not spoken to Mimi when he'd returned. The only response he'd gotten from his father had been a frown and a deep crease in Serzio's brow.

Mimi was going to redeem himself this time. He didn't want to disappoint Serzio again. He'd endured endless days and nights training with him. They'd sparred for hours, usually ending with Mimi on the ground, but he hadn't given up—not until he had knocked his father off his feet. He remembered the wave of relieve that had washed over him when he saw his father's wide eyes look at him. The small grin that had formed across his father's lips had made his chest feel light. He had done it. Even if he'd only won against his father once, it was enough for him.

Mimi tightened his grip around his makeshift spear. He pondered between throwing it at the boar or using the spear in close combat. Based on the size of the creature, Mimi wasn't sure his strength would be enough for the spear to pierce its skin. He wasn't as strong as he'd have liked, since snake chimeras tended to be weaker in comparison to others. But what they lacked in strength, they made up in speed and dexterity.

Mimi took a deep breath before exhaling through his nose. He only had one spear. If he missed or if it didn't pierce the boar enough, the large animal would simply run away.

Close combat. That was the only way he could kill he boar.

Mimi leapt up and ran across the field. His footwork was light, and he made sure he didn't disturb the grass below his feet. The boar hadn't moved from its spot. Good. It would be a clean shot for Mimi. A swift pierce through the neck of the boar was all he needed to finish the task.

Mimi's ankle suddenly twisted, sending him to the ground.

The boar's head snapped up before it dashed away into the maze of trees.

"No!" Mimi scurried back up. He winced as pain shot through his left ankle, but he couldn't let that stop him. He needed to complete his task. Mimi pushed through the pain as he raced after the boar.

Mimi bit his lip every time he landed on his left foot. The pain was starting to become unbearable, but he could see the boar. It wasn't too far off now. He was so close.

But with his injured ankle, he wasn't able to move as quietly as he wanted to. The boar's ears twitched as Mimi grew closer. The creature and chimera made eye contact, and Mimi knew he was going to miss his chance if he didn't do something.

He gripped his spear and let out a yell as he threw it. He was close enough for it to at least pierce the animal deep enough so it couldn't escape far. As long as Mimi could catch up to it, it was enough.

The spear pierced the boar's thigh.

No!

The boar squealed and darted away, ignoring the weapon that stuck out from its body.

Mimi collapsed to the ground. It wasn't enough. The weapon had barely done any damage to the animal. There was no way he could chase after it.

The chimera peered at his left ankle. It was red and swollen. Mimi took in slow, deep breaths. He shut his eyes.

His stomach churned from the pain, and tears threatened to fall.

How could he be the strong son Serzio wanted if he couldn't fulfill the simple task of bringing home prey to feed two families?

Serzio had introduced him to the daughter of another snake family. It was obvious Serzio intended to get Mimi closer to her.

It was unfortunate that Serzio wasn't aware Mimi didn't find females attractive. He'd acted based on formalities when they'd met, but Mimi couldn't even remember the daughter's name or what she looked like.

It wasn't long before the sun set and the cool wind of night blew in. Mimi had crawled to a nearby tree, hoping it would block out some of the incoming cold air. He shivered, and goose bumps grew across his skin. He had failed the ceremony. The time limit was before sunset, and he was still stuck in the forest. Either way, there was no way he was going to be able to return home in his condition.

"Well, well. What do we have here?"

Mimi's eyes widened, and his blood ran cold. He mentally cursed. Why hadn't he realized sooner? He'd been so preoccupied with the coming-of-age ceremony that he had trespassed into human territory.

"Looks like we have a pretty little chimera. How much coin do you think we can get for this?" one of the humans asked. He had shaggy black hair, and his clothes were baggy. Dirt and small holes littered his attire. He nodded to the man beside him. "You think enough to have a good night at the whorehouse?"

"Maybe enough for both of us to last two nights," the other man said. His wavy brown hair was pulled back into a short ponytail. His clothes were in similar condition to the other man's. "An easy catch too. His foot is busted."

"Tonight's our lucky night then. I'm itching to see my beautiful Annie again."

"You know she only flirts with you because that's her job, right?"

The man waved his hand. "The way she says 'Daniel' is enough for me to keep coming back to her. Doesn't Stephanie say 'Peter' in a way that makes your body turn warm?"

"What we do together is none of your business," Peter said.

"Yeah, yeah. 'Til you get drunk and spill me every single detail."

Peter scoffed. "So, we going to spend all night talking, or are we going to take that chimera back and collect our money? Oasis is giving a pretty bounty on chimeras out of their pitiful territory."

"I have a better idea. Why don't we use this one to grab more?" Daniel asked. "It's not like Oasis will know if the chimeras were found within their territory or not. We can just tell them we found them outside."

Peter raised a brow. "You think this one will sell out?"

"Why not?" Daniel stepped forward, crouching down in front of Mimi.

Mimi wished he had the makeshift spear. He would do anything to shank these humans. The way they talked in front of him made him want to puke.

"Do you understand common tongue?" Daniel asked.

Mimi glared at Daniel, scrunching up his nose. The human reeked. How long had it been since Daniel bathed?

"Do. You. Understand. Common. Tongue?" Daniel repeated, pausing after each word.

"I'd rather die than acknowledge you as someone worth my time," Mimi said in chimeran tongue.

Daniel frowned. "So, you don't understand me."

"If he doesn't understand you, then we should just take him and go. He's injured, so let's take advantage of that."

"Fine." Daniel stood, grabbing Mimi's arm and dragging him up.

Mimi tried pulling away, but Daniel kept his grip strong. Mimi hissed, faltering as he accidentally placed pressure on his left ankle.

"I don't want to carry this thing," Daniel said, pulling Mimi up again.

"You want to drag him all the way back?" Peter crossed his arms.

"Throw him on top of your horse."

"*My* horse? Why not yours?"

"I don't want him anywhere near my mare. She's worth so much more than this thing."

"And you think I want him to be near mine?"

"Your mare isn't as pretty as mine."

"What did you just say about my Nana?"

"I'm saying *Nana* is not as pretty as my Wendy. Therefore, Nana should be the one to haul him."

Peter clicked his tongue. "If Nana hauls him back, then I want two-thirds of the money."

"Two-thirds! That's too much."

"If you want two-thirds, by all means, put him on your mare."

Daniel dropped Mimi. He grabbed the front of Peter's shirt, pulling him up to his face.

Mimi tuned out their argument. He needed to return to the chimeran territory. It wasn't guaranteed the two of them weren't going to follow him, but he needed to take that chance. He began crawling back toward the forest and was thankful he still heard their voices as he continued to put distance between them.

A familiar pattern of trees was in sight. He was almost home.

"Where do you think you're going?"

Mimi cried as he felt someone grab his injured ankle, pulling him back.

"If you think you're going to escape from us, think again," Daniel said. He didn't let go of Mimi's ankle, only gripping it tighter as he dragged Mimi back.

The pain sent Mimi into tears. He bit his lip to prevent himself from making any noise. His body began to shake at the increasing amount of agony.

Suddenly, the pressure on his ankle was released, and Daniel's body was sent flying.

Shadows grew across Mimi's vision as he saw another body stand between him and the human. Darkness took over.

When Mimi awoke, he was back home. Serzio was beside his bed. His lips were turned down, and there was a familiar crease in his brow.

Mimi's stomach sank. His father must've found out about his pathetic attempt at the coming-of-age ceremony. Mimi had twisted his ankle, let his prey escape, and nearly been abducted by humans.

"Father . . ."

Serzio smirked, a small chuckle escaping his lips.

Mimi blinked. Serzio never smiled at him unless he had achieved something worth smiling for.

"I'm proud of you."

"What do you mean?"

"Don't be modest, Mimi. The prey you brought back was enough to feed not only us but Serene's family as well. Her daughter's cheeks were red the whole night. Though she was shy and barely said a word to me."

Serene? Where had he heard that name before?

"Are you getting shy yourself?" Serzio reached over, patting Mimi's head. "Serene and her daughter, Kayla, are dying to meet with you. You remember the man of the family, Grant, right? He was telling me the boar you brought home was larger than his."

Mimi gripped his blankets. Right. Serene was Kayla's mother. Grant was her father. Kayla was the female snake chimera Serzio had introduced him to before he'd set off on his task.

But Mimi hadn't succeeded in the ceremony, so why did they think he had? "Father, my memory is a little blurry. What happened?"

"You returned late last night. An ox chimera by the name of Sage brought you and your prey back. He claimed you had already succeeded in killing the boar when humans invaded. You defended yourself and your prey, fighting them off with only a twisted ankle *as a result."*

Mimi swallowed. *"Where did you hear that from?"*

"From Sage. He saw it happen. Claimed the humans were already taken care of by the time he got there."

"And you believed him?"

Serzio smiled. *"I was close friends with Sage's father before illness took over. They're strong and have no reason to lie to me. If anyone else had told me, I wouldn't have believed them."*

Mimi's stomach twisted into knots. He forced the feeling of throwing up down. His success in the ceremony was a lie, but he couldn't bring himself to confess to Serzio. Right now, Serzio was proud of him; the sparkle in his eyes told Mimi that. He couldn't take that away. No. He would live with this lie until the day he died. *"I'm glad then."*

One year ago . . .

"What did you say?"

Mimi flinched at Serzio's hard tone. His voice and presence commanded obedience, yet Mimi had just admitted his feelings for another chimera—one who wasn't approved by his father.

Serzio had deliberately set up meetings with Mimi and Kayla for the past year. Ever since the coming-of-age ceremony, Mimi had been forced to spend time with Kayla. Neither of them had the courage to tell Serzio nothing was growing between them. The time they spent together was usually in silence.

"You are fifteen years of age. The Lykrine. You do not have

the luxury of fooling around," Serzio said.

"I am not, Father."

"You are." Serzio narrowed his eyes. His sharp gaze tore through Mimi's resilience, attempting to tear it down. *"Why is it you are telling me you and Kayla have not created a bond? What have you two been doing for the past year?"*

Mimi bit his lip. He shied away, unable to meet his father's eyes. He knew how important it was to Serzio that Mimi had children. The act of passing down "strong blood" was etched in Serzio's belief. It was the only way they could show strength within the chimeran tribe. Without a strong leader, the entire race would be jeopardized.

"I do not have feelings for her."

"So, if you do not have feelings for her, why did you not tell me? I could've introduced you to other candidates."

Mimi took a breath. *"Father, I am not interested in anyone you introduce me to."*

There was a pause. *"Why is that?"*

"I . . ." Mimi cast his eyes down, staring at Serzio's desk. He knew he needed to come clean with his father, but he hadn't imagined how nerve-racking it would be. He had done everything in the past year to achieve everything Serzio had envisioned for him. He'd grown stronger, quicker, and braver. He'd trained to be able to wield any weapon with either hand. He'd achieved everything . . . except falling in love with Kayla.

Serzio leaned back in his seat. *"I'm waiting."*

"I'm in love with someone else."

Serzio pressed his lips into a straight line. *"You are aware it is your duty to pass down our blood. Our strong blood."*

"I know, Father."

"And I arranged you and Kayla together because I know she is from a strong family."

"Yes, Father."

"Then why did you spend your energy falling in love with someone else?"

Mimi balled his hands into fists. "Because I cannot control what my heart says."

Serzio let out a sigh. "Who is she?"

Mimi bit the inside of his cheek.

"Well?"

"The person I am in love with . . . is not a she."

The silence between Mimi and Serzio was deafening. The air was completely still. Mimi could feel the intense gaze of his father burning holes through his body.

It felt like an eternity before Serzio spoke.

"Not a she, you said?"

Mimi nodded once. "Correct, Father."

"You do know I will not accept that."

"I am aware, Father."

"You are aware. You are knowing. You claim all this, yet you still defy me?"

"Father, I—"

"Who is it?" Serzio's voice was oddly calm, yet his eyes bore pure rage and hatred. "Who is it that set your path astray?"

"I can explain—"

"I do not want your explanation. I want to know who exactly persuaded my son to walk away from the path I set out for him."

Mimi's voice was stuck in his throat. He opened his mouth, but he couldn't utter a response. Was he so fearful of his father's reaction that he couldn't confess with whom he had fallen in love?

"Mimi, answer the question. Who is it?"

Mimi looked down at his feet. *"S-Sage,"* he whispered.

"Sage?" Serzio stood, slamming his desk. *"You are telling me you are in love with Sage? Does he even love you back?"*

"H-he does."

"That is impossible. I do not believe it."

Mimi looked up, immediately flinching at Serzio's glare. He knew his father wasn't going to approve of their relationship, but he couldn't hide it from Serzio any longer. Time was running out for Mimi before he needed to take leadership, and in order to do that, he needed to have a wife.

But he couldn't have a wife if his heart belonged to someone else.

"I will not have you two in a relationship." Serzio sat down. He rubbed his temple. *"When tomorrow comes, I will order Sage into an arranged marriage with Amelia."*

"No! Father, please don't do this!" Mimi leaned against the desk. He couldn't bear the thought of Sage being in a relationship with someone else. It would kill him.

"You are in no position to speak. From now on, I will ensure your relationship with Kayla proceeds as planned. You are not to speak with or see Sage ever again. Do I make myself clear?"

Mimi felt like his entire world was crumbling apart. Memories of him and Sage flashed before his eyes, from their first moments together when Mimi had first met him to when they'd confessed their feelings. He'd cherished every passing moment he had with the ox, knowing one day they would come to an end.

His chest tightened, and he choked back tears. He bowed

his head. *"Yes, Father."*

Though Mimi had initially agreed to Sage's engagement with Amelia and to stop seeing the ox, it hadn't taken long for Mimi to snap. The last conversation he'd had with Serzio was an argument, and then he and Sage had left the tribe in search of new lands.

Mimi hadn't had a chance to apologize, and now he never would.

He hated it. He hated how he couldn't be the son Serzio had wanted. Mimi wouldn't have been surprised if his mother was disappointed in him. If she could see him now, would she be disgusted? Would she be disappointed with who he'd become? Mimi knew Serzio had done what he could to raise a strong, respectable son, but Mimi had thrown it all away. He'd thrown it away to be himself. Did that make him selfish? As Lyeokee, Serzio must have made numerous sacrifices. As Lykrine, had Mimi made any sacrifices? Had he made any worth noting? Mimi couldn't say he had. He'd only brought shame.

Mimi bit his lip. His vision blurred as his eyes stung. He collapsed, his knees digging into the dirt. His chest ached with tightness, and his stomach clenched. He held himself, leaning forward.

Should he allow Sage to fulfill his engagement with Amelia? Would that be the best choice? There was no one left. The only ones who weren't feral were the seven of them. It made the most sense. But Mimi couldn't do it. The mere thought of it made his throat close. Made his heart twist and shatter. Made his body tremble.

But maybe it was a small sacrifice he had to make for the greater good.

42
SPLIT

Minari's brow furrowed as he watched Mimi walk off, ignoring Amelia's family. He had tried to listen to their conversation, hoping there would be moments when they used common tongue, but they had exclusively kept to chimeran tongue. Whatever they'd been conversing about, Mimi didn't seem pleased. Him storming off was a clear indicator. Minari wondered if it was wise to leave Amelia and her family alone with them.

Sage stood. "I'll go see what happened."

"Stay," Amelia said, taking hold of Sage's wrist. "The sun has set. It's not safe to leave."

"Which is why I should go." Sage frowned.

Amelia kept her hand on his wrist. "He's the Lykrine. You don't trust he'll be fine?"

Sage broke free of Amelia's hold. "That's not the point."

"What is going on here?" Nero asked. Amelia's family gathered around them, seemingly uninterested in Mimi.

"Father," Amelia said. She smiled. "Nothing."

One of the younger chimeras looked up at Anna, asking a question with a tilt of his head and pointing in the direction Mimi had disappeared in. Anna shook her head, patting his shoulder.

"What were you talking about?" Minari asked.

There was a slight twitch in Anna's fingers as she pressed them against her son's shoulder. She put a smile across her face, but her eyes were full of suspicion. "Why?"

"The matter concerns you not," Nero said. "Not to outsiders."

"We're not outsiders," Elliot said. "Mimi is our friend, and he's important to us."

"We aren't a threat to you," Hiro said.

Amelia rolled her eyes, scoffing.

Minari couldn't read the situation. He had thought Amelia trusted Elliot, which was why she'd trusted the rest of them. Unless she was faking it. But what was the reason for her to fake it? Their tattered appearance alone explained their hardships. That certainly could not have been faked.

"Do you trust us?" Minari asked, testing the waters.

"We trust you enough to allow you to stay close to our Lykrine," Amelia said.

Minari narrowed his eyes. So that was it. They'd risked themselves. They didn't care what they had to do as long as they could get close to Mimi. Mimi was precious to them, maybe more so than the connection between Mimi and them. It would be troublesome if they tried to persuade Mimi to stay with them. Mimi was a warrior, a vital person to the prophecy. Minari's role was to ensure Elliot succeeded in fulfilling the prophecy. He could not let that happen.

"I don't like how Mimi is out there alone," Sage said.

"You should not pamper our Lykrine," Nero said.

"I'm not pampering him."

"The way you follow him everywhere, I say it's the opposite," Amelia said.

"So what? You want me to pamper you instead?" Sage's voice rose. "You know that's not going to happen."

"It was the will and order of our late Lyeokee. You mean to dishonor it?" Nero matched his voice with Sage's. "You're bringing shame to our kind!"

Sage's hands balled into fists. "I am fully aware of what he wanted."

"It's best you honor it." Nero's voice had lowered, as if warning Sage. "This is what's left of us. You cannot ignore your duty any longer. Nothing will come out of the relationship between you two."

It was as if someone had blown out the warmth in their small campfire. The crackling of the flames went silent. Amelia's, Nero's, and Anna's intense gazes were locked on Sage, waiting for a reaction.

The ox's expression darkened. He scowled, and his brows dug into his eyes. He stared straight at Nero. "You. Have. No. Right. To. Tell. Me. What. To. Do." The words narrowly escaped his clenched teeth.

"What you two share is not natural," Anna said. "Everyone knows it."

"Isn't that why you left?" Amelia raised a brow. "You two

left because you couldn't handle your duties."

"We've spoken to Lykrine. He agreed to proceed with the engagement between you and Amelia," Nero said.

"What?" Elliot blurted.

Their heads snapped toward him, as if they'd just realized they had an audience.

"What engagement?" Elliot asked.

"Mimi's father arranged a marriage between Sage and my daughter," Nero said. "As the male of the family, it is my duty to see it through. Mimi agreed to it. He believes it is the best thing we can do for our kind."

"I don't believe that's true," Elliot said.

"What makes you think so?" Nero asked, arms crossing. "You're an outsider to us chimeras."

"I've been with Mimi and Sage long enough to see how much they care for each other. I doubt Mimi would just . . . agree and allow something like this."

Minari shifted closer to Elliot. He could see the slight tightening of Nero's jaw and the way his eye twitched every time Elliot spoke.

"Elliot means no harm," Hiro said, putting himself in front of Elliot. "Just stating what he has observed."

"And why should we trust you, *human*?" Nero's voice was full of venom.

"We have our reasons, just like you have yours," Hiro said.

"Why are you all with our Lykrine and Sage anyway?" Nolan asked, his big eyes darting between the two groups. "It's kind of weird."

"Weirder than how Lykrine and Sage look at each

other," Zale added.

"Mimi and I are drawn together because of the prophecy," Elliot said. "I know it's not commonly known with the chimeras, but I'm the oracle, and he's a warrior."

The oxen stiffened, their eyes bulging.

"Prophecy . . . ? Oracle . . . ? Did I hear you correctly?" Nero whispered, as if not wanting anyone to hear him utter those words.

Elliot nodded.

"And you say . . . our Lykrine is *part* of this prophecy?"

Elliot nodded again.

Rushed whispers in chimera tongue were spoken between Nero, Anna, and Amelia. Nolan and Zale grabbed their mother's legs, tears welling up in their eyes.

Sage spoke, but Nero snapped, interrupting him. Sage began again, but Nero kept stopping him, his voice rising each time. What could have triggered their fearful reaction? The two younger chimeras had begun trembling, pushing themselves against Anna as if trying to hide from danger. Anna rubbed circles on their backs, whispering words Minari assumed were meant to comfort them.

"They're the same!" Amelia screamed. "The same as the ones who slaughtered our tribe!" She pointed at Elliot and Minari. "You two . . . You tried to pretend you weren't the same, but you are!"

"Wh-what?" Elliot said. "What do you mean? Minari and I—"

"No!" Amelia shrieked. She continued in chimeran tongue, screaming rapidly.

"You guys better leave," Sage said, his voice calm. "They

think you're together with the ones who destroyed the tribe. I'll take care of this."

"What do you mean?" Elliot asked. "That can't be true."

"They saw what they saw, and they believe what they believe. The only thing that can calm them down is you being away from them," Sage said.

"Will you return?" Minari asked. He did not like the idea that Sage may not be able to reunite with them. He knew Mimi would have a difficult time coping without Sage.

That was, if they reunited with Mimi as well.

They would need to track down the snake chimera and inform him of what had happened.

"Worried about me now?" Sage smirked. "Don't worry. We'll see each other again."

43
DESOLATION

Sage made sure the others were out of earshot before he gave Amelia and her family his full attention. It was clear to him now. The reason Mimi had walked off was because Nero had been egging him into getting Sage and Amelia to proceed with their engagement. Sage knew Mimi didn't want this, and neither did he. Sage loved Mimi deeply and knew he wouldn't be able to betray his feelings for him, even if duty called.

Sage didn't care for honor. He didn't care for Serzio. The Lyeokee had been a thorn in his side, and if he was honest with himself, he was a bit glad that he was dead. The stone-cold snake chimera had wanted nothing but Mimi's misery when the two of them had still been living in the chimeran tribe.

"You've got it all wrong," Sage said. *"They have nothing to do with it."*

Nero's face scrunched up. He had relaxed after Elliot and

the others had left, but Sage could still see Nero's muscles tense slightly. *"You say that, but you don't know what we experienced."* He waved his arms, gesturing to his family. *"The day Lyeokee died was the day the pointy-eared assassin declared war upon the oracle, declared that anyone associated with him is their enemy and they will murder us in cold blood. Friend or foe, it does not matter."*

"What?" Sage didn't know what to think. At first, he had thought Elliot and Minari went to the lower lands to find a new home, like him and Mimi. Once he'd learned of the prophecy, it had made more sense. But he was not aware of any other elves traveling to the lower lands. Elliot and Minari hadn't mentioned others traveling down with them. It didn't make sense.

"Those people cannot be trusted. And the fact they have ex-Oasis captains . . . Sage, you are smarter than this."

"Luka and Owen were under Namir's spell," Sage tried to explain.

"Namir? You mean that cat who was cast out?" Anna asked. *"What does Namir have to do with any of this?"*

"You mean you don't know?"

The other oxen looked at one another. None of them seemed to remember having seen Namir and shook their heads.

"There were only humans and those two ethereals that were apart of Oasis," Amelia said. *"Did your memory and sanity leave you when you left the tribe?"*

"No. She was there." Sage frowned. He was sure he hadn't imagined Namir being in the hideout. It was possible they hadn't recognized her because of her transformed appearance, but they'd mentioned there were only humans, Luka, and

Owen. Had Namir been able to mask her scent? Sage reached up and pinched his brows. It could've been a reason. Sage couldn't remember if he'd been able to realize Namir was a chimera based on her scent or not, but he did remember seeing her face and immediately recognizing who and what she was.

"You have to leave with us, Sage," Amelia said. *"We need to find Lykrine and leave. Staying with them brings us misfortune."*

"Your association with them is the reason our home was destroyed," Anna said.

"That's not for me to decide. Mimi will have to decide that himself."

Amelia scoffed. *"Again with this. You've lost your backbone. An ox should not be following a small snake chimera."*

"You know what he means to me."

"And we've told you what he decided for us. There's no reason for you to follow him around anymore."

"I won't believe it until I hear it for myself."

"Are you going to wait around until he returns then?" Amelia asked.

"I'll wait as long as I need to. I will not abandon him."

"Your devotion to him is for the wrong reasons." Nero shook his head. *"It's a shame."*

"My devotion to him is out of love, just like it should be."

"No, your devotion to me should be out of love. Your devotion to Lykrine should be out of duty and respect," Amelia said.

Sage bit back the bubbling heat that was rising in his chest. He closed his eyes and inhaled deeply, focusing on the cold night air, attempting to cool his boiling blood. He clenched and relaxed his fists a few times. He couldn't see red. Not now. He needed to remain calm. As much as he wanted to punch Nero, Anna, and Amelia in the face, he couldn't. If he did that, he would be reverting to his old self.

And he'd worked hard to move on from old habits.

Sage opened his eyes, vision still clear.

"I will stay indefinitely. If Mimi confirms our engagement, I will stay and fulfill the late Lyeokee's wish. If he says otherwise, then you are on your own."

"What do you mean we're on our own?" Nero asked.

"If Mimi says otherwise, then it's likely he has chosen his path as a warrior over his duties as Lykrine. I will follow him wherever he goes, until he dismisses me."

"So, if he still continues with his . . . other duties and abandons his role as Lykrine but also chooses to have you fulfill your engagement, then what?" Nero asked.

Sage hoped Mimi wouldn't make that decision. He believed the snake chimera wouldn't, but there was always a chance it could happen, no matter how slim. And if it did happen, then Sage would comply. He would let Mimi go and honor his duty as a male ox chimera. Just imagining life without Mimi made his stomach tighten and churn. His throat closed up, but he wanted to gag at the same time. Sage didn't know if he could survive the heartbreak that would come with that decision, but if it was Mimi's wish, he would do his best.

"If Mimi wishes for me to stay with Amelia, then I will stay."

44

BLAME

"You're picking your fingers," Minari said.

Elliot's hands froze. He looked down. The skin around his nails was raw and pulled back, allowing blood to ooze from the open wounds.

"Worried?" Hiro asked. He handed Elliot a handkerchief.

Elliot took it. "Thank you," he mumbled. He dabbed the soft cloth over his wounds.

"I believe we do not have anything to worry about," Luka said. "The strings of fate that attach you and Mimi are strong. He will not abandon you."

Elliot clutched his chest. He felt like there was so much he didn't know about the prophecy and how it could cause a ripple effect with others. There had to be a reason Nero and the others knew of it. But how? There weren't many who knew of the prophecy. The only ones Elliot knew of who knew were Ragnar and the council.

Elliot's eyes widened.

Necromancers.

They knew of the prophecy. It was possible a Necromancer had told them about the prophecy and destroyed the tribe. But they'd said the attacker had looked like Elliot and Minari. That would mean a Necromancer was an . . . elf? No. No. No. That couldn't be it. That couldn't be true. There was no way an elf could be a Necromancer. They were all human, surely. Based on Vylantra's tale, it wouldn't have made sense otherwise.

"Ow!" A sharp poke brought Elliot out of his thoughts. He rubbed the middle of his forehead.

"Stop worrying," Hiro said, his hand in front of Elliot's face, "or I'll flick the thoughts out of your head again." He smiled. "Believe in them. They'll come around."

"Y-yeah . . ."

"Hmm? What was that?" Hiro moved his hand closer, ready to send another flick against Elliot's forehead.

Elliot backed away, swatting Hiro's hand. "Fine! I'll stop worrying."

Hiro grinned. "That's more like it."

"I'm assuming the plan now is to wait," Minari said.

"Right. We can't leave Mimi and Sage."

"But we don't know how long we'll be waiting for," Minari said.

Elliot placed a hand on his chest. He could still feel Mimi's connection with him. He wasn't far, and he could feel a sense of distress coming from the chimera. But it wasn't a feeling of danger. There were hard decisions he had to make, and he needed to make them on his own. As much as it worried Elliot, he knew it wasn't his place to interfere.

"Do you feel him too?" Luka asked, his voice soft.

"I do. He isn't far from here."

"But you will leave him alone."

Elliot nodded. "When the time is right, he'll be ready."

"You think he will choose his role as a warrior over his role as the son of the leader of the chimeras?" Minari asked.

"I don't think," Elliot said. "I know he will."

"Wait! Mimi!"

A voice broke off into the distance. It was early morning. The sun had barely risen. There was fresh dew on the blades of grass, dampening Elliot's shoulder and side. He pushed himself up. Minari was already on his feet. Hiro's eyes snapped open. He sprang up into a sitting position.

"Something's not right," Minari said.

Luka and Owen roused from their sleep, but it did not take long for them to be on full alert.

Rushed footsteps grew closer and louder.

Minari's body suddenly shifted. He pulled out two of his daggers in time to block Mimi's incoming attack. He had his rapiers drawn, blades being deflected by Minari's defense. Mimi's skin and body were covered in blood, and a deep scowl was etched into his features. His eyes were full of fire.

"Why? Why did you do it?" Mimi seethed.

"What are you talking about?" Minari asked.

"Don't play dumb with me!" Mimi pushed forward. "Why did you kill them?"

271

"What?"

"Don't pretend you don't know!" Mimi gave Minari another shove, pushing himself back. He pointed his blade at Minari. "Why did you kill them? They did nothing to you. Or are you actually with the elf who killed my entire tribe?"

What was Mimi talking about? Minari had been with Elliot and the others the entire evening.

"Mimi, wait. I think you have it all wrong," Elliot said.

Mimi turned to Elliot. His lips were trembling, and his yellow eyes were glassy and swollen with red. "I know what I saw, Elliot. There were . . . There were stab wounds and clean gashes across their necks. I tried—" Mimi's voice cracked. "I tried to save them, but it was too late."

Sage appeared through the dense trees. His chest heaved as he tried to catch his breath. "Mimi, wait." His clothes were also soaked in blood, but there didn't seem to be any wounds on him.

"I will avenge them, Sage. You can punch him after I cut his head off his neck."

"Mimi! Wait. Please." Elliot stepped forward. "Could you tell us what happened?"

"Why don't you ask *him* that?"

"I don't even know what you're talking about," Minari said. "I was here the whole time."

"You're lying!"

"What reason do I have to kill Amelia and her family?" Minari asked.

"Oh, I don't know. What reason did you have to distrust me or Sage?" Mimi asked. "You've been distrusting of us ever since we left Valquent. I don't know what we did, but it gave you no right to murder my family and tribe!"

Minari's mouth opened and closed, but only spurts of noise left his lips.

"Don't have an answer? Well, it doesn't matter to me. Either way, I will avenge them."

"Wait," Elliot said. He looked over at Minari. "Minari, throw out your daggers."

Minari looked at Elliot like he had just suggested something bizarre. "Why?"

"To prove you didn't do it."

"But—"

"Please," Elliot said. He knew forcing Minari to disarm himself made the older elf feel vulnerable. Elliot wasn't even sure if Minari knew how to fight properly without them. "If there isn't any blood on them, then it proves you didn't do anything.

Mimi lowered his rapier. "I'll accept he's innocent if we find his blades clean."

Elliot nodded at Minari, urging him to throw out his daggers.

Minari didn't move at first, but he eventually threw the two weapons he had in his hands on the ground. He slowly drew each of his daggers from his waist. One by one, he tossed them in front of him. Each of them was clean. With four of them on the grass, he pulled out the last two that were attached to his thighs.

Minari threw them onto the grass.

But they weren't clean like the others.

45
HIDDEN

Elliot stared at the crimson-lined daggers. The blades that were supposed to be silver were stained with red. He was at a loss for words. His mind was blank. His eyes grew unfocused. "Minari, you . . ." Elliot was barely able to mutter those words.

Minari seemed as surprised as everyone else. His mouth was agape, his eyes wide. He shook his head slowly. "This can't be right. I didn't leave."

"The blood on your daggers proves otherwise," Mimi said. His shoulders shook. "I didn't want to believe it, but it's true. You actually murdered them. And everyone else!"

"I didn't!"

"I was asleep when it happened," Sage said. He cracked his knuckles. "To think I'd wake up to Mimi's sobbing . . . Why did you leave us? Why kill everyone else but leave Mimi and me alive?"

"I didn't kill anyone."

"You keep denying it, but the truth is right in front of you!" Mimi yelled. "I can't believe I trusted you. I can't . . . I can't believe I trusted you . . ." His grip slackened, and he dropped his rapiers to the ground. Mimi collapsed onto his knees, head pressing against the ground. He sucked in a loud breath, sobs escaping his trembling body.

"It wasn't me," Minari said. "There's no way I would do something like that."

"We don't need to hear your excuses." Sage marched toward Minari, kicking his daggers out of the way before grabbing a fistful of his coat, pulling him up. Sage chortled. "You think punching you will make you remember?"

"What—" Minari's voice was cut off as soon as Sage's fist met his cheek. Minari stumbled backward, his back colliding with a tree. His face began swelling from the impact.

"You son of a bitch," Sage said. "You have their blood on your collar. You can't hide it anymore. You killed them."

"I-I what?" Minari placed a hand over the collar of his coat. He pulled at it, attempting to see what Sage was referring to.

"Hold on," Hiro said. He moved between Sage and Minari, arms outstretched. "Let's hear what he has to say."

"Why? It's not like he cared what Amelia, Nero, and the others had to say. It's not like he cared what *we* had to say before he murdered everyone."

Minari shook his head. "I didn't—"

"Cut the bull!"

"I don't remember—"

"Oh, you don't remember? How convenient. Do you want us to forget that you killed every last chimera there was? Zale and Nolan were *calves*, and you had the audacity to slit their throats in their sleep. Ha. Maybe I should thank you for giving them a peaceful end instead?"

"Minari," Elliot whispered. He couldn't stop his voice from shaking. "Did you do it? Did you . . . do it?"

"No! Elliot, please believe me!"

"Then why is there blood all over your clothes?" The more Elliot looked at Minari's form, the more his vision blurred in and out. But each time it cleared, he could see splotches of blood on his coat, on his pants, on his boots, on his cheek, in his hair. He could see Minari's expression shifting between confusion and something sinister. Minari was denying everything, yet he did it with a smile on his face. A smirk. A smirk of someone who was proud of what they'd done, like they had achieved something great.

"Huh? What are you talking about, Elliot?" Minari's voice was high-pitched, frantic. He patted his hands over his body as if attempting to cover up the blood that had already stained his clothes.

Hiro crouched in front of Minari, his head scanning up and down. "If you're the killer, you did a pretty good job hiding it. But I can still see traces of where you couldn't clean the blood off you."

"But I . . . I didn't do it . . ."

"Why?" Mimi's voice cracked. "Why? Tell me why!"

"There is no reason," Minari said. "I didn't do it."

"You hate us that much, huh?" Sage said. "Hate us so much you went after our kind. The reason you didn't kill

Mimi or me is because you need Mimi for the prophecy. As a warrior, he is important. And you kept me alive because I'm his lover. A pillar of support for him."

"That makes sense," Elliot uttered. "Minari, you are tasked with ensuring the success of the prophecy. To ensure I fulfill it."

Minari's eyes widened as he looked at Elliot. "What are you saying?"

"You'll do whatever it takes to make sure I succeed, right? As the oracle. You also are here to ensure my safety. Did you see them as a threat?" Elliot chuckled. "Minari, you've changed."

"Elliot, please! It's not what it seems!"

"I don't want to hear your excuses, Minari." Elliot's voice was barely above a whisper.

"May I suggest something?" Luka said.

"What is it?" Hiro asked.

"I believe Minari was framed."

"Based on what?" Sage asked.

"This could merely be Ragnar's doing. Perhaps he hired a skilled assassin to murder Amelia and the others in a way that appears to look like the work of Minari."

"And what of his daggers?"

"They could've slipped blood onto them and sheathed them."

"Minari is a trained scout," Elliot said. "There's no way someone could've crept up on him."

"Unless they are as skilled as me," Hiro said. He picked up Minari's daggers. "How about this. Until we find the original attacker, I'll hold on to these. It's not like he can fight without them anyway." He turned to Elliot. "What do you say? Is that fair?"

"Minari, did you do it? Please answer truthfully," Elliot said.

"I didn't do it," Minari said. "Please believe me. You know I wouldn't do something like this."

Elliot knew Minari wasn't someone who would murder an entire family in cold blood. Not unless they posed a direct threat. He wanted to believe Minari. He wanted to believe his childhood friend and confidant wasn't the one who'd killed the chimeran tribe, wasn't the one who'd murdered Amelia, Nero, Anna, Zale, and Nolan.

Minari wasn't heartless.

So, why couldn't Elliot see past the bloodstained grin of a murderer as he stared at Minari?

"I believe you."

"He gets to walk free, and my kin get killed?" Sage asked.

"No, we can still find the murderer," Hiro said. "You were heading toward the chimeran tribe, right? Maybe we can find clues there. I leave the call up to Elliot."

Elliot nodded. "Yes. Maybe we can find survivors." He walked to Mimi, who was still hunched over on the ground. Silent tears fell from his chin. Elliot placed a hand on Mimi's back. The touch was enough for Mimi to move. The snake chimera buried his face into Elliot's chest. Elliot wrapped his arms around Mimi's shaking body.

He hoped there were survivors or clues of who'd done it. But at the same time, he was afraid to find the truth. Luka had mentioned it could've been the work of a hired assassin. But who the assassin could be sent chills down Elliot's body. The assassin had been stealthy enough to take Minari's daggers and frame him. The assassin was also probably stronger than Hiro if they'd been able to keep themselves hidden from him.

And the only person Elliot could think of was a Necromancer.

46
GEMME

Chloé couldn't take her eyes off the man before her: the all-too-familiar burgundy hair, brown skin, and piercing crimson orbs.

"Chloé," he said.

Chloé squeaked, jumping from the voice she hadn't heard in ten years. He sounded just like she remembered. "F-Father?"

The male nix outstretched his arms, a warm smile forming on his face. "Come here, love."

Yes.

It was him.

Chloé's body felt light as she dashed across the field. Her chest bubbled as she wrapped her arms around Gerald. She couldn't stop the tears from falling, smearing them over his coat.

Gerald stroked Chloé's hair and rubbed circles against her back. "Shh . . ."

Chloé had so many questions. She wanted to know where Gerald had been for the past ten years. What had happened the night Elizabeth was murdered? How had he even found her? Did he know what had happened with her and the council? Did he know about the prophecy too? Was that why he'd gone missing?

Gerald pulled away, placing his fingers underneath Chloé's chin and tilting her head up. "You've grown. You're much bigger than when I last saw you."

Chloé chortled. "You last saw me when I was eight. I'm eighteen now, Father."

"Ah, I remember when you still called me 'Daddy.' How I miss those days."

Chloé chuckled. He hadn't changed. It was then Chloé realized he was wearing the same clothes he'd worn ten years ago, before he went missing. His black coat still looked pristine, the small frills neat. His shoes lacked any sign of wear. "Father—"

Gerald cleared his throat.

"Daddy."

Gerald nodded.

"Where have you been the past ten years?"

"Has it been that long already?"

Chloé frowned. "Yes. I had to take over the council duties after you went missing."

Gerald frowned. "I thought I told them not to do that."

"Not to make me a part of the council?"

"You wanted to travel Etheria. Remember? I wanted to

make sure you did that before you had to join the council."

"But . . . you went missing."

"I didn't. I reported to everyone in the council that I was looking for your mommy's killer."

What? What was that supposed to mean? "Everyone . . . knew? Everyone knew why you left?"

"I even told Cecilia, but I ordered her not to tell you."

"But they made me a member anyway." Chloé was at a loss for words. Not only had the entire council lied to her, but this fact had been kept from her for ten years. For ten years she had been in the dark, hoping to see Gerald one day, hoping he wasn't *dead*.

"I'm sorry I didn't tell you. You were so young, and I didn't think I would be gone for this long."

Chloé shook her head. "No, it's all right."

"So, you're a part of the council now?"

Chloé held back a wince. She didn't know how to tell him. He must not have known what had happened recently if he was asking her. "Y-yeah."

"I hope they aren't giving you a hard time. Some of them can be a little nasty."

"It's okay. Honestly. Did you manage to find Mommy's killer?" Chloé asked, changing the topic.

The corner of Gerald's lips curled up. "I didn't find them, but I know who did it. And the reason."

"Who?" Chloé's eyes widened. "Who did it?"

"The oracle."

"What?" Chloé couldn't move. Her body was frozen, breath stolen from her.

"The oracle." Gerald's smile turned into a frown. "I know

you know who I'm talking about."

Chloé backed away. "What do you mean the oracle killed Mommy?"

"I guess not him directly. Someone close to the oracle did it."

Close to the oracle? Was he talking about Minari? But she was sure the two of them were the same age. Was Gerald insinuating Minari, at eight, had been able to come to the lower lands, infiltrate their manor, murder Elizabeth without anyone seeing him, and return to the mountains?

"That was all the information I'd gathered until I caught wind of what happened in Valquent."

Chloé's throat tightened. She forced the lump in her throat down but couldn't find the voice to respond. So, he *did* know.

"The council contacted me, you know. Informed me of . . . your escape." Gerald stepped forward, placing his hands on her shoulders. "Why did you do it? Why did you allow yourself so close to the enemy? And on top of that, you took their side? You escaping only further proves your betrayal to the kingdom."

Chloé couldn't do anything but shake her head. Words escaped her, and she only managed to utter a few noises.

Gerald sighed. "Chloé . . ." He paused. "They told me they revoked your status as a council member."

That did not come as a surprise to Chloé. She knew that was going to be the result after she escaped with Bunnie and Lavender.

"And that's not all." Gerald took a deep breath. He removed his hands from her shoulders. He placed his hands on his hips and began pacing.

"What is it?" Chloé whispered. "What is it, Daddy?"

Gerald clicked his tongue. "I hate to do this to you, Chloé."

"What? Please tell me."

"The disgrace you've brought to the Gemme family. I can't have that tarnish our reputation. Our family gemstone is the opal. Opals are meant to be pure. We are to uphold the righteousness of our kind. What you did . . ."

Chloé's body began to shake, and her chest felt heavy. She couldn't believe what Gerald was saying. What he was about to say. What he was about to do.

"I'm sorry to do this to you, Chloé, but you aren't a Gemme any longer. Your status as a council member has been revoked, and I've disowned you. You are no longer Chloé Gemme, but just Chloé. You belong to no family. Prim and Rose have also been returned. Their materials are to be remade into new weapons other nixen can use."

"Why?" Chloé's vision blurred, her breathing coming in quick bursts "Why!" Warm tears fell down her cheeks.

"I've already told you." Gerald pressed his lips into a thin line. "You've disappointed me, Chloé. I raised you better than this. Elizabeth would've been horrified by what you've become."

Chloé collapsed to her knees, sobs racking her body. She hugged herself, shaking her head. She didn't want to believe anything Gerald had said to her. Every word had cut her deeply, digging and twisting into her heart. She'd done her best to make her parents proud. It was the least she could do after taking over the Gemme house.

But she couldn't do it.

So, what was she good for?

"Chloé," Gerald said, kneeling before her.

Chloé bit her lip, attempting to keep it from trembling as she looked up.

"I love you, you know. And so did Elizabeth." Gerald placed his hand over Chloé's eyes. "This is for your own good."

Hot, piercing, burning pain exploded in her chest.

Chloé screamed.

The pain traveled from her arms to her fingertips, from her legs to her toes. Her body tingled with a horrid sensation that felt like a thousand needles coursing through her, seeking an exit. Her skin prickled with torture.

And then everything grew numb.

47
TAKE

Oliver knew he was going to get scolded by Deveran and Bunnie when he returned. They'd agreed to be gone for no more than ten minutes, and it had surely been longer. Each passing second made his skin itch. With Ragnar and the Hunters looking for Chloé, it was important they stayed together. They were stronger as four than split into two groups.

Oliver hadn't the slightest clue how he'd lost sight of Chloé. She'd been within arm's reach before vanishing into the trees. The dense forest looked the same no matter where he turned.

"Miss Gemme, where are you?" Oliver mumbled. He looked up at the darkening sky. He was sure it was just midday. When had it started getting so late? The chill air bit into his clothing, sending goose bumps across his skin. He continued to weave through the forest, hoping to find signs of the pink-haired nix.

Oliver's chest was about to burst from anxiety when he spotted a familiar figure lying in the grass. His heart dropped as she rushed toward Chloé. He sighed in relief as he noticed there weren't any wounds on her.

Chloé lay on her back, her hair spread neatly around her head. One of her hands rested on her stomach while the other rested on the ground. Her chest rose and fell with each breath she took.

Had she just fallen asleep? Casually? While taking a walk? Had Oliver taken so long to find her that she'd just ended up taking a nap? No, that didn't make any sense.

Oliver shook Chloé's shoulder gently. "Miss Gemme, wake up." He frowned when Chloé didn't stir. He tried again with a little more force, but there was still no response.

A nearby hoot caught his attention. A Nighthawk owl perched on a nearby branch with a small parchment tied to its leg. Oliver raised his arm, and the owl flew to him. He slipped the note off and read the contents before crumpling it up and tucking it into his pocket.

Based on the coordinates, Bunnie and Deveran weren't too far from them. Oliver would need to carry Chloé.

He slipped one arm underneath her knees and the other behind her back. With a single lift, Oliver held her close to his chest. She was light—a lot lighter than Oliver had expected. He quickly headed toward camp.

"What happened?" Bunnie immediately asked, standing up.

"I don't know," Oliver said. "We got separated."

"You got *what?*" Bunnie narrowed her eyes.

Oliver flinched. An angry Bunnie was never a good one. "We got separated . . . I don't know how it happened. By the time I found her, the sun had already set, and she was like this."

"You two were gone since the afternoon," Deveran said, tossing a piece of wood into the campfire. "How did you lose her for that long?"

"I . . . I really don't know." Oliver frowned. He still couldn't figure out how a few hours had passed so quickly.

"Bring her over here." Bunnie gestured toward the fire.

Oliver laid Chloé gently on the ground. Her expression hadn't changed since he'd found her. It still looked like she was sleeping peacefully.

Bunnie pressed her hand against Chloé's cheek and then her forehead. "She doesn't appear to be sick."

"I don't know why she won't wake," Oliver said. "I've tried waking her up."

"Oliver," Bunnie said, her voice strangely level.

"Y-yes?" Oliver gulped.

"When you found her, did you notice anything?"

"She was sleeping. On her back. On the ground?" Oliver wasn't sure what Bunnie was asking. He did find it strange she'd been lying almost artistically in the grass, but he'd thought nothing of it. Perhaps the nix had done it herself.

"You don't notice anything different about her?"

Oliver shook his head.

Bunnie huffed. "Typical men."

"Oliver," Deveran began, "Miss Gemme's opals are gone."

Oliver furrowed his brow. He glanced at Chloé's neck. It

was bare. The red choker she wore bearing her family's gemstone symbol was gone, and the red bow she wore in her hair with an opal in it was also gone. "Oh no," he whispered.

Bunnie shook her head. She sat down, propped her knees up, and rested her elbows against them. "Someone found her and stripped her of her name." She sucked in a breath. "Dammit."

"But how?" Oliver said. "Who can even do something like that?"

Bunnie pinched the bridge of her nose. "I thought he was dead."

"Gerald Gemme?" Deveran asked.

Bunnie nodded. "The last I saw him was ten years ago. When Chloé stepped in as a council member, I was pretty sure he had died. But it was never confirmed. To think he came out of hiding to do this to his only daughter."

"I don't believe he was working alone," Deveran said.

"No," Bunnie agreed. "This is out of character for him. I've only met him a handful of times, but I know this isn't something he would do. I know he loved Chloé dearly."

"Ragnar," Oliver said. "Maybe he's working with Ragnar."

"It's very well possible, but I don't understand *why*. Why would he work with someone who kept his daughter captive in the Valquent dungeons?" Bunnie said.

"Ragnar is a powerful ethereal. Maybe he did something. Earlier, when I lost Chloé, I could've sworn only a few minutes had passed, but before I knew it, it was past sunset."

"Hmm." Bunnie shifted her gaze toward the fire. "So, time had somehow frozen for you."

"I don't suspect Sir Gemme to have that sort of power."

"I haven't heard of anyone who is able to manipulate time, but that is probably beyond my knowledge anyhow," Bunnie said.

"Given Ragnar's age, it's a toss-up," Deveran said.

"I agree. At any rate, if it was Ragnar, then he knows where we are. I don't know what his plans are, but he didn't kill Chloé. Maybe that wasn't his goal to begin with. Either way, the only thing we can do now is wait for her to wake up. We stay here until then."

"Boss!" Oliver and Deveran said.

48
NEW

"Everyone still in favor of venturing to new lands?" Errol asked.

"Still in favor," Silas said.

Stella nodded. "I haven't changed my mind."

"It's still early in the day, so if either of you change your mind—"

"We aren't going to change our minds," Silas said, smirking. "We've talked about it with each other, and we still agree it would be the best for everyone."

"I've already discussed it with a few other elves, and they seem excited for a little adventure. They're growing tired of hiding away in fear. They want to be proactive in defending themselves, and searching for a new home is a way of defense."

Errol smiled, bubbling with pride. He had been afraid—terrified—Stella would walk down the path of darkness, allowing herself to wither away. But she hadn't. She'd stayed strong, just like her mother. The fact that Stella had made the proactive call to ask other villagers what they thought told him everything he needed to know.

Stella wouldn't need Errol to watch over her for long.

Errol looked out the window. It was still the afternoon, probably around three or four. Alder hadn't specified a time to meet him, so Errol just assumed it was before the day ended on the seventh day.

"I suppose we should take the time to inform the others we'll be moving," Silas said, turning to Stella.

"It wouldn't be a bad idea."

"You sure—"

"Yes," Silas said, cutting Errol off. He walked around the table and placed his hands on Errol's back, then pushed him, forcing his feet to move. "Now go and meet with Alder. We'll take care of everything here. Don't think for a minute you're on your own. We're here to help.

"All right. All right. You can stop pushing me."

"Not until I force you out."

"Force me out? What do you—"

Silas gave Errol one last shove, literally forcing him out of his own tent. "We aren't changing our minds. And the earlier we get all the preparations ready, the better it will be for everyone. Now go." Silas waved before disappearing back into Errol's tent.

Errol sighed. When had his commander gotten so pushy? "Since Alder is expecting me, it would be rude to keep him waiting," he said to himself.

Errol walked up the stairs. The last time he'd done this,

his heart had felt heavy. His entire body had resisted each step, urging him to go back and hide, to welcome the looming darkness. But this time, his body was light. His heart did not ache as much, and he knew there was hope.

The inside of the Moon Shrine had changed. The thick vibrant vines that wrapped around the walls had withered, and the two rivers that flowed inside were still. Life inside seemed empty.

Alder stood in the center of the room, his back toward Errol. The demigod didn't turn as Errol walked up. It was then Errol realized Alder was not alone.

The figure was similar in size to Alder, and both were childlike. She had long wavy teal hair that covered her chest. Scales of green and blue littered her skin. It was Ara, the demigod of water. Their hands were intertwined, and their foreheads were pressed together. A soft glow emitted from the point of contact.

As if finally sensing Errol's presence, Alder and Ara separated, their eyes opening and hands unlinking.

"You're here," Alder said.

"Yes."

"So, you have decided."

Errol nodded. "It wasn't my decision alone. Stella, Silas . . . everyone. We believe it's best if we seek new lands."

Ara smiled. Her clear aquamarine eyes sparkled at Errol. She put her hands behind her back, tilting her head. "It was a decision we knew you would make."

Errol blinked. "How?"

"History likes to repeat itself in various ways," Ara said.

"It will take three to seven days to travel to the base of the mountains and to the coast," Alder said. "But you will need to prepare for sea travel."

"Boats will need to be made. They don't need to be complicated. Rafts can even work. Anything that will carry food, water, and the elves," Ara said. "I will keep the waters clear throughout the journey, but I'll still use the wind to help drift the waves."

"How long will we be out at sea for?"

"No more than two weeks."

"How much time will you allow us to prepare?"

Alder and Ara looked at each other before returning their attention to Errol.

"How long will you need?" Alder asked.

"Well, we've never made boats before . . . I'd have to—"

"I mean how long do you need to say goodbye?" Alder said. "You will not be returning to these lands. Once you leave with Ara . . . it is goodbye."

Errol paused. It was obvious they wouldn't be returning, but for some reason, he hadn't fully digested the fact. He hadn't realized this was a one-way ticket out and there was no turning back from the decision. Alder wanted to give him and everyone else time to return to Mistfall and see if they could find anything of value to them, anything that held precious memories. The chances were slim, but they would take any chance they had. "Maybe three days on top of however long it will take us to build boats for everyone."

"I can give you four weeks to prepare. But beyond that, I cannot guarantee anything."

"That's more than enough."

"The next time we meet, it'll be on the coast!" Ara said.

She waved her hands. "I will take my leave here. Alder, please take it easy." She gave one last wave before skipping toward the river and jumping inside.

"There's something we need you to do for us when we leave," Errol said. "Your familiar. Are you able to communicate with Minari to let him know where we went?"

"You want Redd to wait in Mistfall for their return?"

Errol nodded. "No one really knows of your familiar, right?"

"Lily has seen Redd, but perhaps that will not be a problem. There is no distinct design in Redd that makes him look any different compared to other songbirds."

"Then you'll do it?"

Alder didn't respond right away. His gaze moved from Errol to behind him. It was as if Alder's mind had wandered off from the conversation.

"Yes," he finally said, his brown orbs looking back at Errol. "I can tell them."

49
GRIM

The looming moon and clear skies couldn't hide the horrors of the tribe.

It was in shambles. Debris was scattered across the blood-stained ground. Huts were smashed in.

There were dead bodies everywhere.

No matter where Mimi turned, he suffocated in the number of unmoving kin who surrounded him.

His stomach clenched, and he forced back a gag. Mimi pressed his hand against his mouth. He couldn't believe the gruesome scenery before him. It was just like when he'd found Amelia, Nero . . . their family.

But worse.

Some chimeras' faces were disfigured. They were unrecognizable. Mangled limbs twisted in odd directions around them, some completely severed.

Mimi's legs refused to move.

Sage wrapped his arms around Mimi's trembling body, bringing him against his chest. Mimi heard the racing of Sage's heart, how much his chest expanded with each deep breath. Sage was trying to keep his rage at bay. Holding Mimi was keeping him grounded, ensuring he didn't go berserk on the nearest person—or elf. Their rage from finding Amelia and learning Minari was likely the killer had not quelled.

"This is unbelievable," Elliot said. "Mimi, I am so sorry."

"There may be survivors," Hiro said. "We shouldn't give up hope, no matter how bleak the situation."

"You think there's anyone here?" Sage asked, his voice bitter.

"We won't know unless we see for ourselves. And like we discussed, we may find clues about Amelia's and her family's killer."

"The killer is standing right next to you," Sage said.

Mimi pushed himself from Sage and pressed a hand against his chest. *"I'm okay,"* he said in chimeran tongue. *"Calm down."*

Sage frowned. *"You are not okay. You're pale."*

"As long as you're with me, I'll be okay. He's right. We should look for any survivors."

Sage didn't say anything, only nodded.

"Even though the tribe is small, we should split into groups," Mimi said, shifting to common tongue. "I don't want to stay here longer than I have to."

"Understandable," Hiro said. He pointed at Minari. "You will be with me."

Minari, seemingly snapping out of a trance, turned to

297

Hiro with wide eyes. "What?"

"You're coming with me."

Minari looked over at Elliot, who did not meet his gaze.

"You're still our prime suspect, and I am the only one here who can really stop you if you do anything." Hiro crossed his arms. "I'm not budging."

"Elliot shall be together with me and Owen then," Luka said.

"Meet back here in an hour," Mimi said.

The snake chimera knew exactly where he wanted to go.

Mimi went straight for Serzio's hut. Sage followed behind him, but it didn't take long for Mimi to outpace the ox. The hut was in the heart of the tribe, and the number of dead bodies Mimi passed grew the closer he got to the hut. With no breeze, the smell of rotting flesh had stayed stagnant in the air.

Mimi found it hard to breathe.

But he couldn't stop—not until he saw with his own two eyes the answers he desperately sought.

The Lyeokee's hut was surprisingly undamaged. Compared to the others, it was like no one had even touched it. Mimi slowed his pace, the blood rushing to his ears. He reached for the drape and pushed it aside.

Serzio sat in the center of the hut. His legs were crossed, palms in his lap, eyes closed. There was a large bloodstain on the front of his shirt.

Mimi rushed forward, halting into a kneel. "Father!" He placed his hands on Serzio's shoulders. "Father, are you all right? What happened?"

Serzio's reaction was slow. He tilted his head up before his eyes cracked open.

Staring back at Mimi were empty sockets. Serzio's eyes had been ripped out.

Mimi staggered backward, his breathing coming out in rapid gasps.

Serzio's head twisted to the side, his neck cracking with each jittering movement. His mouth opened, and he croaked.

Mimi couldn't take his eyes off Serzio. His heart was beating so fast he was sure it was going to burst from his chest. His legs and arms felt weak, and he couldn't move. He watched as Serzio's crackling, creaking body slowly hunched over and began crawling toward him.

Mimi wanted to scream.

But his throat closed up, trapping his voice. He was frozen in place.

"Mimi!" Sage shouted. He grabbed Mimi's arm, lifting him up. Mimi leaned into Sage, his legs still refusing to move and his eyes refusing to leave the crawling Serzio. "I'm sorry about this, Mimi." Still holding on to Mimi, Sage kicked Serzio's head. It snapped to the side, and he stopped. Sage pulled Mimi outside. He tapped on the smaller chimera's face. "Hey. Hey, are you okay? Talk to me, Mimi."

Mimi was at a loss for words. He could only shake his head as tears fell from his eyes. He had no idea what he'd just seen. He knew there was no way Serzio could've been alive, but how had his body been moving? It was as if he'd been waiting for Mimi. He'd responded to Mimi's voice and fear. Mimi deeply wanted to erase the vision from his mind, but he couldn't shake it from his memories. The hollow figure of his father crawling toward him, reaching out to him.

Who could've done such a thing? Mimi was certain now

it couldn't have been Minari. The elf wasn't capable of doing something like this.

Like raising people from the dead.

A slow clap echoed from across the plains. Mimi and Sage turned toward the noise.

"Did you like my present? I thought you'd appreciate it."

Aiden. But how? He was dead. Sage had killed the Oasis captain back in Oasis's hideout. He could vividly recall how Sage had stood above Aiden. How he'd pointed the sword over the human's chest, taunting him, asking if he had any last words. And how Sage had driven the blade into Aiden's chest without hearing an answer. So, how could he be here? But that wasn't all. There was something different about Aiden. The air around him . . . and his scent. It reeked of death.

"Long time no see." Aiden smirked. "Miss me?"

"How are you . . . ? I killed you." Sage stared at Aiden, eyes wide like he had just seen a ghost.

"I guess I shouldn't be surprised that you two are surprised to see me. Last you chimeras saw me was quite some time ago. When I was alive. When I was human."

When Aiden was alive? Was he saying he wasn't alive now? And not human . . .

"I came to get revenge on my sister." Aiden put his hands on his hips. "But I see the whore of a woman isn't here with you. I was hoping you'd meet up with her before you came here. So, I guess I'll take my revenge out on you two instead." Aiden snapped his fingers.

The roof of Serzio's hut burst open. The centipede monster from before stretched its body from the small confinement.

300

Mimi's heart dropped.

Was his father the centipede monster from before? Had it not attacked him or Sage because his father was aware of who they were? But that didn't make sense. It was clear to Mimi that Serzio had not cared for him or Sage when they left the tribe. He'd made it clear they weren't welcome.

Had that all been an act? Had it been a front for Serzio to appear strong in front of the other chimeras?

"Have fun." Aiden vanished.

The centipede's antennae twitched, its pincers clasping. It twisted its body, its face looking at Mimi and Sage.

And it shrieked, its voice piercing through the night sky.

50
DOUBT

Luka was beginning to worry about Elliot. The elf was young and had yet to experience many things in life. To have his most trusted friend be accused of murder and to experience the demise of a single race was surely taking a toll on him.

Each passing moment grew dimmer and dimmer. The chance of finding a single soul alive was bleak.

"Luka, it's been about an hour," Owen said.

"I agree," Luka said. Luka and Owen stopped, but Elliot kept walking. Luka frowned. Elliot's mind was certainly wandering. "Elliot," he called out. When the elf didn't stop, Luka called out to him again.

"Huh?" Elliot turned. "Why are you two way over there?"

"Elliot, it's time to head back," Luka said.

"But we haven't found anyone yet."

Luka shook his head. "Unfortunately, I do not see a possibility of any survivors."

Elliot hunched his shoulders. "If Minari did this . . ."

Elliot was still doubting Minari. Luka found this out of character for Elliot, given his relationship with Minari. "Do you think he did it?"

"Don't you?"

Luka shook his head. "I do not believe Minari did it."

Elliot blinked. "Why? The evidence was all there."

"From my time spent with everyone, I can see Minari isn't the kind of person who would do this," Luka said.

"I agree," Owen said. "Minari is caring. Yes, he is strong and skilled, but this was not done by him. The way everyone here was killed . . ."

"Messy," Luka said. "Brutal."

"I agree with Luka that Minari was framed," Owen said. "Whoever is behind it may have wanted to pit us against one another, but we should stay strong."

"When we regroup, perhaps it would be wise to speak with him alone," Luka said.

"You really think he didn't do it?"

"No." Luka smiled. "Look deep into your heart, Elliot. What do you feel?"

Elliot placed a hand over his chest. "I want to trust him. I want to believe him. But . . ." He clutched the fabric of his top. "I can't shake this feeling of doubt and distrust."

Doubt and distrust.

Namir's dark matter may have been playing a role in Elliot's judgment. His mind was being clouded with darkness. If Namir was a Necromancer, then it made sense for her to want to create a rift between Elliot and the others.

Luka outstretched his hand. "Elliot."

Elliot looked at the offered hand. "What?"

"Take my hand."

Elliot hesitated. He kept looking between Luka's hand and Luka, as if trying to see if Luka was planning something. The distrust was starting to spread to him as well. It could've been because Elliot doubted Minari and Luka had confessed he didn't. Elliot may have been wondering if Luka and Minari were working together. Luka hadn't been very open with the group, but Elliot was surely aware of how much more experience and magical power Luka had over Elliot and Chloé.

Elliot stepped forward, his hand lifting. But before their fingertips could brush, a strong gust blew past them. Elliot retracted his hand, covering his face.

"Luka. Owen. My old companions."

Namir.

Luka grabbed Elliot's arm and pulled the elf behind him, then grabbed the hilt of his sword. "What are you doing here?"

Namir had her hands crossed with her palms against her elbows. She strutted, walking around them in a circle, her sharp golden eyes never leaving them. "I came to see how everyone was doing."

Luka narrowed his eyes.

"Ah, a look of defiance. I remember when I never had to see it. It was pleasant to have you and Owen do as I asked every time. Obedience without question."

Luka and Owen kept silent. They both knew the cat chimera enjoyed listening to herself talk. The way her voice rolled off her tongue was seductive and alluring, as if she was trying to use it as a distraction.

"Oh, come now. Remember the times we had together?" Namir stopped, popping her hip out as she shifted her wait onto one leg. "We achieved so much together. And we can achieve more. Do you not want to see Maxwell again?"

There it was. She was using Luka's brother as a seed, tempting Luka to listen to what she had to say. Luka deeply wanted to find his brother, to uncover the truth about their mansion's attack twenty years ago. But Luka needed to push his personal agenda aside. He could not jeopardize Elliot's safety for his own gain.

Namir frowned. "You will not listen?"

Luka flicked his thumb, allowing a small portion of his blade to peek through its sheath.

"Threatening me, are you? Such a shame." Namir lifted a hand, and a dark shadow began to form around it. "You are already aware of my dark matter, correct? I don't need to be anywhere near your precious oracle to release more of it into him. I can simply send some more . . ." Namir twirled her hand.

Elliot grunted. He clutched the front of his shirt, hunching over.

"The process is painful, I hear. Forcing a large amount of dark matter into him rather than slowly sending it into him could cause some damage."

"Stop," Luka said. He kept his eyes on Namir as he reached for one of Elliot's hands. He slowly pushed his own stamina into Elliot, trying to counter the increase of dark matter from Namir.

Namir tilted her head. "And why should I?"

"What are you aiming for?" Luka asked.

Namir's hand stilled. "What do I want? I simply want to obtain eternal beauty."

Namir's desires had not changed. Luka remembered her obsession with looking beautiful.

"And the only way for me to achieve eternal beauty is to offer souls to Father Mykronos. But"—Namir dropped her hand—"it seems my supply of souls has . . . been compromised."

Based on Namir's statement, she hadn't been in charge of the large attack on the chimera tribe, which meant she may not have been aware of who'd done it either. But the criminal always returned to the scene of the crime. Who exactly was she working with?

"What will I do without chimeran souls to achieve beauty, hmm?" Namir began circling around them once more. Her hips swayed side to side with each step. "What can I do but look to those who were born with natural beauty?" She glared at Luka and Owen. "You ethereals were blessed by your gods, granted the ability to live long lives and have everlasting beauty until your death. Tell me why we chimeras weren't blessed with this. Tell me why we were forsaken with such disgusting attributes."

Was Namir looking to kill Luka and Owen? Was she hoping their souls would grant her the same blessings they'd been granted? But if that was the case, why hadn't she done it to begin with? Offering numerous chimeras to Mykronos seemed like an efficient way to achieve her goal. There had to be something else.

"I was hoping you would be more entertaining to me,"

Namir said. "But I guess I will just move ahead with what I was ordered to do." She yanked the fang necklace off her neck.

Luka's eyes widened. Was she trying to kill herself? He had to stop her. If Namir died, the dark matter within her body would have no choice but to reunite with the dark matter within Elliot. "Wait!"

Namir paused. "Hmm?" She smirked. "You always were a smart one, Luka. But no matter. Nothing you do can stop me. This is farewell." In one swift movement, she stabbed her heart with the fang. Her skin went ashen. Cracks grew across her arms, neck, and legs. Her once bright hair began to blacken and twist. A grin crept across her lips before her face cracked. With a snap, her body crumbled, disintegrating into dust.

Luka's head snapped back, checking to see if Elliot was affected by Namir's self-inflicted demise. But it didn't seem like the dark matter within Elliot had changed. There was no increase and no decrease. "Elliot, how do you feel?"

Elliot swatted Luka's hand away. "I'm fine."

"I feel fine. I don't know why you're worried about me."

"It is unknown to us what Namir's true intentions were," Luka said. "She had a piece of herself inside your core."

"I don't feel any different."

"I think it would be wise to keep watch in case anything changes," Owen said.

"Okay, but I feel fine. Maybe Namir knew she couldn't do anything anyway."

Elliot's behavior had definitely changed from before. He seemed rushed. Cold. He was brushing the situation off and not caring how it may affect him or the prophecy. As the oracle, he was vital to the prophecy's success.

"You said we should head back?" Elliot asked.

"Yes, that is correct," Luka said.

"Then let's go."

Luka followed as Elliot led the way.

51
TRUST

Minari felt like Hiro was burning holes into his skull. The way he stared at him made him feel like he was trying to read his mind, figure out how Minari ticked. It sent shivers up Minari's spine.

"I can see how tense you are," Hiro said. "I'm not going to bite you. You can relax."

Minari turned his head, looking behind him. He frowned at Hiro. "You say that, but I can see in your eyes you mean something else."

Hiro smirked. "What do you mean?"

"I didn't do it." Minari had checked his clothes numerous times after Sage and Hiro had claimed there was blood on him, and no matter how closely he'd looked, he hadn't found a drop of blood on him. When he looked at his blades, they were clean. It was like everyone saw something he didn't.

Hiro shrugged. "You keep saying that, but the evidence is there. I just expected more finesse when it came to you."

"You make it sound like I'm some natural-born killer."

"Aren't you?"

"No!"

Hiro tilted his head. "We only crossed blades once, but I could tell by the way you moved that you are very skilled."

"I am not a killer."

"Have you ever taken the life of a person before?"

Minari clenched his fists. He pivoted, returning to the task at hand. He wasn't about to play into Hiro's mind games.

"Based on your reaction, I say yes," Hiro said, keeping up with Minari's pace.

Minari clenched his jaw, forcing himself to remain silent. They shouldn't get distracted. They needed to either find the killer or anyone left alive.

He hoped to find the killer.

The moment everyone believed Minari had killed the ox family and refused to believe anything he said, he'd felt as if the world were crushing him. He was confused. To be accused of something so drastic . . . It was as if they wanted to get rid of him. Now that the hero had been found and almost all the warriors were gathered around Elliot, did they have need of Minari? Hiro was more than capable of protecting Elliot, and Minari had done nothing but screw everything up.

He was a failure.

Minari didn't know how he could face his mother. What would Mayleen even say to him? She'd done her best to raise him into someone she could be proud of, but he knew he'd been anything but since Elliot had awoken to his oracle powers.

But to accuse him of being a ruthless killer . . . It hurt. His heart ached deeply knowing Elliot doubted him. Minari promised he would do *anything* to keep him safe since he was the oracle. It was true, yes, Minari would utilize any means to protect Elliot, but it wasn't because he was the oracle; it was because they were best friends. Minari cared deeply for Elliot.

It was then Minari remembered the birthday present Lily had carved for Elliot: a wooden leaf pendant. He still had it, tucked away inside his coat. He still hadn't found the right time to give it to Elliot and wondered if there was ever going to be a right time. He hadn't even told Elliot about Lily, or the death of his mother and grandmother, or how Mistfall was in ruins. Minari was quickly realizing how Elliot had every right to distrust him.

"I know you didn't do it." Hiro's sudden voice broke Minari out of his spiraling thoughts. "You've probably been framed."

"By what?"

"A Necromancer."

Minari's blood grew cold, his eyes widening. A Necromancer? But if it was a Necromancer, then . . . was it Lily? Sage and Mimi had said Amelia and the others had a clean slit to the neck done by a thin weapon like Minari's daggers. And if Lily was the one who'd done it, did that mean she'd done all of this too? Was she still around?

Was she after Elliot?"

"We need to head back."

"Whoa there." Hiro grabbed Minari's wrist, stopping him in his tracks. "Why?"

"If you think this was done by a Necromancer, then we aren't safe here—not this spread out."

"Elliot is with Luka and Owen."

Minari bit his lip. He wasn't sure if Luka and Owen would be able to keep up with Lily. It was also very likely she wasn't working alone. There was no way she could've done this by herself in one night.

"Do you think you're worrying a bit too much?"

"Do you think you're worrying a bit too little?" Minari snapped. "Don't you care about Elliot?"

Hiro's expression darkened. "Of course I do. Something like that should never be questioned, especially not by someone like you."

Minari furrowed his brow. "What's that supposed to mean?"

"Regardless of your offending question, I have trust in Luka and Owen and in Elliot's own abilities. He's not defenseless, you know. Unlike you, they can all wield magic."

"I don't need magic to fight!" Minari pulled his arm free of Hiro's grip.

"No, but you need your daggers to fight. Or are you well acquainted with your fists?"

Minari glared at Hiro. He was still in possession of his daggers. The mere mention of it was like rubbing salt on a wound.

"Put more trust in them," Hiro said, "and they will trust you in return."

Hiro's words echoed in Minari's mind. It was something so simple, something that happened naturally. It wasn't because Minari didn't trust them. No. It was because Minari was scared. He was scared to lose Elliot. He was scared of losing his memories of Elliot.

Minari didn't have much recollection of the events surrounding his father's death or much of his time with his father. It was like his time with Melvin was one big blur. Minari assumed it was his mind's way of defending him from walking down the path of darkness, preventing him from losing his light due to Melvin's death. And if Elliot were to lose his life, Minari was sure every memory he had of Elliot would disappear.

That was something he would never wish for. He would rather die than lose the memories he had together with Elliot.

A piercing shriek cut through the night. Minari immediately recognized the noise.

It was the centipede monster.

52
FREE

Emptiness. Hollow. Bare.

Light.

The first thing Chloé noticed when she drifted from her sleep was how incredibly weightless she felt. Her chest felt open, and each breath was clear. The grass that poked against her skin was more prominent than usual. She could hear the distant chirping of birds and feel the prickle on her skin as a soft breeze blew by.

It was an odd sensation.

Why was Chloé able to feel everything so much more? She opened her eyes, squinting when her vision didn't clear. Strange. She leaned up and rubbed her eyes. Everything was still hazy, but she could make out a burnt-out campfire and the bodies of Bunnie, Oliver, and Deveran.

Wait.

Why was she here? Where was Gerald?

Chloé's head snapped around, searching for her father. She scrambled to her feet, hoping he was nearby, but she didn't see any other figures. Had she dreamed everything? No, it couldn't have been a dream. It had felt too real to have been a dream.

Chloé's body froze as she recalled Gerald's last words to her. She quickly reached up to her neck.

It was bare.

She reached up into her hair.

There was no ribbon.

Chloé's knees grew weak, and she collapsed to the ground. Gerald had taken her opals. He had really meant she was no longer a part of the Gemme family. Her whole identity and lineage had been stripped, taken away from by her own father. She dug her nails into the ground, biting her lip so hard she could taste warm blood. Her shoulders shook as she silently sobbed.

Nothing. She was nothing. She was a nobody. Everything she had worked hard for had been for nothing. How could she ever face any of the Nighthawk members again? The only reason they were even with her was because of who she was and what she could do for them. And now that she was a nobody, would they cast her aside, just like her father? Was Chloé to face abandonment once again?

Gerald hadn't just taken her opals from her. She realized the empty feeling in her chest and the blurry vision were side effects of her core having been destroyed. The unbearable, excruciating pain from before had been Gerald forcibly making her core shatter. With nowhere to go, the stamina had left through her skin. She remembered the raw, hot sensation that had threaded across her body. It had been like she was on fire.

Not only was Chloé a nobody, but she was also powerless. There was absolutely no way she could possibly still be a warrior. Elliot would surely discard her as well. Warriors needed to be strong, not weak like Chloé.

"Chloé?" Bunnie's voice cut through Chloé's silent sobs. "You're finally awake. What's wrong?"

Without looking up, Chloé shook her head. There was no way she could face Bunnie—not after everything she'd done to get her this far.

The nix heard the crunching of grass as Bunnie walked over. She dropped to one knee and placed a warm hand on Chloé's shoulder and gave her a soft squeeze.

"Hey, it'll be okay," Bunnie said, her voice soft.

Chloé shook her head again. She didn't know what to say to Bunnie. How could she confess she wasn't who they wanted her to be? She was no longer part of the council. No longer a Gemme. No longer a warrior. No longer anybody.

"Hey, look at me." Bunnie gave her shoulder another squeeze.

Chloé hesitated before tilting her chin up. Bunnie smiled. She delicately thumbed the small wound on Chloé's lip.

"It'll be okay," Bunnie said softly. "We're in this together. No matter what."

Chloé's lips quivered as she tried to hold back her tears. How could Bunnie even mention something like that? Surely the older woman knew what her missing opals meant. Did she not care?

Bunnie opened her arms. "Come."

Chloé pushed herself off the ground and into Bunnie's arms. She pressed her face into Bunnie's chest, letting her cries free. Bunnie stroked her head. "You're still important to me. To all of us. Don't for a second think otherwise."

Chloé's stomach clenched at the thought of telling Bunnie she didn't have her core and what it meant for someone like her.

But . . . Bunnie deserved to know.

Chloé pulled away, wiping her tearstained cheeks. "There's something else . . ."

"Hmm?" Bunnie kept smiling, waiting for Chloé to continue, never rushing or urging her to speak.

"I . . ." Chloé placed a hand against her chest. "I . . ." She took a deep breath. Her heart pounded loudly against her chest. "I . . . I was disowned by my father. I saw him earlier . . . and he took my opals. But . . . that's not all he took." Chloé paused. "My core. He shattered it. I don't have the ability to use magic anymore."

Bunnie didn't say anything. She kept her lips curled and her eyes softened.

"Is that all?"

Chloé's eyes snapped up. Deveran and Oliver were walking over, both stretching out their arms. How long had they been awake for?

"Something like that doesn't bother us," Oliver said.

"You are still important to us," Deveran said.

"B-but I can't do what you ask of me anymore! I'm not a council member."

The twins smirked.

"We already had a feeling the council wasn't going to let you back in after the escaping fiasco," Oliver said.

"I know we've mentioned it before, but you've become much more than a mere council member," Deveran said. "You're Chloé."

Chloé blinked as her cheeks warmed. She hadn't expected the mention of just her first name in a casual way to affect her like that. It made her feel . . . welcome. Like she wasn't someone of higher status they needed to be polite to. Now, it felt like they were closer, like she was someone they could truly put their trust in. The absence of her last name did not bother her as much as she'd assumed it would.

"And there you have it," Bunnie said. She stood, her hand outstretched to Chloé. "Simply put, we couldn't care less about your status or your inability to use magic. I've actually been meaning to ask you something."

Chloé accepted Bunnie's hand, and Bunnie helped her up. "What is it?"

"Would you like to join the Nighthawks? Become an official member of my guild?"

Chloé's eyes widened, and her jaw dropped. She looked at Bunnie. At Oliver. At Deveran. They were all smiling at her, waiting for her response. They truly did not care that Chloé had fallen from grace, and they would help her find her wings again as a member of their family.

More tears fell from Chloé's eyes, but this time they weren't from sorrow. She nodded. "Yes."

53
BREAK

The distant bellow shook the air around Elliot, Luka, and Owen. Though Elliot had only heard the noise a few times, he knew exactly what sort of monster was able to emit such a sound.

"What was that?" Luka asked.

"That sounded like no animal," Owen said.

"A monster," Elliot said. "We have to head back. The others are probably under attack."

Luka and Owen didn't question Elliot. They ran toward the heart of the tribe.

The ground shook, nearly throwing Elliot off-balance. Mimi, Sage, Hiro, and Minari were already by the monster. Hiro had his sword drawn. Minari still didn't have his daggers, so he was limited to merely dodging the monster's attacks. But Mimi and Sage didn't appear to have the intention of attacking the monster. It was as if they were doing what they could to run around in circles.

"What are you doing?" Minari yelled. "You're going to get us all killed!"

"Don't hurt him!" Mimi yelled back. The ground rumbled again, and Mimi jumped out of the way. Pincers erupted from the ground, clawing at the air before diving back into the earth below.

The ground emitted a low rumble, and the monster pierced the sky, its long body curling as it dug its legs into the ground. Its pincers vibrated, and the deafening shriek happened once more.

Elliot's vision blurred, and a sharp, piercing shriek stabbed through his skull. He clutched his head as he tried to block out the noise.

Luka bit his lip, squinting as he drew his sword. He nodded at Owen. The feathers on Owen's head began to glow. Luka dashed, heading straight for the monster. In one single swipe, he severed four legs from the giant centipede.

The monster screamed, and its body twitched. Luka immediately held up his arm, unable to react quick enough. The monster slammed its body into Luka, sending him flying across the field.

A gurgling, crunching sound sent chills down Elliot's body. Black ooze dripped from the missing limbs. The muscles pulsated until four new legs ripped through the skin of the monster.

Immobilizing the monster with brute force wasn't going

to work. They had to use magic. Elliot could create a shield *around* the monster, trapping it inside. It might work.

Maybe.

It was worth a shot.

Elliot shook his head. He didn't have time to second-guess himself.

He moved his hands in front of him and tapped into his core. He reached inside, drawing out his stamina, urging it into his fingertips.

Elliot gasped, clutching the front of his shirt. The mark of the oracle burned against his wrist. He took deep breaths as he tried to subdue the agonizing pain that had exploded in his chest. It felt like someone had grabbed his heart and was squeezing it, their sharp fingers digging into the delicate muscle, threatening to crush it if he attempted to call upon his core again.

What was happening to him?

"Elliot!" Hiro called out.

Elliot snapped his head up in time to see a shield form around him, protecting him from an incoming body slam from the centipede. The shield shattered upon impact, and the force blew Elliot off his feet.

Elliot grunted, the ground sending slight tremors of pain through his body. It still hurt to breathe, even after he'd pulled away from tapping into his core.

Minari was suddenly at Elliot's side. He eased Elliot up. "What happened? What were you trying to do?"

Elliot pushed Minari away, glaring. "I don't need your help."

Minari's hurt expression formed a lump in his throat. No.

He couldn't rely on Minari. Not after what had happened. He needed to learn to defend himself and not rely on the help of a merciless killer.

"I still don't have my daggers, so I can't—"

"Good," Elliot snapped. "Stay out of the way, and maybe fewer people will die."

"That's not the point!" Minari grabbed Elliot's arm. "Mimi is insisting we don't harm it. We all know how to stop it, but he refuses to let us destroy the tail and its mouth."

If they destroyed its means of attack—the pincers in its mouth and the ones on its tail—it would die. It wouldn't be easy to stop the monster—not when it could regenerate its limbs. The only way they could stop it was bind it. Elliot could see the monster burrowing into the ground if either set of pincers was to get destroyed. With it hidden safely below, it would have enough time to regrow a new set.

They would need to destroy the two sets at the same time. Minari looked over at Luka. Owen was already at his side, sending stamina into Luka's body so he could recover. Mimi was hesitating to attack the monster, which meant Sage wouldn't harm it either. Hiro could likely sever one pair of pincers, and Luka could sever the other. But someone would need to keep it from moving. But who? Elliot couldn't tap into his core.

"I'm sorry, Elliot." Before Elliot could move, Minari dug into Elliot's pouch, taking Lily's dagger. With a single blade in hand, Minari darted toward the monster's head.

"Minari!" Elliot yelled. What was Minari thinking? Was he trying to get himself killed?

"Hiro!" Minari yelled. He held up Lily's dagger for Hiro

to see.

Hiro nodded, heading to the opposite end of the monster.

"Wait!" Mimi yelled. He stepped forward, but Sage held him back. "Please wait!"

The monster moved, emitting another deafening shriek, but it didn't hinder Minari or Hiro. They pushed through, ignoring the paralyzing noise.

Hiro swung his arm, his blade following the movement, and in one swing, the pincers flew off completely.

Minari jumped, hands outstretched, and grabbed one of the pincers. He dug the blade into the flesh of the monster numerous times. The giant centipede threw its head down, pinning Minari against the ground. Its body twitched as Minari ripped off one pincer. The centipede's movements were more subdued now, allowing Minari to continue stabbing at the other pincer with the drenched dagger.

"Please . . . Please stop!" Mimi cried. He clawed at Sage, but the bigger chimera wasn't letting go.

"Mimi, please. You know that's not him!"

"No, no! Minari, stop! Please! That's my father!"

Elliot's blood grew cold. *That* was Mimi's father? But how?

The centipede let out one last howl as Minari tore off the last pincer. Its body stilled before disintegrating into black dust.

Hiro jogged over to Minari, who was covered in the remains of the monster. He swiped off the dust and pulled Minari into a sitting position. "You are one crazy elf."

Minari coughed, giving Hiro a weak smirk. "I protect

my friends."

Finally breaking free from Sage, Mimi ran toward Minari and Hiro. He grabbed any black dust he could catch.

"Why?" Mimi whispered. "Why did you kill him? Were the others not enough?"

"Mimi, that wasn't Serzio. You know that," Sage said.

"Shut up! He was all I had left! And Minari. You—"

"Mimi." Sage placed a hand on Mimi's shoulder. "Let it go."

"He murdered my father, Sage!" Mimi screamed. His chest heaved as he stared at Minari. "I wish it were you instead."

"Elliot?" a familiar voice said.

Elliot's eyes widened. His heart raced.

That voice. He knew that voice.

He slowly turned.

"Lily?"

54
CONFESSION

Minari tried to yell at Elliot to move away from Lily, but when he opened his mouth, he couldn't speak. He tried to stand, but he found his body wasn't listening to him. His heart began to race as he realized he had been poisoned by the monster. He had been moving solely on adrenaline.

And Hiro didn't seem to notice, his attention now on the female elf.

Lily was still wearing her scout's uniform, and her eyes were bright green.

Elliot and Lily ran to each other, and they locked in a tight embrace.

"Lily, what are you doing here?" Elliot asked, pulling away.

"I couldn't stay still anymore. I had to go looking for you and Minari. To make sure everything was going okay."

"Elliot," Luka said, his hand pressing against his side. "Who is she?"

"This is Lily, my and Minari's childhood friend."

"Her clothes are similar to Minari's and not yours," Luka said.

"They had the same training," Elliot said. "They worked together to defend our home."

Luka nodded, not asking any more questions. He kept his gaze on Lily momentarily before continuing. "Luka Yunmei." He tilted his head down in a small bow.

"Owen Ko."

"Lily."

"No family name?" Luka asked.

Lily shook her head. "There is nothing special about me to be deserving of a family name." Lily's and Minari's eyes met, and a flash of red flickered in her orbs before they settled back into green. "Minari!" She rushed to him.

Mimi moved out of the way, allowing Lily to kneel beside Minari and Hiro.

"Who are you?" Mimi asked, a trace of disgust in his voice.

"Minari, are you okay? What happened to you?" Lily asked, ignoring Mimi. She pressed her hands delicately against Minari's chest.

Minari hissed, eyes shutting. Pain radiated from the open wound as Lily's fingers touched the open skin.

"You're burning up," Lily mumbled.

"The monster must've poisoned him," Hiro said.

"Is there anything we can do?" Lily asked.

Luka looked at Mimi, but he only turned away. Mimi

must've been hesitant to help Minari a third time, especially after Minari had supposedly killed Mimi's father.

"I cannot heal him with my magic," Luka said. "I can heal flesh wounds, but I cannot cleanse his blood of poison."

"Mimi," Elliot said.

Mimi ignored Elliot.

"Mimi," Sage said. "You know that wasn't him. That was an empty shell that took on the form of a monster."

"You weren't there, Sage," Mimi said through clenched teeth. "You weren't there when I saw him."

Lily cupped Minari's cheek, running her thumb over his left eye. Minari's vision was blurry, and his hearing was muddled. It was getting difficult for him to focus on the voices around him.

Minari knew this had to be a trap. There was no way Lily would be here, acting the way she was, without an ulterior motive. She was a Necromancer. There was no denying it. Yet the way she was acting, the way she spoke and how she appeared—it was like she wasn't. It was like she was back to her normal self.

"Minari, it's really you! Please, before she comes back, kill me. I can't hold her for long!"

Maybe Lily had found a way to push back the Necromancer's soul within her. Was that the reason she was how she was now?

A chill ran through Minari's body, and he shuddered.

Suddenly, he was placed against the ground, no longer being held up by Hiro. He could only see blotches of color now, but he was certain he saw Mimi looming over him. The chimera's sand-colored hair was all he saw moving around. He felt warm liquid fall on his face and chest. Mimi must've caved and decided to save Minari.

Minari's senses slowly returned. His vision sharpened, and his hearing cleared. The chills and tremors coursing through him subsided.

Mimi pulled his arm away, pressing a hand against the gash.

"Thank you, Mimi," Elliot said.

"How does that even work?" Lily asked. "Is your blood like a magical antidote?"

"In a way . . ."

"Ah! I'm sorry. Where are my manners? I'm Lily."

"Mimi."

"Sage," Sage added. "Are you related to Elliot and Minari?"

"We're childhood friends!"

"I'm Hiro."

"Pleasure to meet everyone," Lily said.

Minari sat up. The world swayed, and he pressed a hand against his head. He didn't recall having been this dizzy after being cured. Then again, he had been asleep during the whole process. "L-Lily." Minari coughed. It was still difficult to speak. It was like his throat tightened every time he tried.

"I hope you've been doing your job and keeping Elliot safe." Lily smiled. "It's been busy back home without you."

Back home. Was Lily referring to Mistfall? She should've been well aware of what had happened to the village.

Unless . . .

Unless Lily had truly returned to her normal self. Was it possible that when she purged the Necromancer's soul from her that the memories had gone with it too?

"What are you doing here?" Elliot asked. "How did you find us?"

Lily blinked, her smile vanishing. "Minari didn't tell you?"

"Tell me? What was he supposed to tell me?" Elliot asked, his attention now on Minari.

Minari's eyes widened. No. This Lily wasn't the same Lily he and Elliot knew. This was the Necromancer. Minari knew it for certain.

Minari tried to get up, but his legs went slack. He fell to his knees, hands pressed against the ground. His arms trembled as they struggled to keep him up.

"He didn't tell you what happened?" Lily asked.

Elliot shook his head. "What was he supposed to tell me?"

No! Minari needed Elliot to get away, but he couldn't force his body to move.

"Necromancers attacked. Our home was destroyed. Everyone was taking refuge in the Moon Shrine." Lily paused. She reached over and held Elliot's hands. "Elliot . . . Estelle and Elder Lyla . . . are gone."

Elliot didn't say anything at first. He could only stare at Lily. "What?"

"Elliot," Minari whispered. He needed to stop this. But how? How could he when he couldn't move or speak? The only thing he could do was watch.

"Lily, what do you mean?" Elliot asked.

"They were killed, Elliot. I'm so sorry"

"But . . . But how? How did they find them? How did the Necromancers reach Mistfall?"

"I'm sorry, Elliot. I thought you knew."

"Minari, he . . ." Elliot looked at Minari, eyes full of disbelief. "He didn't tell me anything. He said everything was fine."

"I didn't think Minari would lie to you," Lily said.

"I trusted him . . ."

"If he lied to you about that, then he might as well have lied about everything so far," Mimi said. "We should've let him die," he mumbled.

"Minari, why?" Elliot asked. "Why? Did you think I couldn't handle it? Did you think I was weak?"

Minari shook his head. "Ell . . . iot. Please . . ."

"Please what, Minari?"

"Do . . . n't. Don't . . ."

"Don't *what*?"

Minari wheezed, gasping for air. He couldn't say it. Why? Why did his body refuse to listen to him? Why was it taking so long for Mimi's blood to cleanse the poison?

"It doesn't matter anyway," Lily said. She snapped her fingers. A strong gust blew in, and dark clouds appeared. They collided with Elliot, Mimi, Sage, Luka, Owen, and Hiro, knocking them away from Lily and Minari. A black feathered cloak materialized on her shoulders, draping over her back. She blinked once, and her eyes transformed from green to red. The whites of her eyes were now black.

Lily pressed her foot against Minari's shoulder, forcing him down. "I wanted to thank you, you know, for saving me back in the Moon Shrine. Alder had a pretty tight cage on me."

"How . . . ?"

330

"How what? How did I find you?" Lily raised a brow. She reached into the inside pocket of Minari's coat, pulling out the pendant she had carved for Elliot. "This." She chortled. "I don't know how it came about you having this since it was supposed to be for Elliot, but it didn't matter." She tossed the pendant on the ground. She hunched over, her finger tracing across Minari's chest. "Because I'm here for *you*."

Lily unsheathed the dagger that was attached to her thigh. She twirled the blade in her hand before giving Minari one last smirk.

The blade plunged into his chest, straight into his heart.

Minari heard Elliot's distant cries before everything grew dark.

55
FOUND

Ragnar's knife paused. The prongs on his fork sank into his steak. Blood pooled in his dish. His lips curled into a smile.

The End

CPSIA information can be obtained
at www.ICGtesting.com
Printed in the USA
LVHW110704161122
733228LV00012B/154/J

9 781956 501032

AR Level _____ Lexile _____

AR Pts. _____ RC Pts._____